Right then, a
how much he

He would've do
around. What we
was pregnant? He didn't know.

"You've done well with her," he said quietly.

"Thank you for that," she said. "But Travis had a lot to do with it."

Travis. This must be her husband. Neil was surprised at the sudden pang in his stomach.

"What's he like?" he asked. "He's a good dad?"

"He was the best."

Was.

"You're divorced?" he asked.

"No. Travis passed away. Cancer."

He watched Cora closely, unsure of what to say. Ashamed that he'd felt jealous of this poor guy, he was more confused now than ever.

"I'm sorry."

"It's still hard to talk about. But, yes." She looked up at him, her eyes misty. "He was a good dad."

"Is this why Mary wanted to meet me?"

"She's always been curious. I wasn't expecting her reaching out. I'm so sorry, Neil. I didn't mean for you to be hurt."

He was hurt. And angry. But the sight of her crying was more than he could take. Without thinking about it, without stopping to consider whether it was a good idea or not, he reached out to pull her into a hug.

Dear Reader,

Whenever I visit an antique shop and pick up a vintage treasure, I can't help but wonder about its previous owners. What kind of lives they had, what their families were like, if they were happy and if they were loved. When I wrote the Hearts on Main Street series, I wanted to answer those questions for the Sawyer cousins, who took over their grandfather's antique shop and, in the process, were given the gift of coming home again. I wanted them to have the kind of lives you might be curious about, but most of all, I wanted them to be people whose happily-ever-afters you would root for.

With Cora and Neil's story, the sleepy little antique shop on Main Street will close its doors, but I hope your time there will live in your heart for a long time. I know it will in mine—the scent of the musty antiques, the sight of the tourists bundled up on the sidewalk outside and the sound of the December waves crashing in the distance...

Happy holidays, reader! And much love to you.

Kaylie Newell

HER CHRISTMAS FLAME

KAYLIE NEWELL

Harlequin

SPECIAL EDITION

Harlequin®
SPECIAL EDITION™

Recycling programs for this product may not exist in your area.

ISBN-13: 978-1-335-18011-7

Her Christmas Flame

Copyright © 2025 by Kaylie Newell

For questions and comments about the quality of this book, please contact us at CustomerService@Harlequin.com.

TM and ® are trademarks of Harlequin Enterprises ULC.

Harlequin Enterprises ULC
22 Adelaide St. West, 41st Floor
Toronto, Ontario M5H 4E3, Canada
www.Harlequin.com

Printed in Lithuania

MIX
Paper | Supporting responsible forestry
FSC® C021394

For **Kaylie Newell**, storytelling is in the blood. Growing up the daughter of two writers, she knew eventually she'd want to follow in their footsteps. She's now the proud author of over twenty books, including the RITA® Award finalists *Christmas at the Graff* and *Tanner's Promise*.

Kaylie lives in Southern Oregon with her husband, two daughters, a blind Doberman and two indifferent cats. Visit Kaylie at Facebook.com/kaylienewell.

Books by Kaylie Newell

Montana Mavericks: The Anniversary Gift

The Maverick's Marriage Deal

Harlequin Special Edition

Hearts on Main Street

Flirting with the Past
His Small-Town Catch
Her Christmas Flame

Sisters of Christmas Bay

Their Sweet Coastal Reunion
Their All-Star Summer
Their Christmas Resolution

Visit the Author Profile page
at Harlequin.com for more titles.

This one is for all the dogs and cats
that make this world a sweeter place.
Where would we be without you?

Chapter One

Cora Sawyer stood in front of her bedroom window, staring out at the harbor, where fishing boats were making their way back through the choppy water. Back to their slips where the catch of the day would be unloaded—salmon, rockfish, albacore tuna—and the men and women who worked on the slippery decks would shrug their slickers off and go home for the night. Into the coastal winter evening where families or friends waited, if they were lucky.

She sighed and crossed her arms over her chest. *Home.* It was a loaded word. Or, at least, it had felt that way for a very long time. During those years when she'd stayed away from Christmas Bay for so many reasons.

Pain being one.

Secrets being another.

At the thought of her biggest secret, her most important secret, she looked over at Mary's computer. It had been open to her daughter's email account when Cora had pushed the bedroom door open a few minutes ago with a load of lavender-smelling laundry. She'd set the basket down on Mary's bed, curious, but conflicted about looking at the screen, because she was really trying to give her pre-tween as much privacy as possible under the circumstances. It wasn't easy. They shared a bedroom in the small apartment above *Earl's Antiques*. An apartment they also shared with Cora's cousins, Beau and Poppy.

Their grandfather had passed away six months ago, and they'd all come home to run his shop for a year. The length of time he'd asked for in his will, a request they hadn't been able to deny. It had been a calculated move by a man who had wanted his once tight-knit family to come home to Christmas Bay again.

It had worked. The Sawyer cousins were back. They'd mended their once-broken relationship, and were closer than ever, something Cora was eternally grateful for. It would be a gift under the best of circumstances, but was especially precious now that she was a widow with a grieving daughter to raise. They both needed the love and support of their family, and she wasn't sure what she would've done these past few months without them. Especially as Cora was still coming to terms with it all.

She watched the boats chugging through the water, rocking over the late November swells that sparkled underneath the setting sun, and hugged herself tighter. It felt like she'd had a lump in her throat since last spring. She couldn't seem to swallow it down, no matter how hard she tried. The tears were always there, right underneath the surface, threatening at the most inconvenient times. When she was with a customer, or at the grocery store, buying something her husband would have liked. Then reality would hit. Max was gone. Only a couple of months between his diagnosis and his passing. And Mary was without her stepfather—the only dad she'd ever known.

Looking over at the computer again brought her back to the last few weeks. Mary just hadn't been acting like herself. She'd been distant and distracted, her normally sunny disposition clouded by something heavy. Understandable, since she was still struggling with her stepfather's passing, but this change in attitude felt different. Significant. As a mother, it made Cora uneasy, and she wondered for the hundredth time what Mary might be thinking. It wasn't like her not to want to talk about what was bothering her. And on the rare occasions she didn't talk to Cora, she'd almost always talk to Poppy or Beau. She adored her aunt and uncle.

Cora walked over to the computer. The screen saver was on—a picture of Cora and Mary at the beach last summer. It had been taken on Cape Longing, where the scenery was some of the most spectacular in Oregon. The mercurial coastal weather had given them a break that day, a gift in the form of a warm, sunny afternoon. The happy moment—and their smiles, against the backdrop of white-capped waves— preserved forever.

Only now, as Cora touched one of the keys to wake the laptop up, she felt like that smile of Mary's might've been masking something. And any guilt she felt for looking at her daughter's computer was drowned by that worry, that deep-seated instinct to protect her child by any means necessary. Mary had been spending a lot of time on her laptop lately, playing games and looking at social media, all with Cora's supervision. But was there something else going on? Something that was weighing on her?

Swallowing hard, Cora watched the screen saver disappear along with those happy smiles, and saw the Gmail screen pop up in its place. Mary had an email address, but spent most of her time on social media with her friends. Cora had basically forgotten about the Gmail account. Pushing the guilt down, she clicked on the inbox anyway.

And there on the screen, in bold, black letters, was a name she hadn't let herself think about in a long time.

Neil Prescott... Suddenly the room was spinning. Cora put her hand on the rolltop desk, a present from Beau's girlfriend, Summer, who restored antique furniture in her shop outside of town.

"What are you *doing*?"

Cora turned to see her daughter standing there. Eleven-years-old, tall for her age and painfully skinny. Freckles were scattered across her cheeks that were as red right then as a ripe tomato.

"Honey..."

"I can't believe you, Mom! You're reading my stuff!"

Roo, Mary's shaggy Irish wolfhound mix stood leaning against her legs, but at the sound of her voice, turned and slunk away.

"I wasn't reading it," Cora said, trying to keep her voice even and somewhat authoritative. Max had been so much better at this kind of thing than she was. She couldn't help thinking of herself as an imposter sometimes—something she guessed happened when you had a baby so young. In her case, only seventeen-years-old. She was still coming to terms with the harsh realities of parenthood. And now she was coming to terms with them alone. "I was looking because I've been worried about you."

"You were *reading*." Mary had her hands planted on her narrow hips. It was so rare to see her angry that Cora had to take a deep breath.

"I wasn't," she said, "but I probably would have..."

"Because you were worried?"

"Yes."

"You could've just asked."

"I did. I have. You won't talk to me, honey."

"Because I feel *bad*, Mom."

Mary's face crumpled, and Cora took a step toward her. Wanting to wrap her in a hug. Wanting to make the pain go away. But knowing in her heart that this went too deep for a hug to have much effect. This was a lifetime coming.

Mary moved quickly out of her reach, and swiped at the tears that were balanced on her lower lids. She looked like Neil right then, something that made Cora's pulse quicken. She missed Max so much, she ached because of it. He would've known how to handle this. He would've known what to do. Cora felt seventeen all over again, stumbling through adult choices, when deep down, she still thought of herself as a teenager. Like the picture of her and Mary on the beach, a part of her was frozen in time. Her growth stunted because she'd had to walk away from her childhood so young. She'd had to sever that part of herself, and she'd never gotten over it. Not really.

"Mary," she said. "You don't have to feel bad. This is normal. It's natural to want to find your father."

"But I *had* a dad," Mary said, the tears now flowing freely down her face. "And I feel like I'm trying to replace him and stuff."

"Of course you're not trying to replace him. It doesn't have anything to do with how much you loved him." Cora sat down on the edge of Mary's bed. "I just wish you'd talked to me first. It's complicated. Things with your biological dad…"

"What's complicated about it?"

Mary was genuinely confused, it was obvious by the look on her face. She'd always known Max wasn't her real father. Cora had been open about that since she was a toddler. Max had loved her to the moon, so it had never mattered to Mary before. But over the last few years she'd been asking more questions. And now that Max was gone, it made sense that she'd be more curious about Neil. It made sense that she'd be missing that father figure in her life.

All of a sudden, Cora felt a white-hot rush of anger at herself for not seeing this coming. But she couldn't let it show, because her daughter was standing there looking at her, waiting for an answer that she wasn't quite sure she could push past her vocal cords.

"Mom?"

Cora rubbed her temple. "Yes, honey."

"Why is it complicated? I thought he might be happy to hear from me. Maybe he's missed me."

Cora's stomach twisted as she watched her daughter, her beautiful little girl who was on the cusp of her formative teenage years, waiting for her mother to say something, anything that would make sense. Cora knew there was no coming back from this. It was a can of worms that was being torn open now, and all those things that she'd run away from when she was a teenager were going to have to be confronted, once and for all. She'd betrayed the trust of people she cared about. She thought she'd been doing it for the right reasons, but the consequences were the same, regardless. And she was going to have to help Mary through this the best way she could.

"He couldn't have missed you," she said. Her voice was thin and strained. It almost hurt to say anything at all. "He couldn't have, honey, because he doesn't know about you."

Neil Prescott stood there, staring at his phone, unable to process what he'd just read. A fine sheen of sweat had broken out on his forehead, and he reached up to wipe it with the back of his hand.

"Neil. Are you alright?"

He glanced up to see his captain standing in front of him, hands in his uniform slacks, his short-sleeve, navy blue shirt mirroring Neil's.

He nodded, forcing a smile. "Yeah. Fine."

"Sure?"

"I'm sure."

The captain watched him for another few seconds, the way a father might, then turned to walk inside. Presumably to the kitchen, since he was on dinner duty tonight and everyone had requested spaghetti with spicy meatballs, his specialty.

Neil leaned against the cherry red fire engine that he'd just spent the last hour polishing, and looked down at his phone again. *Hi, Dad. It's Mary, your daughter...*

Slowly, he lowered his phone to his side. *Dad...* He'd read that right. He hadn't imagined it, he wasn't dreaming, and he sure as hell wasn't drunk. This was happening in real time. He had a daughter. Or, at least, there was a girl named Mary out there who thought she was his daughter. Either way, it felt like all the air had been sucked out of his lungs.

He looked out to the sidewalk where the tourists were walking by the firehouse. It was a nice evening for being so close to December—barely any wind, which was rare. It was chilly though, and most everyone wore thick, puffy jackets and various kinds of boots—ankle boots, cowboy boots, rain boots, you name it. They held their warm drinks, coffees and hot chocolates, in their hands as the Christmas lights on Main Street began winking on, making the small town look like a greeting card.

Neil barely registered the tourists anymore. Falling back in time, to when he was cocky young kid freshly graduated from high school and on his way to becoming a wildland firefighter. He'd craved adventure, and had left Oregon that fall to fight fires in Washington. But he'd been arrogant and naive, and he'd ended up missing Christmas Bay where he'd spent his summers growing up. He'd missed his friends there, and his family, even though part of the draw of leaving had been putting some distance between him and his incredibly controlling parents.

He'd been sure of his decision to leave—sure enough that he'd been about to break up with his girlfriend, a lovely Christmas Bay local who was a year younger than him. But presumably sensing what was in his heart and mind, she'd left first. She'd had an unhappy home life, and had talked about the possibility of going to live with relatives up north to finish out high school. She'd packed up and left one day, and he'd always assumed that's what she'd done. He'd never heard from her again, even though he'd tried tracking her down in the beginning. Her parents had simply told him she didn't want to see him. And that had been that.

He rubbed the back of his neck. *Cora...* Could she have been pregnant when she left? The thought left him chilled. He'd dated over the years, but he'd been the most serious about Cora. They'd parted ways twelve years ago. He'd wanted a life of excitement and adventure, and she'd wanted the kind of stability and tradition that he'd recoiled from.

"Dude. What's up?"

He turned to see his friend Jay standing there with a Diet Pepsi in his hand. Jay was new to the department, in his early twenties, and Neil's unofficial protégé. But Neil felt more like his big brother most days, when he'd have to remind Jay not to be a dumbass. Easier said than done. But his buddy had a good heart, would step in front of a truck for the people he cared about. And Neil was one of those people.

"I don't know," he said. "And that's the truth."

"Dude." Jay laughed and took a slurp of his soda. "Cap said you were out here acting weird, and he was right. So here I am. Your ear to bend. Your very best bud."

Neil gave him a look.

"Okay. One of your best buds. Lay it on me. What's wrong?"

Jay was a good friend, but there was no way Neil was going to tell him about this. He could barely wrap his own mind around it, let alone explain it to someone else. He needed time to think. He'd be off in an hour, he could think then. For now, he just had to try to act normal, or as normal as possible, so the guys in the firehouse wouldn't try to pry it out of him.

"Nothing, man," he managed. "Just a little overwhelmed with work and life. You know the drill."

"I guess. I don't have women falling all over me like you do, but whatever."

"I don't have women falling all over me."

"Whatever, dude. You know you do. Hello? Allison?"

Neil sighed. He supposed Allison was sort of falling over him, but he'd been clear from the beginning that he wasn't looking for anything serious. He was never looking for anything serious. His standard lines were pretty cliché—*It's not you, it's me. Don't call me, I'll call you.* And so on and so forth.

"We're just having fun," he said.

Jay took another slurp of his soda. "Have you told her that?"

"At length."

"Well, I don't think it's gotten through."

"Why?"

"It's kind of obvious. She calls nonstop. Stops by all the time. She's got hearts in those baby browns."

Neil resisted the urge to groan. Mostly because Jay was right, and he felt bad that he might have been inadvertently leading her on.

"I don't get it," Jay said. "If I had someone that hot chasing after me, I think I'd let myself be caught."

"I'm not good at the girlfriend thing."

"So I've noticed."

The truth was more complicated than not wanting a girlfriend. Neil liked his life the way it was. He thrived on hobbies like skydiving, white water rafting, cliff diving… The list went on and on. To an outsider looking in, it might seem selfish choosing those things over settling down with someone who loved him, but he thought of it as just the opposite. He didn't want to subject someone to any kind of pain of his causing. He'd done that to Cora, and he'd always assumed that was why she'd left.

So he'd grown up, he'd matured and he'd compromised—a little, at least. He'd left wildland firefighting behind—to the endless relief of his parents—and gotten what they thought of as a more acceptable firefighting job in town. But he still lived his life on the edge. He still didn't want attachments of any kind, and he knew the reasons went deep. He understood that what he was really trying to do was prove that he was nothing like his neatly buttoned-up father with every free fall into space. With every breath he held. With every hard, painful landing. He was different. And the world was going to see that he was different, period.

"Chow time," the captain called from inside the firehouse. "Come and get it!"

Jay swigged the last of his Diet Pepsi, then tossed it in the recycling bin a few feet away. "Two points," he said, and burped.

"Nice."

"So you're not going to tell me what's going on with you? No specifics?"

"There are no specifics." He hadn't been friends with Jay long enough for the younger man to be able to tell when he was lying. It was convenient. Neil still couldn't believe what he was lying about. He definitely needed time to think. And a beer. A very big, very cold beer.

"Okay. Whatever you say. Let's go, I'm starving."

"I'm right behind you."

He watched his friend walk inside, his shaggy blond hair brushing his collar. Jay burped again and muttered an "excuse me" before the door closed behind him.

Neil smiled before feeling his lips form a hard line. *Mary...* He suddenly remembered that Cora had always liked that name.

And an ache settled into his bones.

Mary slammed the door so hard, the windows shook. Cora started to go after her, but Poppy grabbed her arm.

"No, sweetie," her cousin said. "I know it's hard, but give her some space."

Anxiety ran in their family, and Mary struggled with it. It was one of the reasons Cora was so worried about her daughter now. Not only was she having to deal with Max's loss, but she was also having to negotiate the terrible world of panic and fear. It was a bumpy road, Cora knew firsthand.

"I don't know," Cora said. "Do you think she's okay in there? I've never seen her like this before."

"I'll check on her." Poppy put an arm around her. "It's going to be okay, she's a tough kid. She knows you've always done your best. And you have, you know. You and Max did an amazing job with her."

Cora managed a smile. "Thank you. I feel like I've made a lot of mistakes."

"We all make mistakes, Cora. You were a kid yourself when you had Mary. Don't forget, you were afraid Neil's parents might've wanted custody, and they could've gotten it, you never know. With all the money and connections they have? You did the right thing."

"But it wasn't the honest thing."

"Well, no," Poppy said. "But sometimes there are gray areas."

"I'm going to have to find Neil. Talk to him. If he'll even see me."

"Do you want me to come? Strength in numbers?"

Cora considered that, and then dismissed it. It was tempting to have her cousin's support, but she knew she had to do this alone. It had been her decision not to tell Neil about his daughter. She needed to handle the fallout.

"I love you for offering," she said. "But no. I'll be alright."

Poppy gave her a squeeze, and Cora felt an ache building in her throat. She wasn't looking forward to seeing Neil again. In fact, she was dreading it, but she had to try to fix this sooner rather than later, for Mary's sake. And of course, it wasn't going to be easy. Or quick.

"I'm going to go in and make sure she's okay," Poppy said. "I'll be right back."

Cora nodded, and watched her cousin knock softly on the door, then open it and disappear inside. She could smell the smoky scent of a lavender candle burning, something that Mary used to calm her anxiety. Her daughter knew she wasn't supposed to be burning candles in the apartment, Cora had gotten her a candle warmer instead, but she decided to pick her battles and bring it up later.

Sitting on the couch, she took her phone off the charger. She'd been very careful not to think about Neil Prescott over the years. When Max had come into her life, he'd been a wonderful husband and father, and she'd been surprised at how much she'd grown to love him over the years, because she'd never thought she could love anyone with her broken heart. Neil was a distant memory now, and that's how she'd wanted him to stay. Of course, she'd known that Mary might want to find her father someday, but she thought she'd have more time to tell her the whole story.

She took a deep breath. She'd track Neil down and see if he wanted to meet her to talk.

For now, it was the best place to start.

Chapter Two

Neil sat at a corner table in the restaurant, nursing his beer. It was a French place in Eugene, very fancy. White tablecloths, snooty servers, ridiculously expensive. Right up his parents' alley.

"Can I get you started on any hors d'oeuvres while you wait, sir?"

He looked up at the young, curly-haired waiter and smiled. He wasn't hungry. In fact, he was unsettled as hell, but he might as well order something for his mom and dad, who were running late. Maybe the food would distract them from going over the list of things they felt he should be doing with his life.

"Uh, yeah," he said. "Can I get the ratatouille with French bread, please?"

"Of course. That'll be right up."

"Thank you."

"My pleasure."

Neil watched the waiter head back to the kitchen, weaving his way in between the well-heeled patrons, and wondered for the thousandth time how he'd ended up Vivian and Richard Prescott's son. Neil liked to think of himself as laid-back, but his parents were the opposite of laid-back. He rooted for the little guy, and they took pride in looking down on people who hadn't done well for themselves. Of course, they would never admit to that, but it was true.

They'd sensed Neil trying to distance himself since middle school, and it had only served to make their grip on him—their only son, their only heir—that much tighter. Cora had been a way for him to rebel. They didn't think her blue-collar, small-town family was up to their standards, which only made her that much more attractive to him. He'd loved how down-to-earth she was, how sweet and relatable. Money hadn't meant squat to her, she wasn't impressed by their summer home on the cape, or the kind of cars they drove, or their family friends. He'd fallen in love with her instantly.

He took a sip of beer and reached up to loosen his tie. It was itchy. He never dressed like this, unless it was for dinner with his parents. Their monthly get-together. Or as he liked to think of it, their obligatory lecture. It was the most he saw of them, outside of holidays and the occasional weekend visits when he'd make the drive into the city during the offseason. Letting them get to him was something he should be well beyond now as a grown man, but somehow wasn't. He wanted to make his own way, but he loved them and didn't want to hurt them, either. It was a tightrope he was constantly walking as their only child. Balancing his own feelings with theirs.

Looking over to the entrance, he saw them come in, and he sat up straighter out of sheer habit. His mother was dressed to the nines in an impeccable cream pantsuit, and his dad looked dapper as always in a navy suit and tie. Commanding attention wherever he went. He was the CEO of a successful tech company, and growing up, Neil hadn't known he owned a pair of jeans, let alone any shorts. He'd just always dressed like this, ready to go at a moment's notice, like he'd be called away to an important meeting at the drop of a hat, and he often was. Because of his busy schedule, Neil had never really known him that well, something he knew his father regretted deep down, but would never admit to out loud.

His mom smiled as they approached, leaning down to give him a kiss on the cheek. She smelled like Chanel No. 5.

"Hi, sweetheart. Sorry we're late. We ran into construction on the highway."

"I saw that."

They sat down, and the waiter hurried over to take their drink order. He seemed to sense that sucking up would pay off well in this case.

Neil sat there, suddenly thinking of Cora, and trying to remember the exact shade of her eyes. He wondered if his daughter had Cora's eyes. At the thought, he tugged on his tie again.

His dad leaned back in his chair. "You look nice, son. I know you don't like dressing up, but when would you ever get a chance to if it weren't for dining in places like this?"

Not necessarily a dig, but Neil was feeling defensive, so it might as well have been.

"Will you leave him alone, Richard?" his mother said. "Just be glad he's here, and we have this lovely dinner to look forward to."

"I didn't say anything. Did I say anything?"

"It's fine, Dad."

He wondered how he would ever break the news if this whole thing turned out to be true. How would they react? He had a pretty good idea, and it wasn't good. They weren't happy with his life as it was. How were they going to feel knowing they had an illegitimate grandchild in the world?

He shifted, more uncomfortable than ever.

"Are you okay, Neil?" His mother frowned and patted his hand. "You look pale all of a sudden."

"It's probably that beer," his dad said. "Too heavy. Why don't you have a nice red for once?"

"I don't like red wine, Dad. You know that."

"It's never too late to try."

His mother cleared her throat. "Let's look at the menu, shall we?"

Neil rubbed his temple. "I ordered some appetizers. But I'm not that hungry."

"Something's definitely wrong," his mother said. "I know it."

"Why?" his dad said. "Just because he's not hungry?"

"He's always hungry."

"But this is French food. I told you he wouldn't like it, but you wanted to eat here anyway, remember?"

His mother's brows knitted together. "Is that why, Neil? We can go somewhere else. I mean, I'm not sure where, all the nicer places take reservations and—"

"No, it's fine," he said, distracted. He couldn't stop thinking about Cora. About all of it. He probably should've canceled this dinner.

His dad gave him a look, clearly trying to decide if he really meant that, and then opened his menu, his readers balanced on the end of his nose.

Neil's phone buzzed from his pocket and he pulled it out, squinting at the text from Jay.

Dude. There was a pretty blonde here looking for you.

He stiffened, staring at the screen. A pretty blonde... That could only be one person. It felt like he'd been strapped into a roller coaster without his consent, and now he was facing that first, stomach-turning drop. For someone who liked adventure so much, he was acutely aware of how terrified he was.

"Neil?"

He looked up. "Mmm?"

"I asked how things are at the fire station," his mom said. "You were talking about a possible promotion?"

He'd mentioned the fact that he was up for driver engineer, and his parents had been thrilled about that.

"Oh," he said. "Yes. Engineer."

"And how's that coming along?" his dad asked.

"Nothing is set in stone yet, but I think that's where it's headed."

"That's wonderful," his mom said. "And does this mean you won't be running off so much? If your job requires more responsibility, you should take that seriously."

"I do take it seriously. But there are other things that are important to me, too."

"Like jumping out of planes?" his dad said. "It's a good thing you don't have a family. I can't imagine a wife being okay with that kind of risk."

"That's why I'm not married."

"Marriage doesn't have to be like that," his mom said, trying to smooth things over before they escalated. "There's give-and-take, Richard."

"Yes, but this is all take and no give."

"Can we leave my hypothetical wife out of this?"

"We're just so proud of your promotion," his mom said quickly. "Let's talk about that, okay?"

"There's really nothing to talk about. Just that it's a possibility."

"A possibility soon?"

Neil pinched the bridge of his nose. "I'm not sure. Maybe."

His phone dinged again, and he looked down at it.

What gives? Who is this girl? And if you're not interested, I am.

"Neil, do you have to look at your phone at the table?" his mother asked. "We only get to see you once a month."

"Yes, son. That's rude."

"It's work," he bit out. Technically it didn't have anything to do with work, but Jay *was* at the firehouse, so it counted. And the fact that he felt like he had to defend checking a text at all made him want to pull his hair out.

He shifted again. So she'd shown up. At the thought of seeing Cora again, his heart did that weird tightening thing that it used to do when he was a teenager. At the anticipation of getting to see her, of getting to kiss her and hold her. She'd had him wrapped around her little finger back then. Well, almost. Not quite enough to change his mind about going.

For a second, he wondered what would've happened if she'd stayed and told him about the baby. How would his life had turned out? Would he have been happy to have a baby so young? Would he have settled down into the safe, predictable kind of existence his parents would've approved of? Or would he have had to fight to have them accept Cora in all the ways that mattered? Would they have ever been able to see her as their daughter? He just didn't know.

"You seem stressed," his mother said softly. "Is everything okay?"

The look in her eyes was one of genuine concern, and he

sighed, then reached out to squeeze her hand from across the table. "I'm alright. Please don't worry about me."

"But I do."

"I know. And I promise everything is okay." That was a lie if he'd ever told one, but there was no helping it right then. What he needed was to excuse himself to go call Jay. He didn't think he'd be able to wait another five minutes.

"But I need to make a quick phone call," he continued. "Would you mind getting me an ice water when he comes back for our order?"

His father nodded. "Of course."

Neil pushed his chair out and stood. Turning for the front door, he tugged on his tie again. First order of business was to call Jay. Second, was to get rid of this tie. If the restaurant required one, he could just eat in the parking lot.

Cora walked out of the fire department and turned to make her way down Christmas Bay's historic Main Street. Pretty soon all the window displays would be Christmas-themed. Mary was excited about a contest the chamber of commerce was having for the downtown businesses—the winner would get to give the cash prize to their favorite charity, and she was already throwing ideas around for the antique shop. She currently had a gigantic crush on Harry Styles, so she was trying to decide between a festive Harry Styles window, or an equally festive Harry Potter window. The jury was still out. Cora thought they'd be fine as long as the name Harry was front and center, surrounded by twinkle lights.

She passed Coastal Sweets on her right, briefly thinking of stopping for a bag of gummy worms—the only thing Mary loved more than Harry Styles—but decided against it. Frances, the sweet, older woman who owned the place, and ran it with the help of her foster daughters, would definitely want to chat, and Cora wasn't up for it. In fact, she didn't think she'd be able to muster a smile right then, so she kept walking, wrapping her soft, oatmeal-colored cardigan tighter around her as the breeze picked up. A few strands of her blond hair had escaped her ponytail, but she didn't bother tucking them behind her ears. Just continued walking with her head down, watching her boots tap against the pavement, feeling like she was making her way through a dream.

It hadn't been hard to track Neil down. Apparently, he was a city firefighter now, so he was right there on the City of Christmas Bay's municipal website. Complete with a picture, just to give her an extra jolt of reality. He'd looked painfully handsome in his uniform, older, with a few noticeable crinkles around his caramel-colored eyes. His smile was the same, vibrant and sexy. Neil had always been able to light up a room with that smile, cliché but true. Cora hadn't been prepared for how her heart would skip a beat at the sight of him. The same but not the same after twelve long years.

Slowing, she put her hands in the sweater's deep pockets. She thought about dinner that night—how she and Mary were supposed to go to Mario's for pizza, but her daughter still wasn't talking to her. She had a right to be upset. She'd had no idea that her father didn't know about her, and although Cora had never outright lied about that, she'd never been forthcoming, either. She thought she'd have more time. She thought she'd have Max here with her when that time ran out.

At the thought of her husband, her chest felt tight. He would tell her to be patient, not to push, to let Mary fig-

ure this out on her own. But Cora had never been a patient person.

"Hey!"

She turned at the sound of a voice behind her. Then saw
a man jogging to catch up. She narrowed her eyes at him.
It was the cute firefighter she'd just talked to at the station.

"Wait up!"

She stood there, watching him approach. He was holding a phone in his hand. He smiled, and she smiled back,
but her stomach clenched. *What in the world?*

Slowing, he held the phone out. "You were asking for
Neil, and he ended up calling me right after you left. I
thought if I could catch you, you might want to talk to
him. It seemed important."

She looked at the cell phone, momentarily at a loss for
words. Neil was on the other end of the line. Her Neil. Although she hadn't thought of him that way for a very long
time. It was strange how fast she'd slipped back into that
habit, given in to that particular tug on her heart.

The young firefighter frowned. "Oh, hey. Listen, I'm
sorry. I shouldn't have put you on the spot like this. I'll
just get your number and he can call you back."

"No," she said quickly. "Thank you."

She took the phone from his hand, feeling her entire
body grow rigid with anticipation. Neil was probably furious, confused, and had all kinds of questions, understand-
ably. Or maybe he just wanted to call her a few choice
names. Or it was possible that he wanted nothing to do
with Mary at all, in which case, she wasn't sure what she'd
tell her daughter. How she'd explain that particular kind of
rejection. She just knew she had to get through this brief
conversation, whatever it held, so she could move on to
whatever was next. She'd take the littlest steps, bit by bit,

until she found her way to the other side. She'd had to learn to do that a long time ago.

"I'll give you some privacy," the firefighter said. "I'll be right over there when you're done."

"Thanks so much," Cora said again. "It won't be long."

"Take your time."

She watched him walk over to a bench in front of the candy shop, and sit, his broad shoulders hunched a little in the chilly breeze.

And then, slowly, she lifted the phone to her ear. "Hello?"

There was a beat or two, and the silence on the other end of the line was deafening. Made her want to walk over and give the phone back to its owner. Made her want to turn and run in the opposite direction. But she couldn't do that. For Mary's sake, she had to see this through. She owed her daughter that much. And she owed Neil that much, too.

"Neil?"

She heard him breathing. Clearing his throat. Her heart slammed against her breastbone as she waited.

"Cora."

His voice was deep, smooth. The way he said her name was so familiar that she had to close her eyes for a second to center herself.

"Yes," she finally managed. "We need to talk. Will you meet me?" There was no point beating around the bush. No sugarcoating this giant, bitter pill they both needed to swallow.

"So it's true, then. I have a daughter?"

She stared across the street, glimpsing azure slivers of ocean between the chalky, redbrick buildings. The sun was low in the sky now, turning it a melted sherbet color. The breeze blew the loose strands of her hair over her collar-bone—feathery kisses from a long-lost lover.

"I need to explain. But I want to do it in person."

There was a long pause on the other end of the line. Long enough that she wasn't sure what he was going to say next. If he'd agree to meet her or not. And again, all she could picture was trying to sit down and explain this to Mary in a way that wouldn't be any more damaging than it already had been.

And then there was the question of his parents. What would they do when they found out they had a grandchild? Neil was an only child, he represented the end of their family line, which had always been important to his father. The question of what they'd do was something that made Cora's stomach turn.

"Fine," he finally said, his voice sharp. "I have the next few days off. We can meet for coffee at Gran's Diner in the morning, it's down the block from the fire station."

"The one with the blue awnings?"

"Yes."

"What time?"

"Ten?"

"Ten works. I'll see you tomorrow."

"Tomorrow," he answered tersely.

And hung up. Leaving her heart squarely in her throat.

Neil dropped the phone to his side and stood there staring at the parking lot pavement like he'd just been hit by a bus. He might as well have been. For the complete fog he was in, for the way his head was spinning like he'd had way too much to drink. Only he was sober, and he wasn't injured. He was just in shock. Complete and total shock.

"A *daughter*?"

At the sound of the voice behind him, he looked up sharply. Then turned to see his mother standing there, white as a sheet. Her cheeks sucked in like she'd just taken a bite of a lemon.

"Mom," he managed. "What are you doing?"

"The ratatouille came, and it was getting cold. You'd been gone so long… A *child*, Neil?"

He couldn't believe she'd walked up behind him, had heard that last part of his conversation, but she had. Obviously. And that's all she'd need to hear.

He scrubbed a hand through his hair, feeling his blood pressure rise. Feeling his face heat, even in the cool evening breeze. A couple walked out of the restaurant hand in hand, and brushed by him with eyes only for each other. He found himself glaring at them as they passed.

"Did I hear that right?" his mother asked.

He forced himself to look at her. "You did."

"What? How long has…" Her voice faded away, and it was clear that she couldn't even pinpoint the right question to ask. He knew how she felt.

"I'm just as surprised as you are, Mom."

She stood there staring at him, and he felt himself starting to sweat. He reached for his keys in his pocket and wrapped his hand around their cold metal. He wasn't staying for dinner. He didn't know where he was going to go, but he couldn't go back inside and pretend he wasn't about to have a stroke or something, because he absolutely felt like he was.

"Who?" his mother asked through tight lips. "Who's the girl?"

"I can't talk about this right now," he said. "I'm sorry, but I can't."

"It's Cora Sawyer, isn't it?"

She said this with disdain. She'd always seen the Sawyers as below them, which was ridiculous, but that's how she felt. She'd never hidden her opinion that Cora wasn't good enough for her son. She had no breeding, no money and no future. At least not with the Prescotts.

Neil found himself prickling on Cora's behalf. Felt his shoulders tense with a heated indignation. Which was strange, considering how mad he was at her right then.

"Don't say it like that," he managed.

"Say it like *what*? How am I supposed to say it? How are we supposed to feel?"

"This is not something you have to figure out. I'm going to take care of it."

She sniffed. "It's a little late for that."

He gaped at her. "What's that supposed to mean?"

"Nothing. It doesn't mean anything. Please, just come back inside. We don't have to tell your father yet, we can do that later."

"*We* aren't going to do anything, Mom. I'll tell him. Or you can tell him if you want. I just need to think. Actually…" He shook his head. "I'm going to go, I'll call you later, okay?"

Her eyebrows shot up. "You're not leaving? Not after this."

"That's exactly what I'm doing."

And then he was climbing into his truck, refusing to look into his rearview mirror, in case she was still standing outside the restaurant's front door watching him. Judging him. Sure he was about to mess up and embarrass the family in some way or another.

He gritted his teeth, started the engine and pulled out with the tires screeching on the pavement.

Chapter Three

Neil was early. Half an hour early, to be exact, but he'd been up since three, and hadn't been sleeping well before that anyway. He'd dreamed of a little girl with Cora's eyes and his sense of adventure, and he'd woken up with his head spinning.

So here he was. Sitting in the parking lot of Gran's Diner, half an hour early, with his stomach still in knots, but his heart remembering exactly how it felt to be in Cora's presence, and it was beating accordingly. Heavy and sure, pushing the blood through his veins with a familiar warmth that was unsettling. He was angry. He was so many things, but he'd be lying if he said he wasn't craning his neck at every car that pulled in, wondering if that was her. Hoping it was, and not knowing what to do with that.

Leaning back, he rubbed the back of his neck, his eyes feeling scratchy and heavy. He probably looked like garbage with the amount of sleep he'd had, but he'd dressed nicely, in a polo shirt and khaki slacks, and had shaved the last few days of scruff that he'd let grow. The fact that he wanted to look decent for her wasn't lost on him. He really shouldn't care, but he did. Inconvenient, but true.

He scanned the road for cars going up and down Main Street, and wondered how long she'd been back in Christmas Bay. Probably not long, since he would've run into her by now. It was a small town, small enough that you couldn't really avoid someone for long, even if you were trying. He'd thought about her over the years, and had tried finding her online, with no luck. Wherever she'd been, whatever she'd been doing, she'd kept a low profile.

He looked up as a white hatchback pulled into the parking lot. He could clearly see a woman driving, with blond hair and a delicate profile. Neil's chest tightened at the sight of her. *Cora...* He could tell it was her before she parked the car. Before she opened the door and stepped out into the bright morning, the sun touching her hair and turning it gold. She took off a pair of dark sunglasses and looked around, and he had to remind himself to breathe, she was so beautiful. She'd always been a pretty girl, everyone thought so. But she'd grown into a woman with lovely features and generous curves, who could stop traffic. And apparently stop a man's heart inside his chest.

He reached for his door handle and waited a beat or two. Time that he hoped would help him relax, to put this meeting into perspective. Would help remind him that she wasn't someone he knew anymore. She'd kept his kid from him. Would he have been a decent father? He had no idea, but the opportunity had been taken from him. He felt cheated and lied to, and all of a sudden, the anger bubbled up again, protecting him from the effects of her beauty and her sweetness and her intelligence, and all of the things that had drawn him to her in his youth. It was like armor, cold and hard, and finally, he opened the door and stepped out of his truck, watching as she turned to settle her gaze on him.

She smiled. It was hesitant, but familiar. He didn't smile back.

"Neil," she said, as she walked up to him. She wore a

pair of jeans, a waist length pea coat, and a chunky blue sweater underneath that brought out her eyes. Her hair was up, showing off her neck, which was long and graceful. She was incredibly sexy. But there was a certain halo of sadness surrounding her now. This was definitely not the same shy girl that he'd fallen in love with all those years ago. This was someone with history. With baggage of some kind, he could tell by the dark circles under her eyes, and the way her mouth tilted naturally downward now. As if smiling were harder to commit to than frowning.

"It's been a long time," she said, stopping in front of him. Not close enough for a hug, or to be touched at all. Which was fine, he hadn't planned on doing either.

Nodding, he put his hands in his pockets.

"Are you hungry?" she asked. "Or would you rather just have coffee? Or maybe we can go for a walk or something. Whatever you're comfortable with."

"I'm not really comfortable with any of this. If you want to know the truth."

"I understand," she said quietly.

She licked her lips, and he willed himself not to be affected by that, either. He was here, he was going to listen to what she had to say. But he couldn't let her in, not where she could do any damage. Falling for Cora had been easy the first time. There wouldn't be a second.

"Why don't we just walk, then," she said. "How about the park on Second? It's just a block or two from here."

"I know where it is."

"Right. I keep forgetting that you live here full-time now."

He watched her, knowing his eyes were stony. What she didn't know was how fast his heart was beating. How his gaze kept wanting to drop to her mouth, where her lips were plump and pink in the morning light. She wasn't biting them anymore, but the damage had already been done.

"Three years now," he said. "Couldn't fight wildfires forever."

"And you like it? Being here in Christmas Bay? I'm sure being a city firefighter feels different..."

"I like it fine."

She nodded, swallowing visibly. He wasn't making this easy for her. He didn't care, that wasn't his job. There was a time when all he'd wanted to do was protect her and make her happy, but he'd failed at that when he'd chosen adventure over loving her. At least, that's how she must've felt, since she'd been here one day and gone the next.

He fell into step beside her, and they made their way to the sidewalk, then turned left toward the park. Tourists walked past them, easy to spot with their coffees and bags from the shops along Main Street. But there were locals too, and they both nodded and said hello to several people as they passed.

Other than that, Cora stayed quiet beside him. He was tall, and she was petite, so it felt like he was hulking over her. He remembered how he used to pick her up so easily when they were kids, she'd barely weighed anything at all. One night before his graduation they'd snuck away to the river, and he'd carried her to the edge of the water, where he'd set out a blanket and some root beers on ice. He wondered if that was the night their daughter was conceived.

He looked over at her now, how her brows were knitted together like she was trying to solve some kind of math problem. This was hard for her, he knew. The fact that she was having to see him after all this time, and explain what she'd done and why she'd done it, would be opening up wounds that had been healed over for a very long time now.

"When did you come back?" he asked, his voice not nearly as biting as it had been a few minutes ago. This is what she did to him. He was like river rock, and she was like the water; beating against him, smoothing him, polishing him to a luster. She used to bring out the best in him when he was a teenager, making him feel like a man long before he'd actually become one.

"About six months ago," she said. "My grandpa passed in the spring and left us his antique shop. Beau and Poppy and I are running it for a while. It was only supposed to be for a year, but I don't know." She shrugged. "We kind of like it. We're surprisingly good at it, and we're glad to be doing this for Grandpa. I know he would be happy we're back home again."

They kept walking, passing the donut shop on the right. It had its front doors propped open and he could smell the warm, sugary scent of donuts wafting out on the ocean breeze. A small, pink Christmas tree glittered in the window. All decked out in donut ornaments, of course.

"I'm sorry," he said. "I know how close you were."

"He had a good life. And he knew how much he was loved. That's the most important thing when you lose someone, right? Being able to look back and know without a doubt that they felt loved."

Her voice broke and he glanced over. He could see the freckles scattered across her nose. A Sawyer trait.

"I wasn't close to my grandparents," he said. "My mom's parents lived all the way across the country, and my dad's weren't…the warmest."

"I remember. They wanted to send you to boarding school."

"You remember that?"

"Of course. You said you were going to run away. You wanted to live in a yurt in Baja."

He snorted. "The grass is always greener…"

"You did get pretty good at surfing, if memory serves. Even if you didn't get all the way to Baja."

"Well, yeah. If there was a way to break my neck, I was going to be first in line."

"And then you found wildland firefighting, and it was love at first sight."

She said it matter-of-factly. There was no bitterness there, no blaming the firefighting for breaking them up. She said it like she knew what made him tick. And he guessed she did, better than anyone he'd ever met.

He slowed. Then came to a stop and turned to look down at her. She frowned, stopping too, probably expecting the onslaught to start. The hurled insults. The fury that she knew had to be simmering just underneath the surface. But he could see that she wasn't the same young girl that he'd carried off to that riverbank, laughing against his chest. She was a woman now, she'd matured. And she was stronger than she'd been before.

"You said you wanted to explain," he said, his voice low. "I'm listening."

She took a visible breath. Maybe what she hoped would be a steadying breath. "You have a daughter," she said quietly. "Her name is Mary, she's eleven-years-old. She's always known about you, that you're her biological father. I never kept that from her."

He let that sink in. The reality of it made his skin clammy. The fact that she was standing here now, telling him what he should've known twelve years ago, made him see a sudden flash of red.

"So, you're saying you could be honest with her, but not with me?" he managed through clenched teeth.

"I know you're angry."

"*Angry* doesn't begin to explain how I feel. How could you do this? How could you keep her from me?"

"What I did was wrong. But I had my reasons at the time. I was young and confused. And I knew you were going to leave."

"You didn't know that," he said.

"I knew you *wanted* to leave, Neil. You were always open about that, you never made me think you'd stay, for me or anyone else."

"I loved you."

"Love isn't enough. You said that yourself. You wanted to leave here, that's all you ever wanted. I wasn't going to tell you I was pregnant so you'd stay. I didn't want that kind of life for her. Or me. Or you, for that matter."

"You had no right to keep this from me," he bit out. "No damn right."

Her eyes were bright. He could smell her perfume, and all of a sudden, he couldn't remember why he'd agreed to this walk. He was thirsty. No, he was actually parched. Every cell in his mouth and throat screamed for water, something cool to relieve the burning ache deep down. But what was he aching for? Cora? Or his baby daughter, who was no longer a baby anymore?

He'd never planned on having kids. He'd never planned on settling down, not really. He hadn't wanted the kind of marriage his parents had—one that seemed transactional half of the time, and almost chilly the other half. He'd recognized it as a boy, had been wrapped in that chilliness, and he'd grown anesthetized to the thought of having a family of his own. He hadn't been able to stand the thought of his life growing cold and predictable. Which was just another reason why he took the risks he did now. He wasn't perfect, but he was anything but predictable.

"I was afraid," she said, gazing up at him. She wore a pleading expression, obviously hoping he'd understand. But he wasn't there yet. He wasn't sure if he'd ever fully get there, it was too much of a betrayal.

"I would've helped you," he said tightly. "I would've been there."

"Would you have, Neil? Because you were pretty clear about what you wanted. I was scared to death, and I felt alone. Not telling you was a mistake, but there were also your parents…"

He stiffened. "What about my parents?"

"We were so young, and I knew how they felt about me, about my family. What if they'd tried to get custody?"

"That wouldn't have happened. You were eighteen."

"I didn't turn eighteen until a few months after I had her. When I found out I was pregnant, all I could think about was protecting her. My parents were so disapproving, I couldn't stand the thought of subjecting her to that every day. And I thought I was doing you a favor, I really did. By the time I'd truly grasped what I'd done…"

He felt the muscles in his jaw bunch as he stared down at her. "How long did that take?" he asked. "Because if my math is right, you've had over a decade to right that wrong."

"I have. That's true."

"Was she ever curious about me? Did she ever want to meet me before this?"

"She knew you were a good person, that we were really young when she was conceived. Too young. She understood all that. But she's gotten more curious as she's gotten older…"

He had no idea how to feel about that, how to act, what to say. So he said nothing at all.

"It was always my intent to find you and tell you. But the timing never seemed right. There was always something in the way, some reason why I felt like I needed to wait a little longer."

He sighed and looked beyond her. His shoulders and back were tense. In fact, they were starting to ache from the way he was standing, with his hands jammed in his pockets. His skin felt tight, stretched over his muscles, and his headache from the night before was creeping back into his temples in steady, pulsing throbs.

"Say something," Cora said softly. "Please talk to me."

"I'm not sure what you want me to say. You want me to be okay with having a daughter overnight? I'm not okay with it. I never felt like I'd be a good dad, and now…"

"Now you'll have someone who loves you unconditionally."

"I don't believe that. It takes a lot more than sharing blood for someone to love you. You have to earn it, and I haven't earned anything."

"Try telling Mary that. She's going to love you, Neil." She paused and bit the inside of her cheek. "That is, if you want to meet her. I won't blame you if you need more time. Or if you decide you don't want this, I'll understand that, too."

"But she won't."

"She'll have to come to terms with it, yes. But it needs to be your choice. You need to want it, or she'll sense it, and it wouldn't work anyway."

She tucked a loose strand of hair behind her ear, and a

small diamond solitaire sparkled on her ring finger. She was married. Despite everything, he felt a strange kind of disappointment at that. A sinking feeling that irritated him because he shouldn't care if she was married or not. Clearly, just being in Cora's presence again was going to mess with his head.

"I know you're mad," she said, "and you have every right to hate me. But Mary is a great kid. Whatever you do, just don't blame her for what I did."

He watched her. Then opened his mouth to answer, but his phone rang from his back pocket before he could. Pulling it out, he saw Allison's name flash across the screen. She'd called last night, and he hadn't called back. He just hadn't had the bandwidth after seeing his parents. But he knew if he didn't answer, she was going to keep calling, and he really needed to put out that particular fire before it got any bigger. The last thing he needed right now was her showing up and then having to explain this to her, too.

"Do you mind if I take this really quick?" he asked.

"Of course not."

He answered, holding the phone tightly to his ear. Cora turned, crossing her arms over her chest to try and give him some privacy.

"Allison. Hi."

"Hey there, stranger. I've been trying to reach you."

"Yeah, I'm sorry about that. Just busy."

"Well, how about a drink? It might help you relax. You promised to take me line dancing this weekend, remember?"

"Uh…yeah. You know, I think I'm going to have to cancel."

"Hey, it's fine. I know you're not big on dancing. We

could just rent a movie and order some pizza instead. I'm easy!"

"It's just not a good time. I don't think I'd be great company anyway."

"How about next week?" she asked, sounding hopeful. Too hopeful.

Allison was gorgeous—long brunette hair, big brown eyes. Jay was in love with her, all the guys at the fire department were. She was smart, well-read, funny—she was also a little clingy. She didn't like Neil's daredevil hobbies—but to be fair, none of the women he'd dated had been comfortable with them. Besides all those things though, there was just something missing for him. There was a reason he hadn't wanted to get more serious with her, but anytime he wondered about that, he'd just dismiss it as a general lack of commitment. He'd never let himself dig any deeper than that, but standing there on the sidewalk, with Allison on the line and Cora standing only a few feet away, he understood exactly why he'd never wanted a relationship with her. She wasn't Cora.

The realization made him wary. Suddenly, all he wanted to do was get in his truck and get the hell out of Dodge. He officially had too many thoughts, too many emotions to comfortably handle at the moment. At least not with any skill whatsoever.

"Allison, can I call you back?"

Cora looked over, and then stared down at the sidewalk. The awkwardness thick and heavy between them.

"Oh. Sure. Call me back. I'll be around, but I work at six."

He'd told Jay that he and Allison were casual, that they were just having fun, but he knew she was hoping for more. That if she held steady, he'd come around. He needed to put the brakes on here, having fun or not. Remind her that he wasn't looking for any kind of relationship, and he was a bad bet anyway. It was true. All of it.

"Alright," he said. "I'll talk to you later."

"Talk soon."

He hung up, and Cora turned back to him. She was so pretty. He remembered that feeling of being knocked flat with one look from her. At the moment, he couldn't quite remember how he'd been able to let her go. But then again, she was the one who'd left. Even as he thought it, he knew she might not have done that if he'd been able to promise her a future.

It didn't matter now. It was all water under the bridge. What mattered now was that he had a daughter. A *daughter*. He was still having trouble wrapping his mind around that one. And at the thought, he was furious all over again.

Cora watched him. "Is everything okay?"

"Fine. Still processing all of this."

"I know it changes everything for you."

That was a massive understatement, and she knew it. Her cheeks colored and she looked away again.

He wanted a better answer from her than she was just young and scared. He wanted this to make sense. He wanted to not be so livid, because it felt like his chest was constricting, like his whole body was starting to collapse in on itself.

"Have you told her that we're talking?" he bit out.

She shook her head. "No, she's really mad at me right now. I'm going to take her to dinner tonight and try to explain some of this."

Mary was mad. And he was mad. He wondered if Cora had any support at all with this, and then remembered her husband. Maybe he was mad, too.

"I haven't answered her email," he said. "I don't want her to think I don't care. I just…"

"I know, you don't have to explain. I'll tell her."

He nodded. Then looked past her to the mountains in the distance. They were beautiful, emerald green against the ocean sky. He remembered when fighting a fire in the woods had made him feel alive. And how it had felt giving it up to come and work in town. It had been the smart thing to do, he wasn't getting any younger and his parents were right, wildland firefighting was dangerous. But it still felt like he'd given in to pressure where they were concerned. If they'd been able to have that kind of effect on him as a grown man, how would Cora have felt at seventeen? A girl who knew she wasn't liked or accepted by them.

He pushed the thought away. He wanted to understand why she'd done what she'd done, but the truth was, being angry at her was a barrier that he needed right now. Not being pissed off meant possibly forgiving her. And forgiving her meant what? A relationship of some kind. After all, she was the mother of his child. She was going to be in his life from now on, no matter what. And what did that look like? He couldn't even guess.

He rubbed his temple, trying to block out the barrage of thoughts that were only making his chest feel tighter, more uncomfortable.

She looked up at him, worrying her bottom lip between her teeth.

"I think," he said slowly, "that this is probably enough for one day."

She nodded somberly.

"Why don't you call me tomorrow," he said. "And we can go from there."

"Okay." She put her hands in her pockets, and looked

up at him steadily. He thought maybe a little courageously, under the circumstances. She knew how he felt. She knew what this secret had done, and how it was rocking his world. But there was a strength in her expression, in her eyes, that he couldn't help but admire, despite himself. He wondered again about his daughter and what she looked like, whose eyes she had.

He hoped she had her mother's.

Cora closed the dog-eared Mario's menu and slid it across the table. "Want to take a look? Or do you want the usual?"

There was a ball of nerves sitting squarely in her stomach. This shadow hanging over them was bad enough. But now she was also a little worried that they'd run into Neil before she had a chance to smooth things out with Mary. Christmas Bay was so small, she wouldn't have been surprised to see him walking through the front door now.

Mary was looking out the window with her arms crossed over her chest. Her face was tight, her heart-shaped lips pursed. She hadn't looked at Cora once since they'd sat down. At one point, her eyes had filled with silent tears, but she hadn't let any fall. She'd just swallowed noticeably until they'd passed.

"Honey," Cora said. "Will you talk to me? Please?"

Her daughter kept staring out the window toward the harbor. It was a pretty evening. Cold, clear. A tabletop Christmas tree sparkled gamely next to the cash register up front. Holiday music played from the jukebox in the corner. A group of elderly women in Christmas sweaters laughed from their table across the room. They all had glasses of wine in front of them, and looked like they were having a great time.

Cora glanced over and smiled, suddenly a little jealous of how happy they seemed. She wished she could join them.

But then she looked back over at Mary, and her heart squeezed. Her daughter was so young, so innocent. She'd started middle school this fall, and was struggling with that. It could be a hard transition for any kid, with friends and boys, and everything that went hand in hand with adolescence, but it had been especially hard for Mary because of her anxiety. And then with grieving her stepdad on top of it, some days it had felt impossible for her.

And now, Neil.

Cora was at the point that if Mary—who'd never gone five minutes without giving her a hug, or kissing her cheek, or showing her a favorite Instagram reel—didn't start talking soon, she didn't know what she was going to do. She had the distinct feeling that she was in over her head here. She needed a sounding board. Poppy and Beau weren't just her cousins, they were like her siblings, but they didn't have kids. She felt like she was navigating this alone, and it scared her.

As if reading her mind, Mary finally looked over. Her pretty blue-green eyes locked with Cora's and softened some.

"I'm sorry, Mom," she said. "I know you feel bad and stuff, but I'm just... I'm just..."

And then fresh tears filled her eyes.

Cora reached across the table and took her hand. "Oh, honey. Please don't cry."

"That's the thing, I don't know *why* I'm crying."

"Is it your dad?"

Mary looked at her, perplexed. "Which one?"

It was such a simple question. But the reality of it hit with the subtlety of a baseball bat.

Cora frowned. "Your stepdad."

"Yes. I mean, I'm always sad about Dad. And I guess that's kind of why I'm crying, but there's other stuff."

"Neil?"

Mary sniffed and swiped at her tears with her free hand. "Yeah."

"You know he just needs some time with this, right? It's not that he doesn't want to meet you." The words slipped out before Cora could stop them. She hoped and prayed Neil *would* want to meet Mary. If he didn't... Well, she was going to try her hardest not to think about that.

"I know," Mary said. "But I feel weird about it."

"Weird how?"

"I don't know. Just weird. What if he hates me? What if he doesn't want a kid?"

Cora swallowed hard. All valid questions. All questions that had kept her up for the last several nights. But as many questions as there were, she couldn't bring herself to believe he'd hate his own child. Resent what she represented? Cora could see that. But she knew Neil would never *hate* Mary.

But getting her to understand that wouldn't be easy. At the moment, Mary was going to be feeling all the things, and nothing Cora said or did would make it any easier. The only thing that would ease her mind was going to be meeting her father in person. And even then, it wouldn't be the fairy tale she was probably picturing. This was messy. This was life.

Cora squeezed her daughter's hand. Mary's fingers were long and slender. She had chipped pink polish on her nails. A friendship bracelet on her wrist that her best friend had made her before she'd moved to Christmas Bay. It was blue and yellow, their old elementary school colors. Cora remembered that Max had always wanted her to play soccer when she got to middle school like he had, but Mary liked volleyball better. Max had been such a good dad. Neil wouldn't know it of course, but he was going to have a hard time measuring up if he wanted to be a part of Mary's life. It wasn't fair to him, but then again, neither was keeping his daughter from him in the first place.

"He's not going to hate you," Cora said softly. "That's not possible."

"It is, though."

"Nobody hates you, Mary."

"Mom, get real! Riley Abbot hates me."

"Who's Riley Abbot?"

"She's the most popular girl in school. Like, everyone loves her."

Suddenly, Cora was thrust back in time. Walking the shiny halls of her own middle school with the warm smell of Tater Tots from the cafeteria in her nose. With her belly in knots because things were okay when you were eleven... until they weren't. And when they went sideways, they usually went *really* sideways. Or at least, that's how it felt to most eleven-year-olds.

"Why do you think she hates you?" Cora asked carefully.

"Because I'm friends with Jessica, and she and Jessica used to be friends in fifth grade, and she thinks I stole her away or something. It's so dumb. And so is Riley. I can't stand her."

"Okay...well, maybe if you and Riley had a talk..."

"She won't talk to me, Mom! She hates me, remember?"

Cora sighed. It felt like no matter what she said these

days, it was the wrong thing. She just wished Mary could see how wonderful she was, and that this angst, this ever-present preteen stress, wouldn't last forever. But that was wishful thinking, of course. To Mary, it was all-consuming.

Her daughter sniffed, somehow holding the tears back, but Cora knew they could overflow at any moment. She was prepared. She had two packs of travel Kleenex in her purse.

"Why didn't you tell him?" Mary asked. And Cora knew this was where it was going to get hard. Or harder than it already was.

"Honestly?"

Mary nodded.

"I was scared, sweetheart. I should've told him. I should've done a lot of things differently. But I was really young and his parents didn't like me, and I just felt too overwhelmed with all of it."

Mary frowned. "They didn't like you?"

"No."

"Why not?"

"I don't think they thought I was good enough for their son. Our family lived on the other side of the tracks."

"Wait. What kind of tracks?"

Cora laughed. "That's just an expression. It means they had money and we didn't. At least not nearly as much as they did."

"So what?" Mary said, clearly defensive. "That's like, the *worst* reason for not liking someone."

"Well, you're right about that. It's not a good reason. But to be fair, I never gave them a chance. It could've been okay."

"They sound mean."

"Listen to me," Cora said, putting some steel into her voice. "They're your grandparents, and I know it's hard not to form an opinion by what I'm telling you, but I want you to keep an open mind about them. They were kept in the dark just like your dad was. You need to give them a chance."

Mary huffed. "If they'll even claim me."

It was a mature statement for a young girl, and an inconvenient truth. Cora stiffened at the thought of her daughter being rebuffed by the Prescotts. It was that agonizing feeling of Cora's own parents not accepting her all over again. What a mess this was. But like she'd just got done telling Mary, they needed to keep an open mind. It was too early to see how any of this was going to unfold.

Mary chewed on one of her fingernails for a second, looking thoughtful. "I can't believe you got pregnant at seventeen, Mom."

Cora's cheeks warmed. She'd been honest with Mary from the beginning about her past. Mostly because she'd hoped that Mary wouldn't make the same mistakes. Not that her daughter was a mistake, of course, but being a teenage mother was harder than she ever could have imagined. Her parents were split up by that point, and her mother had been too involved with her own life to be that present in Cora's. Except when it came to her judgment—Cora had felt that part well enough. They'd been ashamed of her deep down, and they'd never said or done anything in the years following Cora's pregnancy to make her feel that she and her daughter were loved and accepted. As a result, the distance between them had grown into an estrangement that continued to this day. She'd hoped that eventually they'd see Mary as the incredible gift that she was, instead of just an illegitimate child, an outdated and painful way of looking at a human being, but that had never happened. A grim reality.

"I know," she said. "I was very young. Too young."

"Were you scared?"

"Yes."

Mary's eyes grew serious. "Did you ever not want me?"

Cora felt her lungs constrict. They were shrinking as she sat there, and she couldn't get a full breath. The question made her physically hurt from a place that was too deep to fathom. How could she ever explain to her daughter how much she was loved?

She got up and came over to Mary's side of the booth. "Scootch," she said.

Mary scooted over, and Cora sat beside her, pulling her into a hug. "There was never one moment, not one single second, that I didn't want you. You're the best thing that's ever happened to me. Don't you know that?"

Mary let out a little sob, and Cora's heart broke in half. She rocked her daughter gently, remembering when Mary was a newborn, and would wake every few hours with frantic cries. Cora had been so tired, she could barely keep her eyes open to nurse. Her parents had been furious with her, and hadn't shown a lot of interest in seeing Mary, much less with helping with her. But they'd cared enough—or felt guilty enough—to give Cora money in the beginning, so she could afford a rental, which they'd co-signed for, and childcare, so she could work. She'd been lucky. She knew she wouldn't have been able to make it otherwise. Those days had been so hard that thinking about them now filled her stomach with a strange weight. It had been the hardest thing she'd ever done, having a baby so young. But she'd never regretted it. Ever. The love for her child was unlike anything she'd ever known. Sometimes it scared her, it was so strong, so sure.

Mary sniffed, seeming to process what she'd just said. Seeming to accept the words for what they were, and Cora was relieved. It was the first time she'd ever asked if she was unwanted, a natural question for a kid with her history, and Cora had been dreading it.

"I wonder if Dad will feel the same way," Mary said, her voice small. "Or… I guess I should call him Neil, huh?"

"You should call him whatever you want to call him."

"But what should I call him to his face? I mean, if I see his face. In person."

"I'm sure he'll want you to call him whatever you're comfortable with." Cora smiled and kissed her daughter on the temple, but deep down she was worried that Neil wouldn't want to see her. Maybe he'd end up being like her parents, and would give her money in place of a loving relationship. The thought was almost too much to bear.

Again, Cora pushed it aside. He'd given her his number, and she was going to call him tomorrow, like they'd planned. As if he were just an old friend that she was going to reconnect with. If only it were that simple.

She swallowed hard, the smell of Mary's shampoo filling her senses. Until that phone call, until she knew what Neil was thinking, she was just going to have to hide these doubts at all costs. It was what she'd always done, it was how she'd learned to protect that newborn baby in her arms.

Only some of those secrets were coming back to haunt her.

Chapter Four

Neil sat on his favorite deck chair with his coffee, looking out over the beach at the white-capped waves crashing against the rocks. It was cold, but not unbearably so, and honestly, it felt good after the night he'd spent tossing and turning, feeling like he was coming out of his own skin.

He'd worked hard for his house on the beach, it had been a long time coming, years spent saving and working overtime. He'd done it on his own, but he was well aware that he'd been able to do it because he'd come from a place of privilege. A family that hadn't let him struggle with things like a car payment and insurance when he was young, and had sent him on student trips abroad so he could have one amazing experience after another. He'd been given all the opportunities growing up, and every door that he'd come across had always swung conveniently open, and he'd just walked right on through.

He was grateful. No more so than now, sitting here, thinking of Cora pregnant at seventeen. He wondered how much help she'd had. If she'd gone to her parents, or if she'd just packed up and left. He wouldn't be surprised if she had gone it alone. She'd always had an independent streak, been incredibly resourceful as a teenager. The one person she'd leaned on, her grandfather, had been her whole world back then. Well, him and her cousins. She'd been close with Poppy and Beau, too. But her grandpa had been like a father to her. He wondered how Earl had taken it, or if he'd even known at first. All questions that hadn't stopped swirling around in Neil's brain since yesterday, since seeing Cora again. Beautiful as ever. Evoking emotions that had him restless and confused.

Taking another swallow of coffee, he frowned, hearing the crunch of tires on gravel. It was a Sunday, and he wasn't expecting anyone. Except maybe Allison. She'd shown up a few times out of the blue, and his gut tightened. He'd called her last night to tell her that he couldn't see her anymore, at least for the time being. He hadn't gone into detail, but he knew it was the right thing to do. He could hear Jay now, telling him what an idiot he was—and maybe that was true. Or maybe he was just destined to be alone. Some people were. Still, the thought of that made him sad as he pushed himself up from the deck chair and braced himself for seeing Allison. For the heartfelt talk that she might want to have, for the guilt he was going to feel for letting her believe, even a little, that he might've been ready for something more.

He walked into his house, small by most people's standards, but very cool, with an entire wall of windows facing the ocean. It was the house's best feature, other than the deck, and Neil was proud of it. Again, he wondered about Cora's situation. She was grown and married, she probably had a nice life, a nice place to live. But then again, he didn't know that for a fact. He felt like a horrible person all of a sudden, thinking of the possibility of her struggling financially. Thinking of his daughter wanting or needing things that might not have been available to her. All while

Neil was sitting here in his beach house, drinking coffee on his damn deck.

He rubbed the back of his neck and walked toward the front door just as someone rang the bell. He could see the figure of a woman on the other side of the frosted glass, and he took a deep breath as he reached for the handle and pulled it open.

But when he looked up, his stomach dropped. It wasn't Allison like he'd been expecting. Like he'd been bracing himself for.

It was his mother.

She stood on the stoop, her normally perfectly styled hair windblown from her short walk from her Mercedes. She smiled, but there was a look in her eyes that made his chest tighten.

"Mom?" he asked. "What are you doing here?"

She and his dad spent their winters at their house in Eugene. It was rare, but not unheard of, that they'd come to Christmas Bay to spend a weekend at their summer place. Neil had always been embarrassed by that. By the fact that they had a winter place and a summer place, when so many people didn't have a place at all.

"Can I come in?" she asked. "It's so cold out here." She wore a fitted suede jacket with a faux fur collar that had a sparkly Christmas tree pin on it. The ocean mist was sticking to the material like a magnet. As long as they'd been here, his mother had never figured out how to dress for the Oregon Coast.

"Of course," he said. "Come in."

She stepped inside, and he put an arm around her. She leaned into him for a second, and then moved away to unbutton her jacket.

"Remind me to give this thing to Goodwill. It's not rainproof."

He smiled as she shrugged it off. Then took it from her and hung it by the door.

She looked around. He knew she didn't think he was maximizing the small space, and had offered to hire a decorator when he'd moved in, which he'd refused. But she didn't say anything like she usually did. She had bigger fish to fry.

"Can I get you some coffee?" he asked. "Or tea?"

"Tea would be lovely. Thank you. Are you going to put a tree up?"

He walked over to the stove to put the teapot on, glancing at her over his shoulder. She was perched on the edge of the sofa, looking like she might fall off at any moment. His mom had always been thin, watching her weight to an almost obsessive degree. But he thought she looked fragile today. He worried about her. Always going to the gym, always trying the latest diet. Always trying to keep up with the Joneses. It couldn't be a happy place to be. But since when was he an expert on happiness?

"I'm going up to cut one in a few days," he said. "I never got around to it last year."

The truth was, he didn't get around to it most years, which was kind of depressing when he thought about it. As much as he loved it, his house seemed a little cold, a little empty over the holidays, so he spent most of his time at the fire station, which had two Christmas trees and an old fire truck parked out front that was strung with multicolored lights, courtesy of the captain's wife. She decorated everything, and brought pumpkin bread in on the weekends. Overall, it was a nicer place to be over Christmas than his bachelor pad.

The teapot began whistling, and he poured his mom a cup of vanilla chai.

Walking back over, he sat down beside her and handed her the mug. "Careful," he said. "It's hot."

She took it and stared down at the dark, steaming liquid, almost like she'd fallen into a trance. He waited a few seconds, then touched her knee.

"Mom?"

"Hmm?"

She didn't look up.

"Mom."

"Yes, honey."

And then she did look up, and there was obvious sadness in her eyes.

He frowned. She'd looked fragile before, but sitting here now, she reminded him of a bird. So slight, that one wrong move might snap a delicate wing.

"What's wrong?" he asked.

She took a deep breath, closing her eyes for a long moment. He felt a wave of guilt. This could be about anything, but it was probably about Mary, and he knew he shouldn't have left her the way he had the other night. With that bomb being dropped. She'd deserved a phone call at the very least, but he'd been so absorbed in his own thoughts and feelings, that it hadn't even occurred to him until just now.

"I'm a grandmother," she said.

He nodded, watching her. This wasn't the neat and tidy marriage and grandbaby that she'd been expecting someday. It was messy, it was complicated. Mostly, it was a shock that had left them both reeling.

"What are you going to do, Neil?" she asked matter-of-factly.

Leaning back on the couch, he scrubbed his hands over his face. His jaw stubbly and unshaven.

"I don't know," he said. "I really don't."

"You're going to have to help financially."

"Of course."

"Are you going to meet her?"

"Yes."

"When?"

"Soon, I think."

"What's her name?" she asked, looking at him intently.

"Mary."

She let that settle, then nodded. "How old is she?"

"Eleven."

"Eleven… That'd be about right. Cora would have been…" Her voice trailed off as she connected the dots. Probably realizing in hindsight what a scandal it would have been among their friends to have their son become a father so young.

"Why?" she continued, her voice growing chilly. "Why didn't she tell you?"

He took a deep breath, knowing that no matter what he said, it wasn't going to satisfy her. He knew this because he was still grappling with it himself, and this was after he'd talked to Cora, after he'd met with her face-to-face. He was still angry, but at least he could understand part of her decision-making process, whereas yesterday, he'd been unable to understand any of it. So he guessed that was progress.

"She was scared," he said. "She thought she was doing the right thing."

"Keeping a child from her father?"

"She was a kid herself, Mom."

"Yes, but she grew up. She could have told you a long time ago."

"But she didn't."

She pursed her lips. "No, she didn't."

They sat there for a second, the house quiet, the sound of the ocean waves muted through the windows.

After a moment, his mom rubbed her hands down her slacks, her gold bangles clinking together delicately. "How did you find out?" she asked.

"Mary tracked me down. She emailed me."

"So Cora never did tell you?"

"No. But we met yesterday. We talked."

She raised her brows. "You talked?"

"Yes."

"Well," she said slowly. "I have to say, you're handling this better than I would've expected."

He wondered what exactly she meant by that, but he could guess well enough. She thought he'd want to run from it. Maybe this had been Cora's line of thinking when she found out she was pregnant. Assuming she couldn't count on him. Expecting him to be in some kind of denial. He didn't think she would've been wrong to go there, although he liked to think he would have been better than that.

She shook her head. "I'm sorry, I'm just upset. I don't know what to think or how to feel."

"I get it."

"I have to be honest, Neil. I'm angry. I'm angry with her, and I'm angry with you."

He got up and walked over to the window, looking out at the water with his shoulders tight. There was a sailboat bouncing over the swells, its sail stark white against the deep blue water. It looked like a giant shark parting the waves, its fin the color of bleached bone.

Neil watched it, feeling angry too, although he wasn't

sure who he was angry at. His mother? She was just being honest, like she said. Maybe he was just angry at himself. He must've done a lot wrong for Cora to think she couldn't depend on him. They'd been young, sure. But that excuse wasn't going to cut it forever. Sooner or later, he was going to have to take a hard look at what had led to this. And how he could try to mend it, if it even *could* be mended.

"You should've known better," his mom said behind him. "We taught you to be careful, we taught you to be responsible."

He clenched his jaw, feeling a wave of heat move into his face. "Yes, I know. And I screwed up. Is that what you really want to say, Mom? That I'm not the perfect son you tried to raise?" Turning around, he fixed her with a hard look. "How much of this has to do with me, and how much of it has to do with Cora? Would you have felt this way if it had been some girl from the country club? What then?"

"That's not fair."

"Why? Because you did a pretty good job of letting me know how you felt about her from the beginning. She knew it. I sure as hell knew it."

"Well, we were right, weren't we?"

"Because she got pregnant? It takes two to tango."

She sighed. "It never would have worked, Neil. You were too different."

"That's true, we were. But who knows if it would have worked, because she didn't trust me, and she didn't trust my family. I didn't do anything to change that, and now I've got to live with it, but Cora isn't going away. She's always going to be the mother of my child. She's always going to be the mother of your grandchild. And if you and Dad want anything to do with Mary in the future, I'd sug-

gest seeing Cora for the woman she is, and not the woman
you wished she was."

Her expression grew stony, and for the first time in a
long time, she looked her age. She stood slowly, adjusting
her expensive black bag over her shoulder. "I'm not going
to sit here and be lectured by my own son."

She took her coat from the rack and draped it over her
arm, and he sighed.

"Mom," he said evenly. "I think you want to be a part
of her life. Am I right in thinking that?"

She didn't answer. Just watched him with barely contained fury. He'd hit a nerve. Which was fine, she'd hit
one a long time ago.

"All I'm saying is that you're going to have to open
your mind for that to happen. You're going to have to
open your heart."

"My mind is perfectly open. As for my heart, it's always
been vulnerable with you, Neil. When you're a parent, you
never stop worrying. I worry about your job, I worry about
your future. And now I'm worried about what this could
mean for you, for our family."

He frowned. "How so?"

"You don't know Cora now, just like you didn't know
her then. Maybe she wants something. Maybe that's why
this is all happening now."

He stared at her. "Mary reached out to me. Cora didn't."

"Don't be so naive."

"Are you saying this is some kind of bid for money? Is
that really what you're saying?"

She shrugged and looked down at her jacket, smoothing the material over her arm.

He laughed softly. "Well," he said. "If you were hoping

for a relationship with your granddaughter, I'd say you've got a long way to go, Mom."

"All I'm saying is that you need to be aware of the reality here. You want me to be openminded. Well, you should be keeping yours open, too."

With that, she opened the door, letting in the chilly wind with a gust, and then closed it firmly behind her. He watched her climb into her Mercedes and pull out of his driveway with the car's thin sports tires crunching on the gravel.

As she turned onto the sleepy coastal highway, he didn't like the feeling unfolding inside his chest. He didn't believe for a minute that money was any kind of motivating factor for Cora. If that was the case, she would've shown up a long time ago. For some reason, his parents always came back to money. If they were swayed by it, then everyone else must be, too. To Neil, it was an ugly outlook on life.

Still, he had to admit that like his mom said, he didn't know Cora anymore. What was he getting himself into by letting her back into his life so easily? Of course he was going to be responsible for his daughter, try to build some kind of relationship with her, but was it such a good idea to let himself be so open with her mother, too?

He rubbed his jaw. No, he didn't think this had anything to do with money. But other than that, he wasn't sure about anything. Least of all, his feelings for a woman he'd once been in love with. How did he feel about her now? It was complicated.

But he knew his mother had succeeded in planting a seed, like she so often did.

He was going to have to be realistic here. And keep Cora Sawyer at arm's length.

Chapter Five

Cora hung up the phone and stared out the window, feeling dazed. She'd just survived talking to Neil again, which was saying something, considering how hard her heart had been beating the entire time. Her head was dizzy, and she took a deep breath to try to center herself.

"Everything okay?" Poppy asked from across the hardware store, a worried expression on her face.

Cora looked over at her cousin and forced a smile. They'd come over to talk to Justin Frost, Poppy's boyfriend, who was also the owner of Brother's Hardware, about his plans for the window decorating contest that the chamber of commerce was sponsoring. Actually, it was Mary who'd wanted to come over. Since his shop was right across from the antique shop, she considered him direct competition. She didn't plan on being outdone by anything Justin might have in mind.

"I'm fine," she said, hoping Poppy would take that at face value, since she couldn't exactly talk about this in front of Mary.

She looked over at her daughter now, who was listening to Justin tell her about his decorating plans. Something that would involve a giant toolbox—naturally—with gifts overflowing from it.

But before he could go into detail, a customer walked in the door, bringing with him a blast of salty air. He immediately made a beeline for Justin with a question about drill bits.

Mary came over to Cora wearing a smug expression on her freckled face.

"Mom," she whispered. "We've *so* got this. Justin's doing a *toolbox* window."

"What's wrong with that?"

"Well, nothing, I guess. If you're a dude. Who likes tools."

"This is a hardware store, honey. That's kind of his thing."

"Yeah, I know, but *tools*? Over our window?"

Cora frowned. "I forget. Which Harry are we doing again?"

Mary had still been in the decision-making process the last time Cora had checked. She was taking this very seriously. She'd been polling the tourists who came into the antique shop about which window they'd like to see more—one dedicated to Harry Styles, or Harry Potter. So far the two Harrys were in a dead heat.

Mary frowned. "I'm not sure. I can't decide, but I think either one of them will be good. Don't you?"

"Oh yes. Either one."

"But I'd better decide pretty soon because Justin is going to be putting his window up next week."

"What about Frances?" Cora asked. "What kind of window is she doing?"

Mary sighed. The Coastal Sweets window had been the grand champion two years running. "Candy. That's gonna be hard to beat."

"True. But if anyone can do it, you can."

Mary looked happy at that. She put her hands in her

hoodie pockets and glanced at Justin. He was currently explaining the ins and outs of drill bits to the man standing in front of him.

"Justin's nice," Mary said. "He and Aunt Poppy are cute together."

Cora nodded. They were cute together. In fact, Cora hadn't seen Poppy this happy in ages.

"If we win the contest," Mary said thoughtfully, "what do you think about giving the money to the animal shelter? Justin said that's what he's going to do with it if he wins. Or maybe we could give it to that summer camp that Frances's daughter runs. The one for kids who've gotten in trouble."

Cora reached out and tucked a strand of Mary's silky blond hair behind her ear. She was such a good girl. It was just like her to be most excited about where she was going to donate the money if *Earl's Antiques* happened to win.

"I think that's a wonderful idea," she said.

"Frances was telling me about it last week. She said a lot of those kids don't have parents. They're foster kids."

Cora nodded. Frances had Alzheimer's, and her three grown foster daughters had come home to help her run her candy shop. They were such a loving family, and this wasn't the first time that Mary had mentioned them. Cora knew she was taken with how close they were. With the bond they shared. Mary had always wanted a sibling, but it just hadn't happened, even though Cora had hoped for another baby, too.

Mary looked down at her Skechers for a minute, her brows furrowed. When she looked back up again, she wore that familiar expression Cora had come to recognize over the last few days. Serious. Joltingly mature for her eleven-year-old features.

"I know you were talking to Neil," Mary said. "Just now."

It was strange to hear her refer to her dad as Neil. Like a stranger might. But that's what she was to Neil, whether she was blood related or not. Another reminder that this journey wasn't going to be easy. It was going to be full of ups and downs, and they'd just taken the very first step onto that uncertain path.

"I was," Cora said. "I didn't know you'd heard."

"What did he say?"

Cora licked her lips. "He wants to meet you, honey. When you're ready."

"He does?"

Mary sounded surprised. Like she'd been preparing herself for something else, and that broke Cora's heart. But then again, she'd been preparing herself, too.

"Where?" Mary asked quickly. "When?"

"Well, he said the fire department is having their open house tomorrow night. He thought you might like to see the fire trucks up close. It's a Christmas potluck kind of thing, the whole town usually goes."

Mary smiled. Then nodded. "Okay."

"You'd like that? I wasn't sure if you'd want to meet him with a lot of other people around."

"No, I think I'd like that better. It won't be as weird."

It was true. Cora thought the hustle and bustle of the potluck might take some of the pressure off—make the whole thing less awkward. But in the end, who knew. She just hoped it would go okay. She'd had a knot in her stomach since getting off the phone with Neil. He hadn't sounded as chilly today, but he hadn't been warm, either. She wondered how he'd be with Mary—wondered if he'd pull her into a hug, or would keep her at a safe distance at first. Or maybe he'd keep her at a safe distance forever. The whole thing was a giant question mark.

"Okay," she said. "So I'll let him know that we'll be there tomorrow. And if you change your mind and don't feel ready for this, just tell me, okay? We can take it slow. There's no hurry. I know he feels the same way, he doesn't want to rush you."

Mary considered this for a minute, then shook her head. "No, I'm ready. And, Mom?"

"Yes, honey?"

"What do you think Dad would've thought about Neil? Do you think he would've liked him?"

Cora frowned. It was an interesting question. Max and Neil had been so different. In fact, the safety Max had represented had been one of the things that had drawn Cora to him at first. When Neil had been all about excitement and risk, Max had been an anchor for her. She really didn't know if they would've liked each other. But Max had a big heart, and the Neil she remembered had one, too. Maybe that would've been enough. Maybe it wouldn't have.

But Mary was obviously looking for some kind of permission to like Neil, maybe feeling guilty about having another father in her life, whether it was a close relationship or not. She'd adored Max, and Cora knew she'd always be fiercely loyal to his memory.

"I'm not sure," she said, "but I *do* know that your dad loved you. And Neil is going to love you, too. They would have shared that, and that's the most important thing. You."

"Maybe…"

"Maybe, what?"

"Maybe Neil will love me."

Cora stepped forward and wrapped her daughter in a hug. She wished she could take this apprehension, this awful doubt away from her, but she understood it. Of course there was no guarantee how Neil would end up feeling in the long run.

They stood there for a long minute, with Cora's cheek against her daughter's hair. She was so lucky to have Mary. Every day she thanked the stars for aligning like they had, for giving her a little girl, who wasn't so little anymore, but would always be her baby.

"I'll ask him which Christmas window we should do," Mary said against her chest. "If he doesn't know who Harry Styles is, I'm out."

Cora laughed. Then hugged her daughter tighter, overwhelmed with love.

Neil stood looking at his reflection in the window of the firehouse, his chest tight with nerves. His uniform was starched, and his dark hair was a little shorter than usual. It was probably obvious that he'd just gotten it cut. In fact, he thought he looked like he was headed to his senior prom, but he'd wanted to look nice for his daughter. *His daughter...* He still couldn't believe it. He had a kid, and she was eleven, and he didn't even know what her favorite color was.

"Looking sharp, man," Jay said, walking up behind him. "Are you ready for this?" His friend slapped him on the back a little too hard. It left his shoulder stinging. Jay was like the abominable snowman—he didn't know his own strength.

Neil smiled, but his stomach felt a little sick. "Ready as I'll ever be."

"Cap wants to know what's wrong with you."

"What?"

"You're acting all nervous."

"Oh. I didn't know you could tell."

"You've just been quiet and fidgety. And a little weird."

Neil gave him a look. "What'd you tell him?"

"Nothing. You said not to say anything, so I didn't."

Neil had told Jay about Mary, but he was the only person he'd told. None of the other guys at the station knew who was coming tonight. They'd only ask a million questions, and he was anxious enough as it was.

"Okay," he said. "Thanks."

"You know I've got your back, dude. And if you want to sit down and talk about this over a beer or something, I'm here."

"I know. Thanks. I've just been preoccupied, I still can't believe it."

Jay smiled wide. "You're a *dad*, bro. How trippy is that?"

Suddenly Neil felt every bit his twenty-nine years. The word *trippy* didn't even begin to describe it.

"It's gonna be okay," Jay said. "Just be yourself. She's going to love you."

It was a sweet thing to say, but Neil wasn't altogether sure she *would* love him. She was a preteen. Kids that age could be complicated. Even if he knew how to be around kids of any age, which he didn't.

He reached up and straightened his badge in the window reflection, but it had already been straight. He'd just made it crooked. Frowning, he sighed and looked at his watch. Almost six. Cora said she'd be there at six. Only a minute and thirty seconds to go.

"Dude," Jay said. "You've got to relax. If you go out there like this, you're gonna freak her out."

He frowned, turning to his friend. "It's that noticeable?"

"Yes." Jay laughed.

"Are there a lot of people out there already?"

"Oh yeah. You know how these things go. People love to see their tax dollars at work, and we get to show off. Win-win."

Neil smiled. It was true, it was fun shining up the trucks and the station. Most people liked firefighters, so it really was a good time. Well, mostly it was a good time. When you weren't meeting your kid for the very first time.

"I'm not sure I've ever been this damn nervous," he said. "I feel like I'm going to be sick."

"You can call Cora and tell her you need to reschedule. That you need more time because you're going to barf. Better to reschedule than to barf all over your daughter."

Jay said this matter-of-factly, with a shrug that made Neil laugh, despite everything. No, he couldn't call Cora. That would be what she'd expect of him, and he had no intention of proving her right.

"No," he said. "I'm ready. Let's go."

"Are you sure?"

"I'm sure."

Jay nodded and headed through the door that led to the garage where the engines were on display, and all the food was set out.

Neil followed, forcing himself to breathe easy. Sure enough, the station was packed. Full of people laughing and talking, and getting the grand tour. The entire garage smelled like barbecue—the guys had been grilling out back for the last hour or so. There were warm cookies and various pastries set out on Christmas plates, courtesy of some of the wives who always baked for the open houses. Multicolored Christmas lights hung from the ceiling, and a huge Douglas fir stood by the door that led inside the living area. It was all decked out in popcorn strings and paper cutouts of fire trucks, decorated by Christmas Bay

Elementary's first grade class. The space was warm and welcoming, and Neil was proud of it. Happy that the citizens of Christmas Bay seemed proud of it, too. But he was too nervous to pay much attention beyond that.

Slowing to a stop in the middle of the garage, he scanned the space for Cora. And a little girl that he wouldn't recognize if he ran right into her.

And then he saw them. Standing on the far end of the garage, each holding a cookie and a drink. Cora looked beautiful. She also looked as nervous as he felt. Her eyes were wide and dark, and he could imagine that the hand holding that drink might be shaking a little.

His gaze shifted to the little girl beside her. Tall, and painfully thin, she had a pretty face with freckles scattered across her slightly upturned nose. Neil's heart lurched. She looked like Cora. And she looked like him, too. Her coloring wasn't his, but the shape of her face was, and for a second, it was like looking into some strange kind of mirror. One where his reflection had morphed into something dreamlike.

He watched her, his chest so tight that it was hard to breathe.

And then their gazes, both Mary's and Cora's, found his. It was like time had slowed to a crawl, and there was nobody else inside the station but the three of them. This strange, unexpected family.

After a few seconds, Neil cleared his throat and took a step forward. And then another, and another, until he found himself across the garage, and just a few feet from his daughter. He stopped then, and looked down at her. This beautiful child that he didn't know.

Cora put her arm around her. She looked scared to death.

"Mary," Cora said. "This is your biological father. Neil Prescott. Neil, this is Mary."

The little girl stared up at him, her eyes impossibly big. Neil wanted to say something, anything, but he was frozen there for a painful moment, trying to get his mind wrapped around this for the thousandth time. He had a daughter. Her name was Mary. She was waiting for him to speak.

Finally, he stepped forward, and then extended his hand to her. He didn't know if he should hug her or not. He wasn't sure what she'd want, if she'd want to be touched at all. So a handshake seemed safe, if a little formal. He really had no idea what he was doing, and it showed.

"Hi there, Mary," he said, his voice low. The room was humming with people, with activity, but it still felt like it was just the three of them. It was maybe the most intimate feeling that he'd ever experienced. Almost like an out-of-body thing, where he was watching it all unfold from across the station.

Slowly, she put her hand in his. It was small, slender. A little clammy. But she shook his firmly, surprising him. She didn't look stronger than a sparrow, but looks were deceiving. He felt some steel in that handshake, and he was suddenly proud. Someone had taught her that—how to shake hands with confidence. He wondered if that had been her stepdad. He wondered where the guy was, if he and Cora were still together, and if they were, why he hadn't come with them.

"It's nice to meet you," she said.

Again, he felt an unmistakable swell of pride. She was polite, well-mannered. And before he could help it, he thought of how pleased his parents would be about that. She'd been brought up well.

"It's nice to meet you, too," he said.

She took her hand away and leaned into her mother's

side again. But those wide eyes never left his. They were pretty, the color of the ocean.

Cora cleared her throat. "Mary's been looking forward to meeting you. I don't think we've ever been this close to a firetruck, have we, honey?"

Mary shook her head.

"Well, I can show you around if you want. You can even climb inside one of the engines. Look around." Neil felt like he was trying too hard, but he couldn't help it. All of a sudden, he was desperate for her to like him. To trust him. Which was ridiculous, really. She wasn't going to be comfortable with him right off the bat, at least that was what her current expression said. The kid standing in front of him looked shy and withdrawn. It made him angry at Cora all over again. She hadn't had any right to keep Mary from him, no right at all.

"What do you say, sweetie?" Cora asked her. "Want to walk around a bit?"

Mary looked up at her. "Will you come too, Mom?" she asked quietly.

"Of course."

Neil smiled, but his chest still felt uncomfortably tight, his throat even tighter.

He began showing them around, starting with the trucks. He explained how everything worked, what happened when they got a call, his schedule at the station, how they put structure fires out. Mary listened attentively, politely, but he still felt like he was interviewing for a job. If he was interesting enough, maybe she'd want to keep him.

Cora walked quietly beside them, and he could tell she was trying to hang back a little to give them both some time to connect. But there was only so much she could do under the circumstances. Just another reminder of how long this might take. How difficult it could end up being.

"Do you have a dog?" Mary asked, looking up at him. "Like a Dalmatian or something?"

"No Dalmatian, but my buddy Rob brought his bulldog. His name is Truman. I think he's inside the kitchen begging for scraps. He's really sweet if you want to go in there and meet him."

She immediately perked up at this. "We have a dog. Her name is Roo. She's gigantic."

"She is," Cora agreed. "But she still manages to sleep with Mary under the covers. All one hundred pounds of her."

Neil laughed. "That's impressive. How is there room for you in the same bed?"

"There isn't," Cora said.

"*Mom.* There is, too. We just have to be squished a little."

"Or a lot."

Mary pulled away and waved at her mother. "Be right back!"

And then she was off, heading into the kitchen area where Truman would probably try to lick her to death.

Cora watched her go, then turned to Neil with a smile. "She loves dogs."

"Truman loves kids. It'll be a match made in heaven."

"You were really good with her, Neil. She likes you, I can tell."

He put his hands in his pockets and looked down at her. Remembering when she was his girlfriend. Remembering what it was like to kiss her. She was so familiar standing there, that it was strange not having her in his arms. But she was someone else's now. She hadn't been his for a very long time.

"You've done well with her," he said quietly.

They were standing in the corner of the station garage, away from most of the people milling about. The light from the big Christmas tree played on Cora's features, making her blond hair almost glow. She was lovely. And right then he almost forgot how angry he'd been at her, how confused she'd made him. All he could really remember was how much he'd loved her back then. He thought he would've done anything for Cora. Anything but stick around, that is. And again, he wondered what he would have done if she'd told him she was pregnant at seventeen. What the hell would he have done? He didn't know. And that was the truth.

"Thank you for that," she said. She glanced down when she said it, like she might not be able to look him in the eyes. He wondered why. Wondered what she was feeling right then, and if it was anything close to what he was feeling. Overwhelmed with memories—the good ones and the bad ones.

"But I really can't take all the credit," she continued. "Max had a lot to do with it."

Max. This must be her husband. Neil was surprised at the sudden pang in his stomach at the mention of the other man's name. Something that felt a lot like jealousy. But that was absurd. He wasn't a jealous person. Still, there was no denying the feeling, and he swallowed hard, looking at her.

"What's he like?" he asked, his voice flat. "This guy? He's a good dad?"

Cora shifted on her feet. She wore a little snowman pin on her red sweater that sparkled underneath the station lighting.

"He was a very good dad," she said. "The best."

Neil saw her pulse flutter in that hollow spot at the base of her throat. *Was*. The word was heavy with meaning. Heavy with emotion, he could see it etched all over her face.

"You're divorced?" he asked.

She pulled in a breath. Waited a beat before answering. "No. Max passed away last spring. Cancer."

Neil let the words settle. For some stupid reason, he hadn't thought of anything but a separation. Cora was too young to be a widow. But now the puzzle pieces slid slowly, perfectly into place. The sad expression in her eyes. The way Mary had reached out... Of course. She was grieving the loss of her father, and more curious than ever about her biological one.

He watched Cora closely, unsure of what to say. Ashamed that he'd felt jealous of this poor guy, and more confused now than ever.

"I'm sorry, Cora."

"It's still hard to talk about. I know that's normal, that it'll take time, but the pain comes in waves. It's overwhelming sometimes."

"Of course it is."

"But, yes." She looked up at him then, and her eyes were misty. "He was a good dad."

"Did he know about me?" Neil asked. "About Mary?"

She nodded. "Yes. He always knew."

He was glad of that at least. Glad that nobody else had been kept in the dark. At this point, the thought of that just seemed too much, too cruel. Neil had always believed in being honest to a fault, and this was why. Lies only ended up hurting people in the end. No matter why they were told, or who they were meant to protect.

"Is that why Mary wanted to meet me?" he asked. "This must be very hard for her. I can't even imagine."

"She's always been curious about you. I wasn't expecting her to reach out like this out of the blue. I'm so sorry, Neil. I didn't mean for you to be hurt. I didn't mean for..." She let her voice trail off as tears filled her eyes.

He *was* hurt. And he was angry. And he was a whole host of other things, too. But the sight of her crying was proving to be more than he could comfortably take.

Without thinking about it, without stopping to consider whether it was a good idea or not, he reached out to pull her into a hug. Her body was stiff for a second, and then she relaxed into his chest. She lay her cheek there and he lowered his chin to the top of her head. It stirred something inside of him, some long forgotten memory of dancing with her in the beams of his truck's headlights at the river. The classic rock pouring from his stereo, the truck doors wide-open, the stars twinkling overhead. Those had been the best times of Neil's life. He'd been all over the world, done all kinds of crazy things, but those days with Cora had filled him with a passion that he'd never known before or since.

He breathed in the fruity scent of her hair and wondered briefly if that's why he'd spent the last decade trying to find ways to get his heart pounding. Maybe he'd been trying to replicate that feeling he'd had with Cora somehow. Maybe he'd been trying to find it any way he could.

He stood there holding her, feeling her body press softly into his, her curves and angles fitting just right, and it was like no time had passed at all. He felt seventeen again. And like his heart might beat right out of his chest if he wasn't careful.

"Mom?"

He looked down to see Mary staring up at them. She looked confused. Her brows were knitted together, and her eyes were dark.

Cora pushed quickly away like they'd been caught making out. He couldn't blame her—that was kind of how he felt, too. She wiped her eyes and smiled down at Mary a little too cheerfully.

"Hi, honey."

"What are you doing?"

"I was just telling Neil about your dad, and I got sad all of a sudden."

Mary looked at him skeptically, and for the first time he wondered how she'd feel about Cora talking to him at all, much less hugging him. She'd naturally be protective of her stepfather, especially now. He took a step back, putting some distance between him and Cora, as if that would fix it.

"I'm really sorry about your dad, Mary," Neil said.

She gave him what he thought was a brave smile.

"Thank you."

There was an awkward silence for a few seconds and then he cleared his throat. "How was Truman?"

She smiled wider. "He was good. He was super slobbery."

"Yeah, it's pretty gross."

"And he's *fat*."

"Yes. I don't know what Rob feeds him, but he gets too much of it."

"Do you have a dog?" she asked. "At home?"

He'd always wanted a dog, but he worked all the time, and when he wasn't working, he was traveling. He'd never thought it would be fair to one, so he'd held off. Maybe someday.

"No," he said. "But my parents used to have a poodle named Agatha. She could stand on her hind legs and turn in a circle."

Mary laughed.

"Maybe you'll get to meet them sometime soon," he said. And then wished he hadn't, because that would mean bringing his parents into the equation, and he wasn't sure he was ready for that yet. He wasn't sure Mary was ready, either. Cora sure as hell wouldn't be ready for it.

"My grandparents?" Mary asked, her face brightening. "Do they want to meet me?"

Neil hadn't gotten that far with his parents. He hadn't even talked to his dad yet, his mom had broken the news. What would *that* conversation look like? But as disapproving as he knew they'd be, they would never be unkind to Mary. They'd save all their judgment for him and Cora.

"Of course," he said, feeling like he'd painted himself into a corner. All he could hope for was that he could hold this meeting off for as long as possible. At least until he and Mary got to know each other. And until Cora had a chance to get used to the idea of seeing them again.

Cora put an arm around Mary, who'd just finished a sugar cookie. She had a few crumbs on her chin, making her look pretty adorable. But he was biased already.

"What happens now?" Mary asked. "When do we get to see you again?"

Neil smiled. She was starting to come out of her shell a little, which made him feel better. He hadn't known how worried he'd been that she wouldn't like him until right then. Until she'd looked up with that sweet expression on her face, and those crumbs on her chin.

He let his gaze settle on Cora. "What are you comfortable with?"

"Whatever you and Mary want."

He looked back down at Mary. "What if we plan on going to the park next week? You can bring your dog."

"Yeah! You'll like her."

"I'm sure I will."

"And then maybe I can meet my grandma and grandpa."

His gut tightened. "Yeah…"

Cora was watching him closely. She had to be thinking the same thing he was. Suddenly, he wanted to sit down and talk to her, just the two of them. Spend some time with her alone. There was so much he didn't know about her, about Mary. About their lives in general. He wanted to see baby pictures of his daughter. He wanted to know when she'd taken her first steps, what her first words were. And he wanted to know how Cora had managed, if she'd struggled, if she'd ever regretted keeping this secret from him. If she'd ever wanted to tell him before this, or if she'd kept tabs on him throughout the years.

He guessed it was a morbid kind of curiosity, because in the end it didn't really matter. He knew finding the answers to some of the things he wondered about might make him even more unsettled, but it didn't matter. He still wanted to know. If felt like he was standing outside looking in through a foggy window at a family just beyond his reach. He felt disconnected. He felt like an outsider, and he guessed that was exactly what he was.

"Neil," Cora said quietly. "Are you okay?"

"Fine. Just thinking."

"About?"

He buried his hands further into his pockets, feeling his shoulder muscles tighten. Feeling his entire body tense. The fact that he wanted to be alone with Cora wasn't necessarily a good thing. Even if he was convinced it was just so they could talk, it was time alone with her, and that would probably be asking for trouble. He was still attracted to her, there was no use denying that part. No matter how angry he was at her, holding her just now had woken something inside of him. Something that had never really died, but had only been slumbering for the past twelve years.

Cora frowned, watching him. Then looked down at Mary. "Honey, can you go get me a cookie? That one you had looked really good."

"Sure, Mom."

Mary walked over to the dessert table, and started filling up a small plate.

Cora looked back at him. "You're worried about your parents, aren't you?"

He knew she'd be apprehensive about that. Of course she would be. But he was glad she hadn't been able to tell what he was really thinking right then, which was how kissable her lips looked after she'd just licked them.

He swallowed hard. "You know they've always been difficult."

She nodded.

"This is going to be hard for them to accept," he continued. "I wish I could say they'll get over it and move on, but honestly, it might be a little rocky at first. We have a complicated relationship, and they don't love a lot of the choices I've made. It's been a wedge between us for a long time. But they'd never take anything out on Mary. I think they'll love her right away, it's impossible not to."

"But me," Cora said evenly. "They're going to have a problem with me."

"They're not perfect, Cora," he said. "But I can promise you it won't be like it was back then. I won't let it be."

She gave him a small smile. A sad smile. "They'll feel the way they feel. Nothing you do is going to change that."

It was true. But it was hard for him to admit that it was hopeless, this mindset of theirs when it came to certain things. And Mary would be one of those things. Cora was definitely one of those things.

"I think we need to sit down and talk," he said. "I think we need to catch up. To meet each other where we are, and that might take some time. But we'll figure it out."

She gazed up at him, her eyes soft. And nodded.

"Neil?"

They both turned at the sound of the female voice behind them. Sharp, cutting. Familiar.

Neil's gut sank when he saw who it was.

And she had eyes only for Cora.

Chapter Six

Cora smiled at the other woman—dark hair, tall, slender and absolutely stunning. But it wasn't easy because of the expression on her face. She looked almost hostile, which was unsettling.

Mary walked back over and handed her a sugar cookie from her plate. Then looked curiously up at the woman Neil had just called Allison. He didn't seem thrilled. In fact, the whole thing felt incredibly awkward. Cora thought she was probably an ex-girlfriend, or even a current girlfriend, judging by her body language.

"Jay told me where you were," she said, still looking at Cora. "I wanted to come over and say hi. Who's this?"

Neil smiled thinly. "Allison, this is Cora and Mary. Cora is…"

It was obvious that he didn't know how to finish that sentence. Allison was clearly possessive, no matter what her relationship to Neil was, and that was just another reminder for Cora that she didn't know anything about his life. She didn't even know what his relationship status was, which mattered, because if Mary was going to be introduced into the mix, it was going to need to be handled with care.

She stepped forward and held out her hand. "I'm an old

friend from high school," she said evenly. "Mary and I moved to town last spring, and Neil and I were just catching up. It's nice to meet you."

After a few seconds, Allison offered her hand and shook Cora's lukewarmly. "Nice to meet you, too," she said. And then faced Neil, almost turning her back on Cora completely. "Can I talk to you for a minute?"

He glanced at Cora, and then nodded.

They walked over to the other side of the fire station where Allison began saying something with a lot of hand gestures. Cora forced herself to look away.

"Who's *that*?" Mary asked, wrinkling her nose.

"I'm not sure."

"She's rude."

"Well, I think she might like Neil."

"She's still rude."

"I don't think she liked that I was talking to him."

"Gross. That's a red flag, Mom."

Cora looked down at her. Mary was a huge fan of podcasts, and was currently listening to one that gave relationship advice. Red flags were her favorite subject. Red flags for friendship, red flags for marriage, red flags in general. Cora was learning a lot about red flags, and the fact that she apparently missed a ton of them.

"Do tell," she said dryly.

"Well, you know," Mary said. "She's like, jealous. And that's bad. That means she might be insecure and stuff."

"Maybe. We don't know her. Maybe we should give her some grace."

"You're nicer than I am."

"Not nicer, I just know how it is to like someone and be worried they don't like you back."

Mary frowned. "Who did you like that didn't like you back? Not Dad."

"No, not your dad."

"Neil?"

Cora shifted on her feet. "Yes. Neil. I'm just saying, honey, it's not always easy. Sometimes love makes you do and say things that you normally wouldn't."

Mary seemed to consider this. "You loved him?"

"I did."

"And he didn't love you back?"

"It's not that he didn't love me back. It's that we were really young, and we didn't know what we wanted yet. We didn't know how to give and take, and it takes a lot of that to make a relationship work."

Mary frowned, watching Neil and Allison across the station. "I guess."

Cora looked over at them too, feeling tired all of a sudden. The adrenaline and nervousness from before was starting to wear off, leaving her worn out. She wondered if Mary felt the same way, although, by the looks of it, she still had energy to spare. She was munching on another cookie with a twinkle in her eyes.

"I wonder if she's his girlfriend," she said. "Or if she just *wants* to be his girlfriend."

"I'm not sure."

"I wonder if she knows about me."

It was a fair question. If Allison didn't know yet, Cora assumed she wasn't going to be super happy with the information.

"Red flag," Mary murmured, her cheeks bulging with sugar cookie. "I'm telling you."

Sure enough, after another few seconds, Allison threw

her hands up in the air and stormed off. Neil stood there watching her go, his face an interesting shade of red.

"Uh-oh," Mary said. "He doesn't look happy."

"No."

When he began making his way back through the crowded fire station his jaw was set. Cora could see it flexing from where she stood.

"I'm sorry about that," he said, stopping in front of them. "We have some history."

"What kind of history?" Mary asked.

"Mary, that's none of our business."

"It's okay," Neil said. "We dated for a while. It didn't work out."

"Why not?" Mary asked.

Cora bit her cheek. Mary's age was never more apparent than it was right now. Her filter wasn't fully developed yet, and neither was her ability to read the room. Neil looked supremely uncomfortable. But to his credit, he smiled down at her, obviously not wanting to shut her down.

"There were a few things. She didn't like my hobbies, that was one thing. She thought they were too dangerous."

Mary chewed her cookie thoughtfully. "What kind of hobbies?"

Cora waited. This sounded familiar. She'd hated those hobbies, too. But she'd also loved Neil's sense of adventure at the same time. She'd never been able to balance that admiration with the worry of losing him to that adventure. And she'd only been seventeen. She couldn't imagine how a grown woman would feel, a grown woman who might be ready to take the next step and settle down. It would be completely different with a family in the mix.

Neil looked over at her, his jaw bunching, before looking back down at Mary. "I skydive some."

"You *skydive*?"

He nodded.

"What else?"

"I white water raft, climb, cliff dive. Those kinds of things."

Mary's mouth fell open. "Wow. So she said you can't do that anymore?"

"She never said it like that. It was just implied. But we stopped dating, so it's a moot point, anyway."

Mary frowned. "What does 'moot point' mean?"

"It means it doesn't matter."

Cora felt her stomach turn. But it did matter. Mary was just now being introduced to her father. He was going to be in her life, that much was obvious. Which was a wonderful thing, but it could also be a double-edged sword. Cora wanted to protect her daughter from more pain, more loss. And what was it going to look like having a father play with fate like that? She knew it was impossible to keep Mary in a bubble, shielded from all of life's pain, but having a dad who took the kinds of risks he did seemed to go against the laws of common-sense parenting. Some people wouldn't agree with that, but that's how she saw it. And all of a sudden, she empathized with Allison, who might've had a good reason to leave in a huff after all.

"So," Neil said. "Should we make a date for the park? And I can meet this giant dog of yours?"

Mary grinned.

And Cora braced herself. She'd only been in Neil's orbit for less than a week, and it seemed like they were falling right back to where they'd been all those years ago. With the same issues between them.

She just hoped heartache wouldn't end up being one of them.

* * *

Several days later, Neil was stepping inside the still-smoldering doorway of an abandoned shed on the edge of town, his movements feeling exaggerated inside his bulky turnout gear. As far as structure fires went, this one was about as small as he could hope for. No people involved, and that was a very good thing. Or at least, that was the information Dispatch had given them on the way to the call.

But as he narrowed his eyes through the thin smoke, he saw a small, dark shape in the corner. An animal of some kind. The fire was out, but the air inside the shed was hot, and whatever it was didn't look alive.

Turning to Jay, he pointed with a gloved finger, breathing methodically through his oxygen mask. In, out...in, out... It was the soundtrack of his work life, the breaths he took inside his facepiece.

Jay nodded, only his eyes visible inside his own gear.

Neil turned back to the shape and walked toward it, careful to keep an eye on the integrity of the walls around him. When he reached it, he saw that it was a tiny kitten, still as a sack of sugar. It was impossible to tell if it was black, or if the soot from the fire was making it look black. Or worse, if its fur was singed from the fire itself.

Neil bent down to pick it up, its little body limp in his hand. He took another look around and motioned to Jay that he was stepping outside again.

The coastal sun had broken through the mist about half an hour ago, and the morning was bright and calm, with only the smoke from the shed marring the robin's-egg sky.

He jumped over hoses and gear, and jogged to the firetruck where they kept a small oxygen mask meant for reviving dogs and cats. They were lucky to have it, they were hard to come by, and this one had been donated by an animal-loving Christmas Bay citizen last year.

Laying the kitten down on the concrete, he took off his helmet and facepiece, the air cool on his sweaty skin.

"What do we have here?" the captain asked, walking up behind him.

"I don't know if it's alive," Neil said, pulling his gloves off. "But I'm gonna give it a few puffs, and see if I can get it breathing again."

He got the oxygen mask and tank out of the truck, and then came back to kneel down next to the kitten. He lifted its head gently and put the mask over its tiny face. Its body was hot to the touch, and there was some singed fur, but it didn't look too badly burned. At this point, smoke inhalation was probably going to be its biggest problem.

"Cap, can you hand me that bottle of water over there?"

The captain nodded and handed it over. Neil unscrewed the top and poured the cool water over the kitten's little body. Its face was still firmly inside the mask, and Neil began massaging the water into its fur.

"Come on, little guy," he said. "You can do it."

By this time, there was a small crowd gathered around him. A few neighbors watching from a safe distance, and a couple of his firefighter buddies, who'd come over to see what was going on.

Jay knelt down next to him and took his helmet off. "Aww. Poor little dude. Probably feral. The lady across the street says there's a colony around here, thinks the mama cat had her babies in the shed a few weeks ago."

Neil kept massaging its tiny body. It definitely wasn't any older than a few weeks. Would probably need to be bottle-fed, if it even made it.

"Did you see that?" Jay asked.

"See what?"

"It moved. Its paw moved. Keep doing what you're doing, dude, I think it might be working."

Neil leaned closer, the smell of the fire and smoke and singed cat fur sharp in his nose. Sweat trickled down his temples. He was barely aware of the people across the street, some of whom were taking pictures and video now. Mostly he was focused on the little life in his hands struggling to come back. He could feel some of the kitten's energy in his fingertips now. Tiny but mighty.

Neil had seen a lot of terrible things in his career. A lot of people who hadn't made it. Not only in fires, but in car accidents, drownings, falls—all kinds of things. It was hard to accept not being able to save someone, or something, when that was his most important purpose as a first responder. On the occasions when he was able to bring a life back that had been teetering on the edge, well... It didn't matter how small that life was. It counted. They all counted. And as he leaned close to the kitten whose paw had indeed just moved, he said a prayer that it would make it.

Slowly, gently, he took the oxygen mask away from the tiny whiskered face, and rubbed the kitten's ears and shoulders. Trying to get the blood flowing. Trying to get it to rally.

And then, it opened its eyes. Gold, like the winter sun overhead. Neil held his breath until, miraculously, the kitten took one of its own.

Jay slapped him on the back. "Right on!"

The kitten mewed. Surprisingly loud. Its lungs were working after all.

Neil picked it up, its black fur spiked with water. It

looked like a drowned rat. He cradled it in his arms, and its little body nearly disappeared in his turnouts.

Cheers and whistles erupted from across the street, and he looked up and smiled, finally aware of the crowd watching.

The captain bent down and patted him on the shoulder. "Well done, Prescott. Hope you're ready to go viral. This will probably be all over the socials in a few hours."

He laughed, rubbing the kitten's singed ears.

"It's okay," the captain continued, looking over at the crowd with a friendly wave. "Makes us look good. You don't already have a cat, do you?"

"No, sir. I'm not keeping it. I'll drop it off at the vet, they'll contact a rescue for us." Neil looked down at the kitten that was beginning to purr hoarsely. The ends of its whiskers were singed off. It gave it a funny bald look that tugged on his heartstrings.

"Right," the captain said with a knowing grin. "I think that cat has found his new dad."

Cora handed the lady in the pink knit hat and even pinker puffy jacket her bag with *Earl's Antiques* embossed in gold foil on the front. She'd bought her best friend a set of salt and pepper shakers from the fifties that she'd apparently been searching up and down the coast for. She was so thrilled to find them that she hadn't stopped grinning the entire time Cora had been ringing her up.

Tucking the bag underneath her arm, she looked around again. "This place is adorable."

"Thanks so much."

"We drove down here for the weekend. I've always wanted to poke around, but we never seem to have time. I'm so glad I came in, I'll definitely be back."

"Well, we'll be happy to have you. And let us know how your friend likes her salt and pepper shakers. Tag us on Instagram, we love to hear from our customers."

"Oh, I will. She has a lot of followers, they love this kind of thing. She's an antiques nut."

Cora smiled. "My kind of lady."

"And you'll be open over the holidays? I might be able to convince my husband to come back again. I have my eye on that desk over there for my mom."

"We'll be open until the Flotilla of Lights, and then closed until the New Year. My daughter is going to be out of school, so we're planning on spending some time together as a family."

She wasn't used to sharing personal information with their customers, but this woman was very sweet, and honestly, Cora was so excited for the time off with Mary. She and Poppy and Beau were going to kick off their vacation with Christmas Bay's favorite annual holiday tradition, the Flotilla of Lights—a parade of boats that chugged its way through the harbor while strung with lights and lanterns. The Flotilla had been around over one hundred years, and was a hallmark of the holiday season on the Oregon Coast. Mary was beside herself. Well, she was mostly excited for Christmas in general, but the Flotilla was a big deal.

"That sounds lovely," the woman said. "Merry Christmas to you."

"And to you. Drive safe."

Cora watched her walk out the door with her treasures tucked neatly under her arm. She'd been so busy this morning that she'd almost forgotten Neil's phone call earlier. Her heart was still fluttery, and she didn't want her heart to be fluttery where Neil was concerned. She wanted it to be realistic and matter-of-fact, and to beat normally when he said or did things that might be considered sweet.

But that was not what was happening. In fact, when he'd called earlier to tell her that he was going to have to change the plans they'd made to take Roo to the park this evening, her heart sank. For Mary, of course, because she'd been looking forward to it terribly. But Cora was also disappointed, and that was new.

But then he'd asked if she and Mary could come over to his place instead because he was bottle-feeding a kitten that he'd rescued in a fire, and her ovaries had just about popped.

She stood there now, staring out the antique shop's single-paned windows, to the sidewalk beyond. Saw how the Christmas wreaths were swinging from the old-fashioned lampposts in the coastal breeze. How the tourists looked so cozy in their winter sweaters and hats, sipping on their ever-present coffees and hot chocolates as they strolled by. It looked like a Norman Rockwell painting out there, the only thing missing was the snow.

Cora was happy to be home. She missed her grandfather desperately, missed Max every day, but she was so glad to be with her cousins for the holidays. If it weren't for this arrangement at the antique shop, she and Mary would still be in Eastern Oregon, where they'd had no family, and only a few close friends. Where the sadness had been pressing in so heavily, that Cora found it hard to take a full breath.

She sighed softly, taking in the scent of the gingerbread wax warmer next to the cash register, and feeling thankful that she could breathe at all. It had been the worst year of her life. Full of hardships that she never could have imagined. But being back in Christmas Bay was a blessing. And now, things with Neil…

She watched an elderly couple peer through the window at the display of Christmas dishes that Poppy had arranged there, and knew how lucky she was that he was settling into this situation like he was. He was shell-shocked, there was no doubt about that, and he was still angry at her, and he had every right to be. But there was a warmth in his eyes when he looked at Mary that Cora could tell was the beginnings of fatherly love. She hadn't been sure if Neil wanted to be a dad, and maybe he hadn't at first. But it was obvious that something deeper was taking over.

"What are you doing, Mom?"

Mary rolled up to the counter on the skates that Evelyn Frost had given her this summer. Evelyn was Justin's mother, a new friend of their family, and a regular in the antique shop now. Mary adored her. And she adored the skates, which she wore at every opportunity, rolling around on the shop's old wood floors and giving the customers a chuckle. More often than not they gave Cora a headache, but seeing Mary on them was so cute, she'd learned to live with it.

She smiled at her daughter with her freckles and the gap between her front teeth. She had an appointment coming up at the orthodontist for braces, and she was excited about that. Cora was going to miss the gap.

"Just soaking in the Christmassy feeling, I guess," she said. "It's pretty cozy in here, right?"

Mary looked at the multicolored twinkle lights they had strung up, at the Christmas tree in the window, and the fresh pine wreath they had hung on the front door, and nodded. "Just wait until we get our Harry window set up," she said. "It's going to be so awesome."

"Have you decided which Harry?"

She frowned. "I think Styles. I mean, I feel kind of bad not doing Potter. I don't know...what do you think?"

"I think whichever one you go with is going to be perfect. But you do need to decide, because Justin's already got his window up, and it's getting a lot of attention."

Mary gazed forlornly out the window toward Brother's Hardware. Sure enough, there were a few people standing on the sidewalk looking at it now. Cora had to admit, the hardware theme was pretty cute.

"Oh," Mary said. "I *know.* But Uncle Beau said we could set it up this weekend. That's only a few days away."

"Then you'll need to decide on which Harry pretty soon."

"Yeah..." She chewed her cheek, and Cora thought she looked just like her grandpa right then, and her heart squeezed.

"So," Cora said. "Neil called."

Mary looked over, her eyes bright at the mention of her biological dad.

"There's been a change of plan," she said. "But I think you're going to like it."

Chapter Seven

Neil stood in his living room, arms crossed over his chest, contemplating the guinea pig cage at his feet. It had been the best he could do under the circumstances. Judy's Bark and Meow—the most ridiculous name for a pet store ever, but the only one in Christmas Bay—had been about to close, and Judy had been fresh out of crates. She'd insisted that a rodent cage would do the trick, at least for the time being. Until the kitten grew a little and started climbing, that is. And then he'd probably have to go in the laundry room or a bathroom to keep him safely contained until he learned how to use his litter box.

Neil sighed, sleep deprived and gritty-eyed, and gazed down at the tiny feline who was asleep in his plush bed. He was no bigger than an apple. Neil knew it was a he, because the vet who had treated him had confirmed this, along with his probable age, which was about three weeks old. Everything else, Neil had learned from Judy of Judy's Bark and Meow—like the fact that he might be part Persian, if she had to guess. She seemed to know what she was talking about. She'd had little cat earrings on, and a paw print tattoo on her inner wrist. As far as Neil was concerned, she might as well have been a cat PhD, since he, himself, had never spent more than five minutes around cats in his life.

"Now, you're going to have to give him this formula every four to six hours," she'd said matter-of-factly, holding up the tiny bottle.

He'd stared at her. "I work. I can't feed him every four to six hours."

"Well, then, he'll have to go to a rescue, hon. That's the deal."

But it wasn't the deal, because Neil had called all the rescues he'd been given the names of, and they were all full. And he couldn't bring himself to take the kitten to the animal shelter, even though it was a nice place, and was no-kill. He just couldn't do it. When he'd picked the little guy up from the vet, he'd looked up at Neil with his watery yellow eyes, and mewed. And that had been that.

So here he was. With a three-week-old kitten, and no cat experience. But all he had to do was keep him alive for the next few weeks until one of the rescues opened back up to intakes after the holidays. And that was where his daughter came in.

He looked at his watch now. They'd be here any minute.

Walking over to the window facing his dirt drive, he rubbed his chin. He hadn't shaved for two days. He was exhausted, up most of the night—the kitten was definitely not on a four-to-six-hour schedule, more like a two-to-three—and wondered if this was a tiny fraction of what having a newborn felt like. He thought of Cora and his gut tightened. Not even eighteen with a baby to take care of. How had she done it?

Neil stared out the window and up at the slate gray sky, the clouds plump with rain. The thought of her choosing to be alone over being with him, or at least giving him the

chance to be there for her, was a hard pill to swallow. It
hurt going down—it was jagged and chalky. Had he been
that bad? Had his parents been that threatening? They
must've been, *he* must've been, in order for her to take
the path that she had.

The question now was, how was he going to fix it? His
plan for his relationship with Mary was pretty straight-
forward—spend as much time with her as possible. But
he didn't have a plan for Cora, and he'd need one moving
forward. His feelings for her were all over the place, to say
the least. And suddenly, he worried how he was going to
handle this, having a new daughter in his life as well as
her mother, whom he really, really wanted to kiss again.
This kitten and his feeding schedule were probably going
to be the least of his problems.

Outside, Cora's small hatchback made its way down
the drive. He ran a hand through his hair, watching the
car come to a stop next to his front door. Mary got out
and grinned, looking around, obviously impressed with
the house's proximity to the ocean. Neil was too—he was
just steps from the beach, which made for a pretty epic
front yard.

Cora stepped out of the car, too. Smiling at Mary's excitement, she looked beautiful tonight with the wind whip-
ping at her blond hair. She wore a gray rain jacket that was
unzipped, a black turtleneck sweater and jeans that hugged
her curves. Neil's throat went dry just looking at her.

He walked over to the front door and opened it before
Mary had a chance to knock.

"Hey there," he said, looking down at her. "I've been
waiting for you guys. Did you find the place okay?"

Mary nodded. "This place is supercool! You're right
on the beach!"

She came in for a quick hug, surprising him. She looked pretty adorable in a reindeer Christmas sweater that was about two sizes too big for her.

"Come on in," he said. "I'm gonna make you some hot chocolate. Do you like whipped cream or marshmallows?"

"Ooohh. Marshmallows, please." She looked around his entryway curiously.

Cora stepped past him, and he could smell her perfume. She always smelled so good, like flowers and vanilla.

"Can I take your coat?" he asked, feeling like a kid who was trying to make a good impression. He was no kid anymore, but he guessed he *was* trying to impress her. She'd never been to his place before, and he wanted her to like it. He wanted her to leave with a good feeling about him in general, which he wouldn't let himself think too deeply on at the moment.

"Thanks," she said with that pretty smile. "Neil, this place is amazing."

"Thank you. It took a while, but I finally closed on it last year. I'd had my eye on it for a long time. A retired couple were the most recent owners, and when they decided to move across town, I couldn't make an offer fast enough."

"There's a sea lion on the beach!" Mary said, looking out the window.

"Yeah," Neil said. "That's Big Fred. He likes to sun himself on the rocks over there."

Mary laughed. "Big Fred."

"My friend Jay named him. Poetic, I know."

Cora walked over to the kitchen window that Mary was peering out of. "You can see all the way down to the cape from here."

"The best part of the house, as far as I'm concerned."

"I love it," she said, looking around. "When was it built?"

"The sixties. I've done a few things to it, but I've tried not to mess with its character. I like old houses."

"So do I."

He remembered that about her. She was an old soul. She'd always liked old things, which made sense. She'd spent her childhood in an antique shop.

"What's that?" Mary asked, pointing to the guinea pig cage in the living room.

Neil smiled. It hadn't taken her long to zero in. He'd been hoping she would.

"That's why I had to change our plans tonight."

Mary stood there staring at the cage that was next to the Christmas tree he'd cut just a few days ago. She was obviously dying to go over and investigate.

Neil touched her shoulder. "It's okay. Go take a look."

Cora smiled over at him. So far, so good.

Mary walked tentatively across the room, then sank to her knees in front of the cage. "You got a *kitten*?"

"Well, I wasn't planning on it. We rescued him from a fire a few days ago. He's a stray."

"Poor baby. Some of his fur is burned off."

"Yeah, he had to spend the night at the vet. But overall, he's doing pretty well."

The kitten's golden eyes fluttered open and he yawned from his little bed.

Mary just about lost her marbles. "Oh my gosh! He's *so* cute!"

As if on cue, he stretched his tiny legs, his even tinier claws poking from his toes. He looked at Mary and sat up. Then tried crawling off his bed toward her, but tumbled out like a potato bug instead. He went rolling onto the carpet in a ball of floof.

Mary clutched her chest. "Ooohhhh!"

"Um, I think she might be in love," Cora said.

Neil winked at her. "That's what I was planning on."

He'd talked to Cora on the phone about this, asked for her permission, because his plan would require Mary to be at the station while he was working. If she agreed to it, she could help feed the kitten during the day, and he'd pay her like a pet sitter. He'd also get to see her regularly for the next few weeks, which was the best part. Really, it had all fallen pretty perfectly into place, considering how it had started out. He thought Judy of Judy's Bark and Meow would be proud of him, if he did say so himself.

"Are you keeping him?" Mary asked.

"No," he said. "I'm going to take him to a rescue, but they're all full until after Christmas. So I'm going to keep him until then. But the problem is, I work, and he needs to be bottle-fed on a schedule."

"I can help!" Mary said quickly. Then looked at her mom pleadingly. "Mom, can I help Neil? I'm on Christmas vacation, so I don't even have homework. I promise I'll do a good job."

"I know you would, honey," Cora said. "My only worry is that you might get attached when he has to go to the rescue."

"I won't. I promise."

"Because he can't come home with us. We already have Roo…"

"I know."

Cora looked a little hesitant. She'd know if Mary could handle this or not. Neil watched her, wanting to hold his breath.

"Okay," she finally said. "I do think it'll be a good learning experience. And you'll get to spend some time at the station with Neil."

Mary nodded quickly, then looked over at Neil. "Thank you, thank you! Can I hold him?"

"Of course you can. I think he'd be pretty disappointed if you didn't."

Sure enough, the kitten was batting his little paw through the cage, trying to touch Mary's sweater.

She reached in and scooped him gently up. Neil watched her, his chest tightening. She was a good kid. And she was born for this, he could tell.

"I think she might be lost to us for a while," Cora said quietly, stepping next to him.

"You're probably right. Want a cup of coffee?"

"I'd love one."

With one more look at Mary, he walked into the kitchen with Cora following behind.

"Sit," he said. "Please. Make yourself comfortable."

Cora pulled out a chair at the sturdy maple table and sat down.

"I have to admit," she said, looking around, "I didn't know what to expect. But for a bachelor pad, this is pretty cozy."

"Well, it's kind of sparsely furnished, and nothing really matches, but I like to be comfortable. You can't even sit on some of my buddies' couches. I've never liked that cold steel-and-iron aesthetic."

"If I didn't know better, I'd think you had a decorator help you with this. It could be in a magazine or something."

He laughed, looking at her over his shoulder as he got a couple of mugs out of the cabinet. "You can tell my mom that, she's not a fan. I just grabbed stuff that looked cool and didn't hurt my back."

Flipping the coffeepot on, he walked over and sat beside her. At the mention of his mother, her expression had changed, and he wanted to kick himself.

"Hey," he said.

"Mmm?"

"I don't want you to be worried about my parents. It's going to be okay. I'm not saying it's going to be perfect or anything, but it'll be alright."

She didn't look convinced, but she nodded gamely. He glanced down at her pretty hands, folded neatly on the table, and he wanted to take them in his. He wanted to rub his thumbs over her knuckles, trace the graceful length of her fingers.

He felt his jaw bunch as he forced himself to look away. If he couldn't get a handle on this, it wasn't going to end well. He was supposed to be keeping his distance from Cora, at least emotionally. This was not keeping his distance. This was very close to giving in to temptation.

"It was so sweet of you to ask Mary to take care of the kitten," she said. "I think you made her entire year."

He leaned back in his chair as the coffee began percolating, filling the kitchen with its dark roast scent. "I would've been up a creek without a paddle without her. She's helping me out big time."

She watched him, her mouth turned up a little. "But you didn't have to keep that kitten. I'm sure somebody else could have taken it."

"I asked around, believe me. Since he's so little, he requires all that feeding, and there's nobody who can do it right now."

"Not even the animal shelter?"

She had him there, and she knew it. She was smiling a knowing smile. *You're a softie*, it clearly said.

"Okay," he sighed. "I could've taken him to the shelter. And if I'd put out more feelers, I'm sure someone would've taken him. But you have to admit, he's pretty damn cute. And he was looking at me with those big eyes, and I just couldn't do it."

"It makes sense. You saved his life. You're bonded now."

"I wouldn't go that far. He just eats and poops. That's about it."

"Tell Mary that," Cora said, nodding toward the living room, where she was sprawled out on the floor letting the kitten bat at her hair. "She's obviously over the moon."

"Yeah…"

"It's perfect that she'll be able to be at the station some so you can get to know each other. It's really nice, Neil."

His face warmed, and he stood to get their coffee. He wasn't used to this kind of approval with any decision he made. Usually, it was a girlfriend telling him he did dumb things, or his parents telling him he did even dumber things.

He poured the steaming coffee into their mugs, and then put the teakettle on for the hot chocolate.

Walking back over to Cora, he handed her the coffee, his fingers brushing hers. She looked up at him, maybe feeling the same electricity he had.

He cleared his throat and sat, waiting for the teakettle to whistle. A light rain had begun falling outside, tapping softly against the windows. The ocean outside was surly and gray, the waves slamming against the beach with a force only Mother Nature could bestow. A winter storm was blowing in, making Neil think about the inevitable circumstances that would follow—accidents. From rockslides on the highway, to people standing on the jetty when the surf was up and dangerous. All of it. He thought of Cora's cousin Poppy and the car wreck she'd had as a teenager—the one that had killed her high school boyfriend—and he took a sip of his coffee, suddenly lost in memories. Memories of his youth, of being in love with Cora, of navigating his family problems, and her family trauma.

Cora held her coffee in both hands as the steam curled into the air. "Can I ask you a question?" she asked quietly.

He looked over, jolted back to the present. "Shoot."

"Why are you still single? The woman we met the other night sure seems interested."

He watched her, thinking about that question. There were so many ways he could answer. The easiest would be to say that he hadn't met anyone yet that was okay with his lifestyle. But that wouldn't be the whole truth. Because he was starting to realize that after seeing Cora walk across the parking lot at Gran's Diner, he still wasn't over her yet. That maybe he'd been comparing every woman he'd met since to her. That in some crazy way, he'd been hoping she'd come back into his life.

But of course, he couldn't say that. He couldn't even admit that to himself. So, he took another sip of his coffee, thinking carefully before he answered.

"I just haven't met the right person yet," he said, setting his mug down again.

She nodded. "You said Allison didn't like your hobbies. Is that why she's not the right person?"

"Yes...no. No, that's not why. I mean, I'd like to be with someone who understands me, but everyone feels that way. The hobby thing though, the adventure thing, it's not really the relationship blocker that my folks always thought it was. None of the things I do are too important for me not to meet someone halfway."

She watched him, letting this sink in. Maybe wondering if it was true or not. He couldn't blame her, because he'd surprised himself with it, too. He'd never really stopped to think about it in depth before, because he hadn't wanted to go there. To confront the things about himself that seemed to sabotage the important stuff in his life.

The teakettle began to whistle, and he got up to pour Mary her hot cocoa. And not a minute too soon, because the conversation was starting to hit a little too close to home.

Cora shifted in her chair and put her elbows on the table. "I can't believe Mary and I are here. At your place. That we're talking again. It seems surreal."

"It is."

She looked over at him and took a visible breath. "I hope you'll forgive me someday, Neil."

She'd obviously been worried about it. He knew now that leaving here hadn't been easy for her. On the contrary, it must've been one of the hardest things she'd ever done. Still though, he wasn't past feeling betrayed. He should've been a part of his daughter's life from the beginning. She'd taken that experience away from him, and he wasn't sure when the anger would go away, *if* it would go away.

But the expression on her face softened him, like it always seemed to do.

He picked up the cocoa topped with extra marshmallows. "I'll be right back," he said. "Hold that thought."

Walking into the living room, he saw that Mary had curled up on the couch with the kitten in the crook of her arm. She was gazing out the window facing the ocean, looking comfortable, and that did something to his heart.

He could see traces of himself in her features when she turned and smiled up at him. And for the first time, he felt an undeniable wave of love for her. It was so strong, that it almost knocked the breath right out of him.

He handed her the cocoa, and saw that the kitten was fast asleep. The little guy might not have a mother anymore, but there would be no shortage of affection in his life. At least for the time being.

"Careful," he said. "It's hot."

"Ooohh. The marshmallows are all melty. My fave."

"Mine, too. It's the only way to enjoy marshmallows, in my opinion. Melty."

"Maybe I get that from you."

She took a sip of the hot chocolate, mindful of the kitten, not wanting to jostle him. Neil thought that wouldn't be a problem. An atomic bomb could probably go off right then, and this cat was not going to be disturbed.

Maybe I get that from you... She'd said it so casually, but the words were powerful. It seemed like everything she said, everything she did, was affecting him in ways that he couldn't have anticipated. He'd missed a lot. How would he have felt holding her for the first time? Hearing her baby gurgles and coos, or seeing her blinking up at him, her eyes unfocused and impossibly sweet? He wasn't sure. All he knew was how he felt right now, getting to know his little girl at eleven-years-old.

He smiled down at her. "You have everything you need? Your mom and I are just talking in the kitchen."

"Okay, I'm good."

"Are you hungry?"

"Nope, we had pizza at Mario's."

"I love Mario's," he said. "Good choice."

"We have a lot of stuff in common, right?"

"We absolutely do."

"My uncle Beau teases me about pineapple on my pizza, but I like it, it's delicious." She narrowed her eyes, as if testing him. "What do you think?"

"I think it's how pizza was meant to be. Obviously."

This made her giggle, and the kitten stirred, then yawned, looking like a tiny panther.

He walked back into the kitchen feeling like his heart had grown an entire size. A strange feeling. Not necessarily a comfortable one, since Neil was all about control. And this felt like he was losing it in a hurry.

Cora looked up. "How are things in there?"

He sat down at the table with a sigh. "Are you sure you're not in the market for a cat?"

"Definitely no. Roo is all the pet we can handle at the moment."

"Yeah, I get it."

Cora took a sip of her coffee.

They sat there for a long minute with the rain tapping against the window, the muted sound of the waves crashing on the beach. The Christmas tree sparkled from the living room, the light making everything seem softer, more peaceful. The house felt warm and full, and Neil realized that as much as he'd always loved his home, as comfortable as he was here, it had never felt like this before.

He looked over at Cora and was overwhelmed with the need to know more about her. About the adult her, who was making him feel this way. He wanted to know more about what had happened when she'd left Christmas Bay, and what had happened since she'd been gone. He wanted to know all of it, and knew it was going to take more than just an evening drinking coffee with her to satisfy this sudden thirst.

He put his elbows on the table and leaned forward.

"Tell me about when you got pregnant," he said evenly.

Her gaze was hesitant, because this would bring up feelings that would get messy, she'd know that. But it was time, it was *past* time, and she probably knew that, too.

She pulled in a breath, and leaned forward, closer to him. He could smell her hair, smell her flowery scent, and his gut tightened. Her eyes were so blue that they reminded him of how the sky looked over the mountains in the morning. There was a vastness there that shook him.

"She was conceived the night you took me to the river," she said quietly. "The night we danced and had the music turned all the way up. Do you remember that?"

His heart slammed inside his chest, reminding him that he definitely wasn't as in control as he liked to be. Yes, he remembered that night, and then some. In fact, he'd thought about it so much over the years, that it was hard to tell now what was actual memory, and what might've been his subconscious filling in the blanks, giving his heart what it had been yearning for, but had been denied the day she left.

"I remember," he said.

She grazed her teeth over her bottom lip before going on. "Do you remember the fight we had the next day?"

That part was harder to recall. Probably because they'd had more than one fight that year. They'd had several, and they all tended to run together in Neil's mind. They'd been about him wanting to leave. About his parents controlling his life. About Cora loving him and wanting to try and make something work, even though they'd been babies at the time.

He remembered thinking the idea of trying to make anything "work" at barely eighteen was next to impossible.

She might as well have suggested they fly to the moon on the next shuttle mission.

"You told me something your parents said about me, and I had a hard time getting over that," she said. "In fact, I don't think I ever did. It was one of the reasons I decided to leave without telling you, or anyone else, really."

"I don't remember…"

"It was a long time ago."

"But still significant."

She frowned. "Well…yes. Because I'm not sure they feel any differently now."

"What did they say?"

She waited a minute. Long enough that he wondered if she was going to say anything at all. And then she took a breath. "They said I was going to hold you back. It just hit a nerve."

He rubbed his temple. "Good God. Why would I have told you that?"

"We were fighting. I said some things, too. But I've always wondered…did you feel the same way?"

The question cut. He'd known his parents had made her feel small, but he was ashamed that he'd rubbed salt in that wound. Yeah, he'd been young, but he should've known better. He'd loved her. That wasn't how you treated someone you loved. And slowly, slowly, the picture of why she'd left, the circumstances surrounding her leaving, was coming into sharper focus. But it didn't make him feel any better, that clarity. It only made him feel worse.

"No," he said, his answer more forceful than he'd meant. But he wanted her to know. He wanted to be unequivocal about this. "In fact, I felt like being with you might've been life-changing. I could see a future I was fighting against, settling down young, commitment, responsibility, growing up, all of it. And I wasn't ready for that. My parents didn't know you, they had no idea how good you would have been for me, if I'd been ready."

She smiled. "Thank you for that."

"We're not here to blow smoke, Cora. We're here to finally start being honest with each other, right?"

"Right."

"So believe me when I say I didn't feel like you would've held me back. That's ridiculous. And I'm sorry I ever said it."

She nodded, seeming to accept that for what it was worth. It was a start.

"So," he continued, glancing toward the living room to make sure Mary was still busy with the kitten. He was currently perched on her shoulder playing with her earrings. "When did you find out you were pregnant?"

"About six weeks later. I started getting sick. My parents thought I had the flu, and took me to the doctor, but deep down, I knew before we went. It's weird how you know, but you do. Or, at least, I did."

He frowned. "We were careful, I remember that."

"We were. But of course, it's always a possibility, no matter how careful you are. When you're a teenager though, you never think it's going to happen to you."

She could say that again. He was well into his twenties before he realized that he could actually die doing some of the things he did for his adrenaline rushes. Sad, but true.

"So," he said. "You found out at this doctor appointment?"

She nodded. "Yeah. It was pretty brutal. My parents lost it."

"I bet."

"It was a huge fight, right there in the office. My dad

almost got kicked out. We fought all that night, all the next day. They couldn't get where I was coming from, but to be fair, I didn't even know where I was coming from. All I felt was this instinct to protect the baby, and I couldn't verbalize anything at that point. I couldn't talk to my parents in a way that made sense, because what made sense to them was putting her up for adoption."

"And you couldn't tell me," he said quietly. "Because?"

She watched him, her expression grim. Back then, she might not have been able to verbalize the reasons for the choices she'd made, but he was giving her plenty of opportunity to verbalize them now. He needed to know the details. He deserved to know. Even if he didn't agree with her reasons, at least he might be able to understand them better.

"Because," she said slowly. "I couldn't look you in the face and tell you that I was about to change your future as you knew it. I thought about what that conversation would look like over and over again. I couldn't eat, I couldn't sleep. I was so in love with you and…"

She let her voice trail off, and she looked down at her coffee, unwilling, or unable to go on.

He waited a few seconds, composing himself. Because the emotions swirling around in his chest were too much to be able to contain right then. He didn't want to say something wrong. He didn't want to do something wrong. There were too many years stretched between them, too many mistakes made, to make any more now.

"I was in love with you, too," he finally said. "I'd like to think that even though I was young, I would've been present, that I would've been there for you and Mary."

She looked up at him.

"But maybe I wouldn't have been," he finished. "You had a pretty deep instinct about the whole thing, and maybe you were right to leave without telling me. To be honest, I don't know what my parents would have done. Sued for custody? I have no idea."

He'd meant for that to be a joke, but it really wasn't funny. Because there was an element of truth to it that was sobering. Did he think they would've tried to take the baby away from Cora? No. But that didn't mean they wouldn't have interfered, used their power to try to sway her. Or sway him, whatever he'd decided to do.

"Not telling you is one of the biggest regrets of my life," she said evenly. "And I feel so bad about letting Mary grow up without you in her life."

It was true, he hadn't been a part of her life. Until now. And she wasn't exactly grown, she was eleven. If he was going to look at this with a silver lining, it would be that she still had plenty of growing to do. And he was here now.

"I'm glad she had a dad who loved her all this time," he said. And meant it.

She nodded. "He did. He was wonderful. But she should have had both of you."

"When did you meet him?" he asked. "How long were you on your own?"

She looked far away, like she was falling back into those complicated memories. He wanted to put his hand over hers, he wanted to touch her and feel the warmth of her skin, and give her some comfort, but he didn't trust himself to do that. He didn't trust himself with much of anything at this point.

"My parents helped me by giving me financial support for childcare," she said. "So I could work. I wanted to go to school, but that wasn't an option. I needed to support the baby, and I was lucky to get a good job. I worked at Target for a few years and worked my way up. They were flexible with my schedule, and my supervisors were really nice. I was always planning on going to college eventually, but then I met Max. He came through my line one day, and we hit it off. He was a few years older, and we started dating. He loved Mary, she was only two at the time and she adored him right back. It all happened pretty fast. He wanted to take care of us. And even though I was very independent by that point, there was something in me that craved that safety. We got married, and I was a stay-at-home mom, and I was happy."

He watched her. Saw the way her eyes softened when she talked about that time in her life. And he was glad that she'd been happy, and had found safety and comfort when she'd needed it the most. Even so, the anger from before rose up inside his chest. In the process of her finding what she'd needed, she'd left him behind. And yeah, he'd told her that he was going to leave, but all that would have changed if he'd known he had a daughter. Or at least, he thought it would have.

She frowned. "What is it?"

He pushed away from the table and walked over to the window. The rain was coming harder now, streaming down the glass like tears. He watched the foamy waves slam themselves against the beach, and they matched his sudden mood. Dark and turbulent.

Cora got up from the table, and came up behind him. He felt her warmth, smelled her perfume, and it made his throat tight, even as he struggled with the anger he couldn't seem to shake. He still loved her. But he resented her. He wanted to hold her, and he wanted to push her away. She'd stolen part of his life, time with his daughter, but it was more than that. She'd waited so long to tell him the truth, and he wasn't sure she'd even be here now if it weren't for

Mary reaching out. He was having a hard time forgiving that. He was having a hard time with all of it.

She put her hands on his arms. He stiffened at her touch, overwhelmed with the need to distance himself from her. Physically, as well as emotionally.

But then she lay her cheek against his back. She just stood there, half holding him from behind. Waiting for him to soften toward her again.

"What are you doing?"

They both turned at the sound of Mary's voice, sharp and accusatory.

She stood there looking at them with an undeniably angry expression on her face. It was the second time in a week where she'd caught them close like this. She didn't know exactly what was going on between them, but she didn't like it. She didn't like it at all.

Neil understood how she felt, because he felt the same way.

Chapter Eight

Cora drove the road back from the beach slowly, taking the curves more carefully than she probably needed to. Ever since Poppy's car accident back in high school, she'd hated mountain roads. It made it hard to go anywhere outside of Christmas Bay without experiencing a ton of anxiety in the process.

She glanced over at Mary, who was staring out the window. She hadn't said a word since leaving Neil's.

"Honey," Cora said, looking back at the road again. "Are you going to tell me what's wrong?"

She'd been sullen ever since walking into the kitchen, acting like she'd interrupted something intimate. Which Cora couldn't blame her for. It *had* felt intimate. And she'd felt guilty for that. She was a grieving widow, a single mother who had her daughter to think of. Clearly, she didn't have her head on straight. But being in Neil's presence again was affecting her judgment. It felt like her heart, so broken over the last year, was fluttering to life again, and she couldn't accept that he might be the reason.

"Mary."

"What."

"Answer me, please."

"I'm fine, Mom."

"You're not fine. You're upset. Can we talk about this?"

Mary sighed heavily. Then shifted so she was facing Cora in the dim light of the car. The rain had stopped, and the sun had set a few minutes ago, leaving the retreating clouds a dusky purple-gray. Mary's face was bathed in shadow, the lights from the dash playing across her features.

Cora looked back at the road, gripping the steering wheel with both hands.

"Okay," Mary said. "I don't like how you two are acting all of a sudden. Like, close and everything. Too close. It's weird."

Cora frowned. "Do you mean the fact that I was giving him a hug?"

"That, and you were hugging each other the other night, too."

"I was upset about your dad, Mary. He was just trying to comfort me."

"What about tonight?"

"We were talking. It was emotional. It's hard to explain."

"Yeah. Weird."

"Okay. What's weird about it?"

"You *know*, Mom."

"Is this about your dad?" But she already knew the answer to that. It was obvious that it was, and that was like a dagger to Cora's heart.

Mary shifted again and looked out the window. "Whatever," she mumbled.

"No, not whatever. Talk to me."

"Don't you miss Dad?"

"Of course I miss him. I miss him every day."

"It doesn't seem like it."

Another dagger to the heart. Mary was just a kid, dealing with her own pain, and this was her verbalizing it. But it hurt, it hurt a lot, and Cora slowed the car, pulling over at a turnout with her hazards on.

"What are you doing?" Mary asked.

Cora put the car in Park and turned to her daughter with her full attention now. The half-moon hung in the sky above them, illuminating their faces in a silvery light. "I thought you liked Neil," she said.

"I do like him. But I don't want you to like him. Not like *that*."

"Because that would be disloyal to your dad."

Mary nodded, her chin quivering.

"Would you feel this way about any other man?" Cora asked. "Or just Neil?"

Mary frowned and shrugged her thin shoulders.

"Honey," Cora said, putting a hand on her knee. "Nobody is ever going to replace your dad. Ever. Neil and I are reconnecting because of you. We have things to talk about, and some of those things are going to be really emotional. I need you to understand that. I need you to be okay with it because if he's going to be in your life like I know you want him to be, we all have to have a relationship."

"I know," Mary said. "I'm sorry, Mom. I don't know why I got so mad. I do like Neil, I do. But I almost slipped and called him 'Dad' tonight, and that made me sad. It made me sad for Dad, and…and…"

That did it. She choked on a sob, and Cora reached out to pull her close.

"I just miss him so much," Mary said.

"I know you do."

"And we're never going to see him again. *Never*."

"We'll see him in heaven." Cora used to have doubts

about whether or not there was something after this life, but she'd been through things that had given her a personal belief that there was. She felt that there was something good waiting for them on the other side. Something beautiful. She was grateful that Mary believed that, too. It was a comfort, and she sorely needed that right now.

"But we won't see him now, and I miss him now. Sometimes it feels like too much, Mom, like I can't stand it. It hurts too much."

"Oh, honey. I know it does. I know it won't make you feel any better, but it's supposed to hurt like this when you lose someone you love. It's because you loved him so much that the pain is so strong. It means you lost something precious to you, and he will always be precious to you, and he'll always be your dad. Always."

Mary's sobs grew softer and softer, until she was breathing gently against Cora's sweater. When she finally pulled away, there was a wet spot there from her tears.

She wiped her eyes. "I'm sorry I got pissy about you and Neil. I hope he still likes me."

"Of course he does. He knows this whole thing is confusing for you. It's confusing for him, too."

"Did you know that his kitten doesn't have a name yet?"

"Well, I don't think he thinks of it as his kitten. He probably hasn't named him because he doesn't want to get attached."

Mary sniffed, her mouth tilting at one side. "Yeah, right. Good luck with that."

"He's pretty cute, right? You should help name him, you're good at names."

She seemed to think on that. Cora could already see the wheels turning. Neil didn't know what he was in for, but his kitten "that wasn't his kitten" was about to have a name for the ages.

"Feeling better?" she asked her daughter, brushing her hair away from her face.

"Yeah."

"Ready to go home?"

Mary nodded.

Cora put the car in Drive, and turned on her blinker. She thought the odds of this cat being named Harry were pretty good at this point.

Neil wiggled the cardboard roof he'd cut to fit the top of the guinea pig cage, now complete with a kitten-sized litter box in the corner, and stepped back to admire his handiwork.

"He's gonna be out of that thing in five minutes."

This, from Jay, who was standing next to him, staring down at the cage with his arms crossed over his chest.

Neil frowned. It was ridiculous, really, because he could just go back to Judy's Bark and Meow and get something sturdier. But he felt like the more time he spent on this cat and his surroundings, the more attached he was going to get. It was probably futile anyway, because he was already pretty attached. You couldn't save a baby animal from a fire, revive it, and then bottle-feed it for a week and a half, and *not* get attached.

But he was firmly entrenched in denial, at least as far as the enclosure went, and that meant not going back to Judy's, and making what he had work. And right now that was cardboard.

"He'll be okay," he said, rubbing his chin. "Besides, Mary will be here with him most of the time anyway."

He'd finally told the captain about Mary, and the plan

to have her help with the kitten, and his boss had been happy to give the okay. He was a family man to his core. The only rule was going to be that she'd have to stay in the living area of the station, and out of the garage where the trucks and heavy equipment were, in order to keep her safe.

Jay slapped him on the back. "How's being a dad, bro? Are you settling in? Do you know what you're doing yet?"

Neil laughed. "Are you kidding?"

"You'll learn."

"Eventually."

"And what about Cora?" Jay said this with a knowing smile that made Neil stiffen. "How are things with her?"

"What do you mean?"

"I mean, how are things? Are you reconnecting? Are you still pissed at her? Give me the deets."

"There are no deets," Neil said. "Just that…you know. We have history, so it's… I don't know. It just *is*," he finished awkwardly.

"Ooohh, sounds like there might be deets after all."

Neil headed to the fridge for an iced tea. Then handed Jay a soda, hoping it would shut him up. "Here."

"Oh thanks."

"There's nothing to tell," Neil said. "I mean, as far as Cora goes. Were there feelings before? Sure. And are there some feelings now? Yeah. Stuff that's left over from before, but nothing to get all worked up about."

"I'm not worked up," Jay said, after a long slurp of his Diet Pepsi. "You are."

"No, I'm not."

"Okay."

Neil rolled his eyes.

"I'm just saying," Jay went on, oblivious that he might be overstepping. "You obviously love her—"

"Whoa, whoa. Who said anything about love? I mean, I *like* her. Okay, I admit it. I like her. But that's it. I never said I loved her."

Jay grinned. "I was talking about Mary."

Heat crept up Neil's neck. "Oh."

"Yeah. Oh."

"Will you just drop it? Mary's gonna be here any minute, and you're making me nervous."

"And why would that be? Because you might have unresolved feelings for her mom?"

"Shut up."

"You shut up."

Neil laughed, unable to help it.

"You love it," Jay said.

"Not really."

"I'm just here to keep you on track. Make sure you don't mess this up."

"There's nothing to mess up."

"There might be, brother. I've never seen you this invested before."

"I'm invested in my daughter," Neil said. "There's a difference."

"You're just invested, period. In your family. And that's okay."

That was just his friend's way of needling him. But at the same time, Neil felt like there might be something to it, and that had him spooked. He was not the type to get invested, period.

"Look who's here."

He and Jay looked over to see the captain walk in with Mary. He seemed happy to have her visiting. Mary lit up a room.

She grinned from underneath a red knit cap. She wore

matching mittens and a green puffer jacket—all the colors of Christmas, and then some.

"Our firehouse kitten-sitter," the captain said, "and she even brought cookies."

Sure enough, she held up a plate of sugar cookies. Neil could smell their sugary scent from where he stood.

"My mom helped me bake them," she said. "She remembered you liked this kind."

Jay cleared his throat, and Neil shot him a look.

"That's really sweet," he said, smiling down at her. "She's right, those are my favorite."

"Hey, Mary," Jay said. "Are you going to name that cat, or what? Neil hasn't gotten around to it yet, which is just unacceptable."

"I have the *perfect* name," she said.

"What?"

She smiled her gap-toothed smile. "Harry," she said.

Cora pulled up to the fire station at six o'clock sharp. She didn't want to be late, even though she knew Neil was on duty for the next few days. Still, she didn't want Mary to be in the way in case he'd gotten a call or something. He said he'd text and let her know if that was the case, and she hadn't heard from him. But she was anxious to find out how this first day had gone.

She looked up to see him walking through the dusky night, handsome in his dark blue uniform. He made his way down the driveway and past the antique fire truck that was strung with lights. She thought he must be cold in his short sleeves, because he had his hands buried in his pockets and his shoulders hunched against the chilly December breeze.

She rolled her window down with a smile. "Hey," she said. "Where's Mary?"

He leaned down so he could see her better. His hazel eyes looked dark in this light, sexy, and she tried to ignore the sudden butterflies in her lower belly. The instant guilt she felt at noticing his eyes, when she should only be missing Max.

"She's inside," he said, his breath forming a puffy silver cloud. "It's spaghetti night, the captain's specialty. She asked if she could stay."

"Oh...of course." Cora looked at the clock on her dash. The shop would be closing up soon. Poppy and Justin had a date, and Beau and Summer were headed into Eugene to see a movie. Something Avengers related that wasn't playing in Christmas Bay. She'd be on her own tonight, but that was okay. She could rent a movie or something, make some popcorn instead of having dinner. She'd never minded being alone before, but the simple truth was that she wasn't used to it now. She and Mary had always been close, but when Max had passed away, their bond had gotten stronger. They usually weren't far from each other. And if Mary wasn't around, Poppy and Beau usually were.

She looked up at Neil again, and hoped the sudden pang of loneliness didn't show. She was just having a moment. She was happy that Mary was going to stay longer—it obviously meant that today had gone well.

"Just text me," she said, "and I'll come back to pick her up. Are you sure this is okay? She's not in the way or anything?"

"The captain loves having her around, she reminds him of his granddaughter who lives in Washington. She's pretty much charmed everyone else. And we've been able to hang out today, which is nice. Making up for lost time."

"That's good," she said. "I'm so glad."

"Cora…"

He leaned closer to the open window. Close enough that she could smell his faint aftershave.

"Yeah?"

"What are you doing right now? Do you have plans?"

"Me? Oh…no. Nothing exciting. I was thinking about renting a movie. It's the holiday season, my favorite."

"Do you like spaghetti?"

She happened to love spaghetti. Her heart jumped a little at the thought that he might be including her, but this time was for him and Mary.

"I do," she said.

"Why don't you come on in? Have some with us?"

"That's sweet, but you don't have to do that."

"I don't have to, I want to."

She considered that for a minute. The thought of going back to the empty apartment above the antique shop wasn't thrilling her. The fire station looked warm and cozy with light spilling out its windows, and a Christmas tree sparkling next to the front doors. She thought she could smell the scent of warm garlic bread all the way out here, but that was probably just her imagination. Or wishful thinking. Her stomach growled, and she hadn't even thought she was that hungry.

"Come on," he said. "You can park in the employee parking lot so you don't have to find a spot on the street."

"I don't know…"

"Why not? You said you were free. You'd rather watch a Christmas movie than have the best spaghetti of your life with yours truly?"

She smiled. "Well, when you put it that way…"

"Attagirl. Pull around, and I'll walk you in."

* * *

Neil was stuffed. Normally he wouldn't have such a huge dinner, but he'd been busy talking and laughing, enjoying Mary's company, and how she fit so naturally into his surroundings. And he'd been enjoying Cora's company, too. So much so that he leaned against the outside railing of the fire station patio now, sorry that she'd be leaving in a few minutes. Taking Mary home to get some sleep, so she could be back in the morning, bright-eyed and bushytailed, as his mom would say.

At the thought of his mother, he clenched his jaw and tucked his chin into the collar of his fleece. She'd left him a few messages over the last few days, and he needed to call her back. But things had been going so well with Mary that he hadn't wanted to disrupt the delicate balance. That wasn't realistic, though. He had to call her back. He needed to talk to her, to his dad, and let them in on what was happening with their granddaughter.

Cora stood beside him, her hands buried in her pockets, the tip of her nose red from the cold. She was staring out toward the marina where the fishing boats were docked. Pretty soon they'd be all decked out in their finest, strung with lights and lanterns for the Flotilla. But for now, they were just hardworking boats, some of them rusty and paint-chipped where their names had once been proudly emblazoned on their bows.

But that was Christmas Bay. Neil thought the boats matched the spirit of the town—full of character and history. It was what he loved about it, and he wondered now why he'd ever wanted to leave. But of course, when you were a teenager, the grass was always going to be greener on the other side.

"I had a good time tonight," Cora said, looking over at him. "I like your friends. Especially Jay. He's sweet."

"He *can* be sweet. Most of the time he's a dumbass."

She laughed. "But he's your dumbass."

"Exactly."

"I remember you always wanting a little brother. Now you've got one."

Neil smiled. "I guess you could say that."

"I don't really have many friends here yet. In Bend I was a little isolated being a stay-at-home mom. All the friends I made from working at Target eventually moved on or moved away. It was always hard for people my age to understand my situation, having a daughter so young. When they went to parties, I had to go home and pay the babysitter. In a lot of ways it was a relief to stay home, so I didn't have to explain my life to people who weren't there yet."

"But you liked it?" he asked. "You liked being home with her?"

"Oh, I loved it. It was the most amazing thing. I'd get to make her breakfast and take her to the park. We joined some playgroups, she did gymnastics and soccer. All the things."

"And Max was supportive of you. Of what you wanted to do with your future?"

He was only asking because he remembered her being excited for college. And she'd mentioned wanting to go back, but she never had. Why was that? She said she'd been happy, and he didn't doubt that. But he also wondered if she might've lost herself a little along the way. It wouldn't be surprising with all she'd been through.

She smiled over at him. "He was. But you know. Life happens. Whenever I'd get ready to enroll in school, something came up and it never seemed like the right time.

Mary had a lot of anxiety when she was little, she still does, so it was hard to juggle everything. You know…"

He really didn't. He didn't even know Mary had anxiety. He frowned, leaning against the railing, listening to the muted laughter coming from inside the firehouse. Mary was in there, saying good-night to the kitten. Which might end up being a never-ending lovefest. Cora would probably have to go in and drag her out at some point.

"What about you?" she asked. "Do you have many friends outside of work?"

"Some. But the station is my home away from home, we're like family here. And this kind of job doesn't leave a whole lot of time for new relationships. At least it hasn't in my case."

She nodded. "How did you meet Allison?" She didn't look at him when she asked, just kept gazing out toward the boats.

"I met her on a call. Her grandpa was having a medical emergency, and we talked afterward, and that was it. But it was never going to work with Allison. I think she knew that, just like I did. We're too different. She wants a traditional relationship, and I…"

He wasn't sure how to finish that sentence. What did he want? At one point he thought he knew. Now it seemed foggy.

"You don't want to settle down?" she asked. After a minute, she did look over, and her eyes were dark, like the water in the distance.

"Maybe someday," he said. "But I have some trust issues to sort through, Cora."

He hadn't meant for that to sound so sharp, but it was true. If someone that he'd loved as much as Cora could've kept this kind of secret from him, what else would he be in for if he opened himself up in the future? The possibilities seemed endless.

"I get it," she said. "I do."

"I'm sorry."

"You have nothing to be sorry for."

He scrubbed his cold hands over his face, feeling bad for snapping like that. But before he could say anything else, his phone rang.

He dug it out of his pocket, and saw that it was his mom. Sending her to voicemail, he tucked it back in his pocket again. But not before Cora had seen his mother's name on the screen.

Her expression fell. "Why didn't you answer it?"

She probably didn't want to know the real reason—that it wasn't going to be a pleasant conversation.

"I haven't talked to them about Mary yet. I've been putting it off. I know that's selfish, but I can't seem to find the bandwidth right now."

"You have to sort through it the best you can. I'm sure they understand."

"I'm not sure they do."

His phone rang again and he gave Cora an apologetic look. The timing really couldn't be worse. Unless his mother actually walked up behind them. That would be worse.

"You should answer it," she said. "I have to go in and get Mary anyway."

"Are you sure?"

"Positive."

He watched her turn and head for the door, the lights of the boats reflected on the water in the distance. She cut a beautiful silhouette against it, her hair loose tonight, and her profile delicate in the shadows. His throat tightened looking at her. He was in deep here, much deeper than he could've been prepared for when she'd reentered his orbit a few weeks ago. It had happened suddenly, but it had also happened over a series of hours, days, years. She'd been a part of his life for a long time, and now it wasn't just Cora who was a part of it, it was Mary, too. Their daughter. Their child.

She opened the door and stepped inside with one more look at him over her shoulder. And then she was gone, leaving him with his phone ringing insistently.

He raised it to his ear, watching the spot where she'd been like she was a sunspot, burned into his retinas.

"Hello?"

"Neil," his mother bit out. "Why aren't you answering your phone?"

"Hi, Mom. I've been meaning to call you back. I'm sorry, I've been busy—"

"Never mind that. Your father's in the hospital. You need to come home."

Chapter Nine

Neil ran up the steps and through the front doors of the hospital, the antiseptic scent immediately making him queasy.

His dad was apparently stable, thank God, and as far as heart attacks went, this had been a mild one, but he still needed to stay overnight for monitoring. He was mostly tired, his mother had reported wearily, and wanted to go home. The food there wasn't up to his standards. She'd said this with a little laugh, but Neil could hear the fear in her voice. There was no such thing as an insignificant heart attack. It was a warning sign. A sign that his weekends spent golfing—not even walking the course—he drove a cart—weren't going to cut it. He needed some real exercise, and he needed a major diet change, something that Neil had been on him for years about.

He stepped inside the elevator, his heart beating hard in his chest. His mom had called needing him, and he'd actually sent her to voicemail. He was going to have a hard time forgiving himself for that.

He stood there looking up at the red digital numbers change from one to two. And then the elevator stopped with a ding, and two nurses stepped inside. They smiled at him appreciatively. *It's the uniform*, he thought. Always the uniform. But he could barely manage a smile back. He was too busy thinking about his dad, thinking about how this night could've ended very differently. And how life had a way of changing in a heartbeat. Literally.

"Christmas Bay?" one of the nurses asked.

He looked over. "Hmm?"

She nodded at the patch on his sleeve. "Christmas Bay Fire Department?"

"Oh… Yes."

"My friend's brother tried to get on there a few years ago. It's such a nice little town."

She was pretty. Auburn hair pulled back in a pony-tail. A festive green sweater over her scrubs. It brought out her eyes.

Neil nodded. "It is. Very nice."

She and her friend exchanged a look. He'd become used to this kind of interaction when he was younger. And he'd eaten it up. But right then it felt like it was happening to someone else. The subtle flirty exchange, the smiles, the way she kept looking at his badge and waiting for him to say something else. She'd given him an opening after all. But it was all lost on him. Even if he weren't on his way to see his dad, it still would've been lost on him. Because for the last few weeks, he'd been lost in someone else, and he needed to figure out how to find his way out of that particular maze. He didn't trust Cora, and even if he did, he still didn't want to settle down. And she was definitely the kind of woman you settled down with.

The elevator began climbing again, and when it reached the third floor, it stopped again with a ding. He stepped back to let the nurses by with a nod. The one with the auburn hair smiled at him over her shoulder, and then they were gone.

He stepped out and looked up at the signs that would point him to his dad's room. The floor was busy. Doctors were being paged overhead; the phones were ringing in muted tones. Family members and friends walked in and out of their loved ones' rooms, looking exhausted and worried.

Neil swallowed the uncomfortable feeling in his throat and headed down the hallway. He saw his father's room number, and slowed, hearing his mom talking from just beyond the open door.

"Now, honey. You need to at least try to eat something. Anything."

"I'm not hungry, Vivian."

"I know, but still. How about some juice?"

"I don't want juice."

"Richard, please."

"I hate the hospital. It smells in here."

"Nobody *likes* being in the hospital. And it doesn't smell."

Neil smiled, despite the tight feeling that had migrated to his chest. His dad was being difficult, and in Neil's mind, that was a good thing. He still had some spunk, even from his hospital bed.

He knocked softly on the door and stepped inside. "Dad?"

His mother was sitting on the windowsill, looking so different, that for a second, Neil could only stare at her. Her usually perfectly styled hair was flat and a little frizzy. She had dark circles under her eyes, her face free of makeup. She wore jeans—she *never* wore jeans—an oversize sweater and tennis shoes. The tennis shoes were what had Neil the most surprised. The closest she ever got to tennis shoes were boat shoes, and even those always looked stiff and overly white. Despite the tired expression on her face, she seemed comfortable, and that was a good thing.

"Son," his dad said. "You didn't have to come right away like this. I'm fine."

Neil walked over and leaned down to give him a hug. For the first time ever, he seemed vulnerable, with the IV in his arm and his gray hair going in every direction. It was a shock to the system, and all of a sudden, Neil's stomach turned. This was a reminder that his parents were getting older. He was an only child who would have to navigate the future with them on his own. It was a sad thought, and one that left him cold as he stepped over and gave his mom a hug, too.

"Hi, darling," she said. "I'm glad you're here."

"He really didn't need to come," his dad said. "You didn't. I'm *fine*."

"Dad, you had a heart attack."

"A tiny one."

"Richard…"

"Vivian…"

Neil sighed. "Why do I feel like you two are going to need a referee by the time this is all said and done?"

"I'm not used to being confined to bed like this. It sucks."

Neil's mom's eyes widened, and he laughed, unable to help it.

"I don't think I've ever heard you say 'sucks' before, Dad."

"Well, it does. Might as well call a spade a spade."

"He's been like this all night," his mom said. "He's acting like a little boy. Won't even have anything to eat."

"Because I'm not hungry. I'll eat when I'm hungry."

Pursing her lips, she crossed her arms over her chest.

"Mom, I think it's okay if he doesn't eat anything right now. His body has been through a trauma, he just needs to settle for a little bit, okay?"

"See?" his dad said.

"But you really should try to eat something later, Dad." His mother huffed.

"What's going on with you guys?" he asked.

The room was quiet for a long minute, and then his mom's eyes filled with tears.

"Oh, honey," his dad said, reaching for her hand.

It was a rare show of affection from his father, and Neil watched quietly.

His mom got up and went over to sit on the bed. "It was scary, Neil. I thought… I thought…"

"But it ended up fine," his dad said. "I'm okay."

It was starting to sound like he was trying to convince himself. Neil frowned, and sat on the other side of the bed. He was surprised they all fit there, but they did. His family. Small, only the three of them. They'd always felt so dysfunctional over the years. With so many issues left unaddressed—so many things left unsaid. Being so open now felt strange. But it also felt nice.

"I know it was scary, Mom," he said. "And he's going to be okay." He turned to his dad. "But this is a wake-up call. You know that, right? There's not usually second or third chances for this kind of thing. This means going to the doctor for checkups. It means exercise and eating better. All of it."

"I know."

"I mean it, Dad."

"I know. I hear you. I'll be honest… I was scared, too."

Neil's mom sniffed, and his dad squeezed her hand.

"I've been lying here thinking about it, you know?" he

continued. "Life is short. My own dad passed when I was fourteen. He was only thirty-nine."

"I didn't know that," Neil said. "I didn't know how young he was."

"To me, he was larger-than-life. Dads usually are to their kids. I thought he was going to live forever."

Neil watched him. Watched him run a hand through his silver hair, and that spark, that familiar stubbornness was suddenly gone from his expression. He just looked different. He looked so much older.

"Neil," he said quietly.

"Yeah?"

"I want to meet our granddaughter. I want to meet Mary."

Cora stood in front of the antique shop window, her arms crossed over her chest, the blindfold over her eyes slipping so much that she had to tilt her head back in order to keep it from falling over her nose.

"Are you ready yet?" she asked Mary.

"No! Just stay right there. And *don't* look!"

"I'm not looking."

It was the afternoon of the big unveiling. The Harry Christmas Window, the future winner of the Christmas Bay Chamber of Commerce Window Contest, according to Mary. A mouthful.

Other than some kind of Harry gracing the window, Cora really had no idea what to expect. But Mary had been working on it all morning. Poppy was at a doctor appointment, and Beau was Christmas shopping with Summer, so they were going to see it tonight. At the moment, it was just Cora and Roo, who was sitting very patiently by her side. Mary hadn't insisted on a blindfold for the dog, thank goodness.

"Just one second. This one thing doesn't want to stay standing up. I might have to tape it," Mary mumbled under her breath.

Cora shifted restlessly on her feet. She was excited to see her daughter's big creation, but she'd been distracted since last night—since Neil had left the fire station with only the briefest of explanations. His dad was in the hospital, and he'd text her later.

She'd been thinking about him all day, about his dad, and how bad it might be. She'd never been a fan of Richard Prescott's, but she didn't want him to be sick. The look on Neil's face had broken her heart when he'd turned and headed for his truck. She knew that look—it was one of deep uncertainty. Of reality hitting you right in the face. She'd worn that look herself when Max had been diagnosed. She'd walked around in a daze for weeks afterward. There was nothing like a family member being in jeopardy to make you think about the future in a hurry. How much time you might have, what there was left to say and do.

"Okay," Mary said. "Are you ready?"

"I'm ready."

"Alright, you can take your blindfold off."

Cora smiled, lifted the blindfold and opened her eyes. And let her gaze settle on the biggest, brightest Harry-themed extravaganza she'd ever seen.

"Mary!" she said. "You did all this by yourself?"

Mary stood there beaming, her cheeks full of color. "Uncle Beau printed out the pictures and helped me cut out the cardboard to stick them on. Aunt Poppy got the twinkle lights and mini trees and ornaments. Roo supervised."

Cora gazed at the window display with pride blooming

in her chest. Mary hadn't picked one Harry, she'd settled on them both. There was a big, sparkly, glittery sign that said, *Have a Harry Christmas!* In front of it, were various cardboard cutouts of Harry Styles and Harry Potter wearing Christmas hats and sweaters. They were surrounded by miniature Christmas trees, and fake snow and microphones and broomsticks, and everything Cora imagined would be included in a tiny Christmas town full of Harrys. Lights twinkled all around the display, and people were already stopping on the sidewalk to peer inside, smiling and pointing at the creation that was so fun and full of life.

"Honey," she said, pulling Mary into her side. "I am *so* proud of you. This is fantastic! I can't believe how creative it is."

"Well, you said go with your heart, and I love them so much. I had to do both. You don't think it's too much?"

"No way, it's perfect. Justin is going to have a run for his money."

Mary grinned. "I already saw him looking at it from across the street. He gave me a thumbs-up."

They stood there, arm in arm, watching the tourists stroll by. It was a foggy morning, and the lit wreaths hanging from the streetlamps gave Main Street a wintery, magical feeling.

"Mom?"

"Yeah?"

"What do you want for Christmas? I haven't done my shopping yet."

"Oh… You know what, sweetie? I haven't even thought about it. I'm more interested in what you want."

"You always say that. You never ask for anything. You have to want *something*."

She kissed the top of Mary's head. "Okay. I just want

you to have a nice Christmas. I want us to spend a lot of time together over your school break, I want to watch a lot of movies, and bake a lot of cookies, and just hang out. How about that?"

"We do that anyway."

She laughed. "True."

"Mom?"

"Hmm?"

"This will be our first Christmas without Dad."

Cora looked down at her daughter with a sudden ache in her heart. Pretty soon she wouldn't be looking down anymore. Mary was getting so tall, and she wasn't even a teenager yet. The thought that Max would miss that—he'd miss her prom, her graduation, her wedding day, and so much more—made her so sad that it was hard not to cry.

"It will be," she managed.

Mary was quiet for a second, thinking. Her brows were furrowed, and she looked like Neil right then. Cora wondered if he saw himself in his daughter. She wondered if he saw his parents in her, too. She was a perfect representation of her family, near and far. The ones she was close to and the ones she wasn't.

"And the first one without Great-Grandpa, too."

Cora nodded.

"Sometimes I'm excited for Christmas, and then I feel bad for being excited when they aren't here with us."

"No, honey," Cora said. "They'd want you to be excited. And they're here, just in a different way. They're in our hearts, right?"

Mary seemed to consider this. "Yeah…"

"I know it's hard, I'm sad, too. Every day I'm sad. But we'll get through it together. You and me, Beau and Poppy. All of us together."

"And Neil?" Mary looked hopeful.

"And Neil," Cora repeated. "Do you mean Christmas the day, or Christmas the season?"

"I don't know. The season, I guess. But...what do you think he does for the day? Like, Christmas Day?"

"I'm not sure."

"It seems kind of weird that my dad is here, and we wouldn't, like, invite him over for Christmas. Don't you think that's weird?"

Cora could feel her pulse tapping in the hollow of her throat. Could feel her cheeks flushing at the question. She hadn't thought about it, but she guessed it was kind of weird. They were a strange family, she and Mary and Neil. But even strange families got together for the holidays.

"Do you think we can invite him?" Mary asked. "And he could bring Harry?"

"Roo might not like cats." It was the only thing she could think of to say, even though it probably wasn't true. Roo was a gentle giant.

"Yeah..." Mary deflated a little at that. "But we could still invite Neil."

Cora licked her lips, which suddenly felt dry. "Well, I'll have to think about it, honey."

"Why?"

"Because, I just do."

"But why?"

Cora rubbed her temple. "Because Christmas is... I don't know, *Christmas*. It's a special holiday, and inviting him for Christmas might seem...it might seem..."

"Like you like him?"

"What? No."

"But you don't like him, not like that. *That* would be weird."

Cora stared at her.

"I mean, it would be," Mary continued. "But you don't, so it's cool and stuff. You can at least invite him so he knows we want him here. What if he's all alone at Christmas or something?"

"He's got his parents. He wouldn't be alone."

"Geez, Mom. It seems like you don't want to."

"It's not that."

"You always want to ask people over for Christmas. You even made me invite that gross Jordan Thacker in the fourth grade because his dad was out of town or something."

"That's different. He and his mom didn't have anyone to spend the day with."

"Yeah, but he was gross. And you still made me invite him. And Neil is like, my *dad*."

"Okay, okay. I get your point."

Mary watched her. "So you'll think about it?"

"I will."

"Awesome sauce. Do you care if I go down to Frances's for some gummy worms?"

"No, but only if you bring me back some caramels. There's a five in my purse."

"Thanks, Mom!"

"And be careful!" she yelled after her. "Just there and back, no stopping anywhere else, got it?"

"Got it!"

Cora watched her disappear into the back office with Roo at her heels. It seemed like she really did want Neil here for Christmas, and that was very sweet. But there was no way Cora could explain the real reason she needed to think hard about inviting him—she was afraid of her feelings for him.

It was crystal clear that Mary didn't want Cora thinking about anyone else but Max, which was more than understandable. Cora didn't think she should be thinking about anyone else either, but here she was. She remembered her mom telling her once that love didn't operate on a timeline. It just hit right out of the blue, whether you were ready for it or not. She used to think that was silly because if you weren't ready for love, then you could just tell it to kiss off.

Right. How naive she'd been. How young. Her mom had never given her much advice, but she'd gotten that one right.

One hundred percent.

Chapter Ten

Neil sat on his couch with all the lights off except for the Christmas tree. It cast a soft glow throughout the living room, as stormy winter waves crashed against the beach outside. The room felt warm and comfortable, with the kitten in the crook of his elbow, suckling on the bottle with formula all over his chin. But Neil had never been so exhausted in his life.

He blinked down at Harry (the name had stuck) as he neared the end of his midnight snack. He was only taking one bottle at night now, which was a great improvement over the two or three they'd started out with. Especially since Neil had a hard time going back to sleep after each one.

Sleeping tonight was going to be especially hard, since he was so preoccupied with thoughts of his dad. He'd gone home yesterday. The doctor said he was doing well, and was lucky—it could've been much worse. Something that Neil saw he didn't take for granted. There was a funny kind of warmth behind his dad's eyes that hadn't been there before this heart attack. And who knew if it was just temporary or what, but it was noticeable to just about everyone. Even Tammy, his parents' housekeeper, had mentioned it when he'd walked through the door, and had given her a hug, of all things. *Who's this man, and what did he do with Mr. Prescott?* she'd said with a laugh. But Neil and his mother had exchanged a look. It was so out of character that it was hard *not* to notice.

Readjusting the kitten's tiny body over his arm, Neil turned to look out the window. The moon was nearly full tonight, and it shone down on the water with a shimmery brilliance that made him blink at it in wonder. It was beautiful. But he was somewhere else altogether. All he could think about was what his dad had said in the hospital— and twice on the way home. *I want to meet our grand- daughter...*

It wasn't necessarily what he'd said, it was how he's said it. With softness and gentle intention. Neil's mother had stared at him. This had obviously come out of the blue. There was no doubt that this heart attack had given Richard Prescott a jolt of some kind. It had brought everything into clearer focus, whatever that might be.

Neil rubbed the stubble on his chin, and looked past his reflection in the window to the ocean beyond. It was good, all of it. The fact that his parents might be coming around to the idea of having a granddaughter was good. But Neil had experienced a lifetime of their harsh judgment and sharp words. Words that when spoken about people he cared for, cut like a blade. He was finding that he couldn't stand the thought of putting Mary in the same room with them, and chancing even a fraction of that pain. Mostly for her. But for him, too. And then there was Cora…

At the thought of her, his heart beat heavily inside his chest. He and Cora were just now finding their foot- ing again after twelve years apart. He didn't want to risk her running again. He wasn't sure what she would and wouldn't do when it came to his parents, and that worried him. Plenty.

He shifted on the couch and looked down at the kitten, who was snoring now, his little paws in the air.

"And just what am I going to do with you?" he asked quietly.

The kitten's golden eyes fluttered open at the sound of his voice, and then closed again. His belly was so full that it stuck out comically, right along with his paws. Neil stared down at him, accepting the fact that he was now firmly in love with this stupid cat, and he didn't want a cat.

So now he had some decisions to make. Follow through with his original plan of taking Harry to the rescue? *Or* he could find him a home himself, which seemed like a better option at this point. At least he'd have some say-so about who his new family would be. Or he could keep him. Mary would be thrilled. But then he'd have a cat, and again, he didn't *want* a cat. At least that's what he kept telling himself as he scratched underneath Harry's chin and listened to him purr. He had a surprisingly loud purr for something so little.

Sighing, Neil stood up and set the bottle on the end table. Then tucked Harry into the crook of his arm and headed down the hall to his bedroom. The guinea pig cage was officially toast at this point. Harry had figured out how to climb out of it, even with the cardboard top, and that was that. He now slept on the bed with Neil.

He opened the door to his bedroom, and lay the kitten on a throw blanket at the foot of the bed, and then climbed under the covers with a yawn. No sooner had he stretched out and closed his eyes, than he felt tiny footsteps making their way up his legs.

He peered down at the kitten in the shadows.

"Oh no. No way. You're sleeping down there."

The kitten mewed and continued his trek up Neil's thigh.

"No." He sat up and scooped the cat up in one palm, and deposited him on the blanket again. "Stay."

He stared at him for a few seconds, making sure he was in fact going to stay, and then lay back down on his pillow, utterly exhausted.

After a few seconds, the kitten mewed and began walking up Neil's legs again. This time he made it to his stomach before Neil scooped him up and set him back down on the blanket. He mewed, sounding pathetic and tiny and adorable. Also annoying. It was going on two in the morning.

"Listen," Neil said, aware that he sounded like he was addressing a person, but he didn't care at this point. He guessed this was what happened the longer you went without having an actual woman in your bed. "If you're going to sleep up here, you have to stay in your own spot. I have my own spot, you have yours. Got it?"

Harry blinked at him.

"Okay. Good night."

He lay back against his pillow, but waited a few beats before letting himself relax. He was just beginning to touch the feathery edges of sleep, when he felt the tiny footsteps again. The kitten walked up, up, up, until he was on his chest. Then curling up into the crook of his neck with his motorboat purr.

Neil opened his eyes and stared at the ceiling, fully intending to put the kitten right back where he'd come from. But he never got that far. The last two things he remembered thinking were, one, he was losing this battle, and quickly. And two, he was going to have to approach

Cora about introducing Mary to his parents. Sooner rather than later.

But before he could think too deeply on either subject, he was touching those feathery edges of sleep again. With the kitten snuggled as close as he could get.

Cora walked up the driveway to the fire station, holding her bright red umbrella in one hand, and the Tupperware container full of gingerbread cookies in the other. She'd just gotten them out of the oven, and had wanted to bring them over before they cooled. Plus, it was an excuse to see Neil again, and she was starting to grab onto those with both hands. An inconvenient truth that was getting harder and harder to deny. Even Beau had raised his eyebrows when she'd told him where she was going.

What? she'd asked. *I'm just taking them over to Mary.*

Right, he'd replied with a smile. *Sure.*

Her cheeks warmed now at how obvious it probably was. Maybe even to Neil himself, and just what was she going to do about that? He was in her life to stay. She was going to have to figure out how to balance her old feelings for him with these new feelings. And all without Mary realizing what was really in her mother's heart. She felt so guilty, so torn and confused, that she almost turned on her heel and headed back to the antique shop. Beau would be thrilled. He loved gingerbread cookies.

But before she could, the front door to the station opened, the captain appearing there with a smile.

"I saw you coming. And in this weather, too. If you brought baked goods, I might have to kiss your feet."

She smiled back. "I just thought you guys might like some cookies. I've been baking all morning."

"My wife has been baking this week too, but her specialty is fruitcake. Don't tell her, but I'd rather have cookies."

Cora laughed, handing him the warm container. "I actually love fruitcake."

"I'll bring you one. Or three. Come on in."

She closed her umbrella, shook it out and set it down inside the front door. The station smelled good, like they'd just made lunch. Her stomach growled. The only thing she'd had to eat that morning had been cookie dough, despite Poppy's repeated grandmotherly warnings that it could make her sick. Cora figured that if eating raw cookie dough was as risky as she got in life, she'd probably be okay.

"Mary is in the back with the kitten," the captain said. "She just got done feeding him. I'll put the cookies in the kitchen, and thank you so much. They're not going to last very long."

"I'll just have to bring more."

"When you do, I'll have that fruitcake for you."

"It's a deal."

She watched him disappear into the kitchen, then stood there for a minute, looking around. The Christmas tree glowed in front of the window, bright and cheerful against the backdrop of the gray coastal day. She shrugged out of her raincoat and draped it over her arm. It was warm inside the station, cozy. It was no wonder that Mary liked to spend so much time here. The kitten didn't need nearly as much attention as he had even a few days ago, but coming down to the station in the mornings had become part of her Christmas vacation routine. She didn't head back to the antique shop until early afternoon, and always with stories about Neil that his coworkers had shared with her. She was getting to know him by spending time together, but also by hearing about him from his friends, and Cora recognized what a unique blessing that was. Especially since they'd started out as complete strangers.

"Hey, you."

She turned at the sound of the voice behind her, and saw Neil standing there, looking so good in his uniform that her heart skipped a beat.

"Hey," she finally said, clasping her hands in front of her belly. "I was baking this morning, and just wanted to bring some cookies down."

He smiled. "It's good to see you."

He'd called the morning after they'd had dinner at the station to let her know that his dad was recovering at home, thank goodness. But other than that, she hadn't heard from him.

"Mary just got done feeding Harry," he continued. "She's been a lifesaver. I'm not sure what I would've done without her."

"Honestly, I haven't seen her this happy in a long time. It's been good for her, being here. With you."

He nodded, the muscles bunching in his jaw. "Cora, there's something I need to ask you."

"What?"

Putting his hands in his pockets, he rocked back on his boots, looking suddenly tense. There was a scanner in the corner, and the dispatcher was saying something about a police call across town. Code three, whatever that meant. The crackly background chatter was a reminder that no matter how warm and cozy the station felt, Neil could get an emergency call at any time. Something that could end up being life-threatening. Cora remembered being scared for his safety when they were young, and that same feeling rose up in her chest now. It shook her. She didn't want to be scared for him again. She didn't want her heart fluttering at the sight of him. And she didn't want to be falling for him again. But it seemed like all those things were happening anyway, whether she wanted them to be, or not. This was what she got for bringing cookies over against her better judgment.

Neil nodded toward the couch by the Christmas tree. "Want to sit for a minute?"

"Sure."

They walked over and sat, Neil's thigh brushing against hers. It gave her butterflies. She realized then that this was a mistake. Coming here was a mistake, but she couldn't change it now. All she could do was try to get a handle on it before it exploded into something she couldn't control anymore.

He took a deep breath and put his elbows on his knees, his uniform shirt stretching over his muscular shoulders.

She frowned. "What is it?"

"My parents," he said. "They want to meet Mary."

She wasn't sure what turned her stomach upside down more—those words, or the fact that he'd said them with such trepidation.

"Oh?"

"I know how you must feel about my mom and dad," he said. "And I don't blame you."

There wasn't much she could say to that, so she didn't even try. She just sat there with her heart in her throat.

"They have a lot of faults," Neil continued. "Believe me, I know. And I know it probably feels soon to be introducing them to Mary when she and I don't even know each other that well yet. But my dad just had a heart attack..."

Cora let that settle. Then nodded. "No, I agree. It's the right thing to do." She paused, then went on carefully. "I'm not going to lie, though. I'm worried about what might happen. I mean, how they might feel about her. What they might say…"

He clasped his hands together and gazed over at her. His hazel eyes were dark and smoky. "I'm sorry," he said. "I know you're worried about that because of the things they said about you. That never should've happened, Cora."

"It was a long time ago."

"But you still feel it. It still hurts."

The words hit a sore spot that she'd been careful with for a long time. She got up and walked over to the window, not wanting him to see how rattled she was.

He got up too, and walked up behind her. "Just tell me if you're not comfortable with this. I know you'll want to be there when they meet, and if it's too much, just say so. I can hold them off. Maybe we can wait until after Christmas when Mary goes back to school. There'd be less pressure that way, with her routine getting back to normal and everything."

She shook her head. "No, it should be now. If there's one thing I learned from when Max was sick, it's that life is short. Mary wants to meet them, too. She's nervous, but she'll want this, I know it."

He put both hands on her shoulders and squeezed gently. His touch was warm and sweet, and more than anything she wanted to lean back against him. Let him hold her and comfort her and be there for her like she hadn't let him be there when she was pregnant with Mary. She'd been too scared then to need anyone. But had anything really changed? Could she let herself be vulnerable with this man, while at the same time not letting herself love him again? It was a slippery slope, and she closed her eyes, concentrating on her breathing. Concentrating on the beating of her heart against her rib cage.

Behind her, his pager went off. She startled at the sound, and turned to face him. And then the siren in the station erupted, piercing her ears. Suddenly, there was commotion everywhere. Firefighters rushing to the trucks, doors slamming, engines starting. The dispatcher over the radio was relaying the call, and the sound of the emergency tones gave her chills.

"I've got to go," he said. "I'll call you tonight."

She nodded. "Okay."

He gave her one more look and there was something in his eyes that made her more afraid than she'd been in a long time. Maybe since that night when she'd found out she was going to have his baby, and had decided to do it alone. Her pulse raced as she watched him head for the door.

"Neil."

He turned, and she thought that image was going to be burned in her memory forever.

"Be careful," she said.

And then he was gone.

Chapter Eleven

Neil stood by the front doors of the restaurant with his hands in his pockets, waiting for Cora to pull into the parking lot. He was having to consciously keep himself from pacing back and forth. He didn't think he'd ever been this anxious in his life, and the other night he'd escaped a burning building about twenty seconds before it collapsed. So that was saying something.

He looked at his watch. His parents were already seated inside the small Christmas Bay restaurant. They'd gotten a table by the window, facing the ocean. It was an Italian place, something Mary had requested. She loved fettuccini Alfredo and so did his mother, and he was counting that as their first win of the night.

Still, he couldn't seem to relax. He felt like a ton hinged on this meeting—how Mary took to his parents, how they took to her. And how Cora would end up feeling about the whole thing. A lot of that would depend on how his mom and dad treated her. They weren't stupid, they knew how it would end up if they were anything but warm, and she wasn't stupid either—she'd pick up on the slightest bit of resentment in a heartbeat. And if that was the case, the whole thing might fall apart, and his relationship with his daughter was on the line. But his relationship with Cora was too, and that felt significant.

Looking up, he saw her pull into the lot and his back muscles tensed. This was it. Go time.

Mary saw him through her window and waved as Cora parked the car. He walked over, and they both got out, the wind snatching at their hair.

"Hey," Cora said with a nervous smile.

Mary came over and hugged him. He was still getting used to that part, being hugged by his daughter, and he found that it was what he looked forward to most when he knew he was going to be seeing her. He'd missed so many hugs over the years.

Pulling away, she looked up at him. She was nervous too, he could tell.

"Hey," he said. "They won't bite, I promise."

She nodded, but didn't look convinced.

His gaze settled on Cora, who looked stunning in a black V-neck sweater and gray slacks. Her blond hair was pulled back into a messy bun with loose tendrils around her face, and her makeup was understated. She looked mature, but not stuffy. Beautiful but not unapproachable. She looked perfect as far as he was concerned.

"We're a little anxious," she said.

"I think we're all a little anxious. It's okay."

She glanced toward the restaurant. "Are they inside?"

"They are. Best seat in the house."

They never settled for anything less. As soon as he said it, he wished he could suck the words back in. He was trying to make her feel more relaxed about meeting with them, not pile onto the perception that they were snobs. Which, to be fair, they kind of were.

"They have noodles here?" Mary asked.

"They do," he said. "Loads of them, just for you."

Cora put her arm around her daughter. "Neil says your grandmother likes fettuccini, too. It's her very favorite dish."

"I wonder if I get that from her."

"You come from a long line of noodle-lovers," Neil said. "Starting with yours truly. But I lean more toward spaghetti if you want to get specific about it."

Mary gave him a hesitant smile.

"And then, let's see… There was your great-granddad Gerald, that was my mom's dad. He was a great cook. He could make all kinds of pasta from scratch."

Mary brightened up a little more.

"So you come by it honestly. We're eating at the right place tonight."

"What should I call them?" she asked.

Cora's gaze met his. The first test. The people she'd known a decade ago hadn't exactly put out grandparent vibes. On the contrary, they seemed like the kind of people who didn't want to be seen as that old.

"Whatever you feel most comfortable with," he said.

She nodded, leaning into her mother's side.

"Ready?" he said. "Ladies first."

They stepped ahead of him, and he swallowed hard, crossing his fingers that this whole thing would go smoothly. That his parents would behave themselves. That Mary would like them. And that Cora would consider forgiving their behavior all those years ago. There was a lot to forgive.

They walked inside, and Neil breathed in the smell of warm pasta and bread. The space was small and dimly lit, candles flickering on the red-checked tablecloths. A hostess in an emerald green dress led them to a table by the window, where his parents sat waiting expectantly.

He put an instinctive hand on the small of Cora's back, and his mother's gaze dropped there quickly. Her face was a complete mask, her expression devoid of any kind of nervous emotion. Although Neil knew for a fact that she *was* nervous. She was probably beside herself, honestly. But she wasn't going to let it show. She never let anything like that show, especially not at a time like this, when all her defenses were probably up. Neil hoped the years had softened her, and that she didn't see Cora as some kind of strange threat anymore, but he really didn't know what he was up against. Or what Cora was up against. It turned his stomach a little, as he forced a smile.

"Mom and Dad, you remember Cora."

His father stood, straightening his tie, before reaching for Cora's hand. "Of course we do. Cora. How have you been?"

"I'm doing well," Cora said. "I'm glad you're up and around after your stay in the hospital."

He smiled down at her, and Neil thought of Tammy, their housekeeper when she'd said, *Who's this man, and what did he do with Mr. Prescott?* Truer words had never been spoken. It was like he was a different person standing there in front of Cora, with warmth and an easy handshake. But it wasn't enough to make Neil breathe any easier. They had an entire dinner to go, and his mother was still a huge question mark.

His dad's gaze then shifted to Mary, who was looking up at him, scared to death.

"This is Mary," Neil said. "Mary, these are your grandparents, Richard and Vivian."

His mother stood, her perfect composure slipping just the slightest bit. Her eyes were bright, her smile genuine.

"Mary," she said. "You are just lovely. You look like your mother, I think."

Mary smiled, obviously happy with that.

"Hello, Mary," Neil's dad said. "It's nice to meet you."

"It's nice to meet you, too."

"Are you hungry? We hear this place has the best pasta in town."

Mary nodded.

"Your grandmother…err, Vivian likes pasta, too. But I'm sure Neil told you that already?"

"Yep."

"Well, then." After a few seconds he clapped his hands together. "Shall we sit?"

Nodding, Neil pulled out Cora's chair. Then Mary's, and sat beside them, glad there were big glasses of ice water already on the table. He was thirsty, his throat scratchy and dry.

His mom looked over at Cora. "It's been so long, Cora. Neil said you came back to Christmas Bay recently, but I wasn't aware you'd even left."

Her face immediately colored, and she threw him an apologetic look. At this point, he wasn't sure how she really felt—surprised that Cora would actually leave her small hometown, or if she'd meant to be nice, but had sounded condescending instead. Either way, Cora stiffened.

"I did," she said. "We've actually been living in Bend, but my grandfather passed recently, so we came back to help my cousins run his antique shop."

"Oh," Neil's dad said. "Is that the one on Main Street?"

"It is."

"I'm sorry," his mom said. Then looked at Mary. "Were you close to your great-grandfather?"

"He sent me birthday presents, and gave me hard candy, but we didn't get to visit that often."

She raised her brows. "Why not?"

Mary threw Cora a look. Clearly, she wasn't sure how much to say. "Um… I don't think Mom wanted…"

"It's okay, honey," Cora said. "I think they know why I was careful about visiting."

"Because it's hard keeping a secret in a small town," Neil's mother said evenly.

Neil leaned forward. "Mom."

"I'm sorry, Neil, but it's true."

"It's okay," Cora said. "We can talk about it, you have a right to know. But not now. Not here."

"Mom," Mary said. "Stop treating me like I can't handle it."

Neil's dad frowned. "No, Mary. She's absolutely right. There's a time and place, and this isn't it. We're just here to get to know you. We don't want to put your mom on the spot, or make anyone feel uncomfortable, do we, Vivian?"

"No," she said, looking like she was sorry she'd said it. "I apologize."

"It's alright, Mrs. Prescott," Cora said.

She gave Cora a softer look. Neil shifted in his seat, his blood pumping hotly in his veins. He felt like the tension could be cut with a butter knife, and he looked over at Mary, wishing this could all be easier for her.

"Cora," his dad said. "We were sorry to hear about your husband. And your dad, Mary. Our deepest condolences."

"Thank you."

"Max was his name?"

She nodded.

"Well, we're very sorry."

Neil's mother looked at Cora for a long moment. "Cancer?"

"Yes."

"I recently lost a close friend to cancer. It's awful."

"Yes, it is."

"Was he in the hospital long?"

"Not too long," Cora said. "We actually took care of him at home. Didn't we, honey?"

Mary gave her a small smile. "Yep."

"You took care of him?" his mother said. "That must have been very hard on you."

"It was, but it was also a blessing. To get to show him how much we loved him."

Neil's mother watched Cora, and her expression softened a little more. There was common ground here. Some basic understanding that hadn't been there before.

His dad put his napkin in his lap and then took a sip of his tea. He was taking a break from wine for a while, which Neil thought was a step in the right direction. Now, if he'd go to the gym or walk on the beach regularly, he'd be doing everything his doctor ordered.

"Mary," he said, "Neil said you just started middle school. How's that going?"

Mary frowned. "It's okay. Some of the kids are snooty. But some of them are nice."

"Snooty? How so?"

"They think just because they have money and stuff, they're better than everyone else. Especially this girl Riley. She's a real pain in the—"

Cora put her hand on Mary's arm. "Honey."

"Sorry. She's a pain."

"Riley..." Neil's mother said. "Riley Abbot?"

Mary's eyes widened. "You know her?"

"I don't really know her, but I know her mother. We're members of the same country club, and have lunch sometimes." As soon as she said it, she must've realized how it sounded. A little snooty. Not that having lunch with friends at a country club was snooty, but from where Mary was sitting, it was pretty close.

"Oh." Mary nibbled at a piece of bread, looking deflated.

"Just because someone has money doesn't mean..." Cora let her voice trail off as the server came and refilled their drinks.

Neil felt hot and itchy in his sweater. It seemed like everything was going to be a touchy subject. Or an awkward one. Money had always been important to his parents, and it looked like they had no idea what to interject into this conversation that had hit a little too close to home.

"What I was going to say, Mary," Cora said as the server walked away, "is that just because someone is wealthy, that doesn't automatically make them stuck up. Or snooty. Or whatever. Maybe Riley is nicer than you think, maybe people don't give her a chance."

"Mom."

"I'm just saying. Maybe they don't."

Neil glanced at his parents. They were nibbling on their bread, too. Cora took a long sip of her water, and looked at him over the rim of her glass.

"So," he said, anxious to fill the sudden silence. It felt like he'd run a marathon already, and their dinner hadn't even come yet. "Christmas is coming up. Mom and Dad, Mary decorated the window of their family's antique shop for the chamber's contest. It's pretty cool. You should see it."

"Oh?" His mother sat up straighter. She loved antiques.

"Yeah," Mary said, looking proud. "It's a Harry-themed window."

"Harry…" Neil's dad furrowed his gray brows.

"Harry Potter and Harry Styles," Mary said.

"Who's Harry Styles?"

Mary gaped at him. *Who's Harry Styles?*

"You know who Harry Styles is, sweetheart," Neil's mom said. "He's part of that band…" She snapped her fingers. "One something or other."

"One Direction," Mary said. "Only they aren't together anymore. *Sadly.*"

"Oh."

"So you have a Harry window, huh?" Neil's dad looked intrigued. "I'd like to see this window. See if it stacks up against the Coastal Sweets' window."

"You've been to Coastal Sweets?" Mary asked.

"Have I been to Coastal Sweets? Best peanut brittle I've ever had."

"I've never tried the peanut brittle," Mary said. "I like the gummy worms."

Neil's mother wrinkled her nose.

"Mary considers gummy worms one of the main food groups," Cora said.

His mom laughed. Actually laughed. Neil couldn't remember the last time he'd heard her laugh.

"Mary," his dad said, "I'm right there with you."

"Since when do you like gummy worms?" his mother asked.

"Since…since I just do. Only they have to be chocolate covered."

She stared at him.

He winked at her.

Neil wasn't sure who was surprising him more, his

mother or his father. They were both acting like they'd shed some kind of weight over the last few minutes. Since being in Mary's presence. It was like they were younger somehow—or were trying to be younger in order to connect with her. Whatever the reason, it was kind of sweet. He wondered if Cora noticed, or if she was still expecting them to be awful by default.

"Cora," his mother said. "Tell me about this antique shop. You run it?"

"I do. It was my grandpa's and he left it to me and my cousins, Poppy and Beau. We're learning as we go."

"I'd love to come in sometime."

"She's an antique junkie," Neil's dad said.

"I wouldn't go *that* far."

"I would. Listen, when you come home with three clunky typewriters, none of which actually work, I think you can safely say you have a problem."

"That was one time, and they were on sale. I got a great deal."

Mary was watching this with an amused look on her face, her gaze shifting from one to the other, and back again.

Neil sat back in his chair and smiled. Then his eyes met Cora's, and she smiled, too.

"So you're running the shop," his mom said, turning her attention back to Cora. "What were you doing before that?"

"I was a stay-at-home mom. I was going to go to school eventually, but one thing led to another, and well. It just hasn't happened yet."

"I see. And what would you like to study?"

"I'm pretty good at doing the books for the shop. I'm actually interested in accounting and business."

Mary turned to her mom. "You never told me that."

"You never asked."

"When do you think you'll go to college, Mom?"

"I'm not sure. Maybe when we get the shop more established, and I can take some time off."

Neil's parents watched this exchange quietly. He could tell they probably admired her work ethic. Cora had always been a hard worker, but they'd never bothered to notice back then. When she was seventeen, they'd just seen her as trouble, nothing more, nothing less. She represented their son's wild streak, a way he'd let himself be derailed, and had dismissed her as easily as waving their hands.

Now he saw they might be trying to make up for that. It was a start. And Neil found himself sitting back in his chair and relaxing a little for the first time since he'd walked in the door. He looked over at his daughter, who was listening to something his mother was saying about when she was in middle school. And then his gaze found Cora's. They watched each other for a long moment—and he could almost feel the years between them shrinking, growing less significant with each passing second. Was this what it was going to feel like having her back in his life again? Was he going to let her get close, even though he knew that if she left again, this time with Mary, she'd have the power to break him? The thought was sobering.

But as she smiled from across the table, that beautiful, sweet smile, he wondered if the damage had already been done.

Chapter Twelve

Cora rounded the corner of the narrow road that ran parallel to the beach, and shifted her little Hyundai into second. It was raining and the wind was howling—not the best afternoon to be running errands, but she had so much to do leading up to Christmas that she couldn't wait for the weather to clear. She'd just donned her raincoat and comfiest rubber boots, and had headed out, telling Mary, Beau and Poppy that she'd be back later that evening.

She took a breath now, wondering if she was going to regret her next stop. After Mary had asked if Neil could come to their place for Christmas, she hadn't let herself think too much about it. Maybe she'd been afraid of asking, and him saying yes. Would that be a betrayal of Max, since this was the first Christmas after his passing? It was confusing, and she wasn't sure what to do with all the thoughts and feelings she was having lately.

But after she'd left the antique shop, she'd texted Beau and Poppy on the spur of the moment, and had asked if they'd mind if she invited Neil for Christmas morning. So he could be there when Mary woke up, and see her open her presents. It had only taken a minute for them to text back saying it was a great idea, and they'd be happy to have him. The more the merrier.

So here she was, turning into his driveway with her pulse skipping. With her heart doing somersaults in her chest. She wanted him to say yes, but she was afraid. Afraid of it all, really. She kept wondering what Max would think of this, but she knew he'd just want her to be happy—he'd told her as much before he'd passed. Holding her hand, squeezing it in that way that had always made her feel so safe. And he'd want Mary to be happy above all else. Still, she couldn't get past the guilt, and it nibbled at her belly as she pulled up to Neil's little beach house and cut the engine.

Grabbing her umbrella, she pushed the door open into the wind and rain. It immediately snatched at her hair and jacket as she ran up to his front door and rang the bell.

After a second, the door opened, and he stood there in a pair of faded jeans and a Christmas Bay Fire Department sweatshirt. He looked good in it. He also looked surprised to see her.

"Cora," he said, taking her umbrella and setting it under the eaves. "What are you doing here?"

"I was running some errands, and wanted to stop by to ask you a question. Can I come in?"

"Of course."

She walked by him and he touched the small of her back, sending chills up her arms. Closing the door behind her, he turned with a smile. His eyes were darker than usual, and he was so tall that she had to tilt her head back to look into them.

He stepped close, reaching out to brush his thumb underneath her eyelashes.

She startled. She hadn't realized she was so tightly wound, but she was. She was about to come undone standing here in his foyer, with his musky scent flirting with her senses.

"Raindrop," he said, his voice husky. "Sorry."

"No, no. That's okay…"

He put his hands in his pockets. "It's awfully nasty out there. Do you have time for a cup of coffee?"

"Actually, I'd love one. I got some rain down the back of my shirt when I left the shop, and I'm kind of soggy."

"Here," he said. "Take your coat off. You can have my sweatshirt. There's nothing worse than damp clothes."

"Oh, that's okay. I'm fine."

"You can wear it home if you want. I mean, you'll swim in it, but that's alright. At least it'll be warm."

She smiled, shrugging out of her jacket. He took it and hung it by the door.

"Okay," she said. "Thank you."

He grabbed his sweatshirt by the hem and peeled it over his head. His T-shirt rode up with it, revealing his muscled abdomen, and a sexy line of hair that disappeared below his belt. She swallowed hard and looked away.

"Here you go," he said.

She took her sweater off, glad she'd worn a tank top underneath, and then pulled the sweatshirt on. It smelled like him. Her belly tightened.

"Damn," he said. "I don't look nearly as good in that as you do."

Her cheeks heated. "I'm a mess."

"No. You're not. Trust me."

They watched each other for a long moment. There was a fire crackling in the fireplace, and it popped and sizzled across the room. The warmth of it felt good, but not nearly as good as the sweatshirt against her skin.

"Well," he said. "I'll get you that coffee."

He walked into the kitchen, and she followed, running a hand through her hair. Trying to smooth it because despite what he'd just said, she couldn't believe she looked even close to presentable. The rain outside was blowing sideways.

"So," he said, turning the coffeepot on and opening the cupboard for a couple of mugs. "We didn't really get to talk after dinner the other night. Mary texted me a kitten meme that she thought looked like Harry, but other than that, she's been pretty quiet."

Cora felt something soft rub against her ankles, and she looked down to see the kitten standing there, blinking up at her with his big yellow eyes. He mewed, and her heart melted.

"Speaking of," she said, leaning down to scoop him up. He fit perfectly in the palm of her hand, but he had quite a tummy now.

She pulled out a chair at the kitchen table and sat, cradling the kitten in her lap. Then glanced out the window at the stormy waves crashing against the beach. There was a high surf warning this afternoon, and the ocean looked turbulent beyond the rain spattered glass.

"I love the storms here," she said. "I missed them. We don't get stuff like this in Bend."

"No, but you get snow." Neil set her coffee cup down and sat beside her, his knee brushing against hers. "I love the skiing over there."

"The rafting is pretty great, too. So I've heard, anyway. I'm kind of a chicken when it comes to that stuff."

He smiled. "No skydiving for you?"

"No way. I'm scared of heights."

"You'd be surprised. When you're in the plane getting ready to jump, you don't really get a sense of how far up you are. Everything below seems fake, like it's on a Monopoly board or something. It's not as scary as you'd think."

"I'll take your word for it."

"Maybe I'll convince you to jump with me someday. I'd be right there beside you…"

She rubbed the kitten's soft ears, and felt him start to purr. The thought of Neil being right beside her wasn't the worst thing in the world. Even if she was free-falling into space at the time.

She pushed the sleeves of the sweatshirt up, and took a sip of coffee. It was dark and a little bitter, just the way she liked it.

"So…about dinner with my parents," he said, watching her. "How do you think it went?"

She licked her lips and set the mug down. The expression on his face was tight, like he was worried what she'd say. Like he might've been thinking hard on it since they'd pulled out of the restaurant parking lot the other night.

"Honestly?"

"Yeah."

"I think it went really well," she said. "And I wasn't expecting that. I never really got to know your mom and dad before. I think they were trying. I felt like they were, at least."

"They were. I wasn't sure you'd be able to tell, but it was obvious as hell to me." He smiled and took a sip of his coffee. "I mean, it was awkward, right? But I thought it went pretty well overall."

"Mary liked them, Neil. She's been talking about when she can see them again."

He raised his brows. "Really. Because my mom was telling me she wanted to come by the shop to look around.

That's just an excuse, of course. She wants to see Mary again."

Cora let out a long breath and leaned back in her chair, the kitten curled up in a tiny ball in her lap. "Okay. Well, I'm relieved. I was dreading this part."

"Me too," he said. His gaze settled on hers, and his eyes were warm. Full of something that she couldn't quite identify, but that made her stomach clench all the same.

"I'm sorry for how they made you feel back then, Cora," he continued. "You were special, and I can't believe that I messed up with you like I did."

She swallowed hard. "You were so young. We both were. We just didn't know any better."

"But I should've, even at that age. I must've been pretty selfish to make you think I wouldn't be there for you. I screwed up."

"I did too, Neil. I was the one who left, remember? I did exactly what I was afraid of you doing. And I'm going to have to try to forgive myself for that eventually."

The wind blew against the kitchen windows, rattling them. The ocean roared outside, as if it was angry at Cora, just like Neil probably was. No matter how sweet he was being now. No matter how gentle.

He put his hand over hers, and his fingertips were rough and calloused. He rubbed his thumb over her knuckles, back and forth, stoking a fire in her belly. In her heart. It was pounding away, making her head spin.

"Can I be honest?" he asked.

She nodded, bracing herself.

"How do I know you're not going to leave again, Cora?"

The words stung. Because of what they meant—that he didn't really know her at all. She could say it all day long, but he had no idea how terrible she felt for leaving the first time. She'd had a long time to rectify that mistake, but in the end, she'd been too scared. The day she'd found the email from Mary, she'd vowed that she wouldn't let fear dictate her actions ever again. But Neil still thought she was afraid—afraid enough to leave. And maybe take Mary with her. She could see it in his eyes.

Slowly, she moved her hand away from his. Then forced her shoulders back. "I can't blame you for asking me that. It's only fair."

"Yes," he said quietly. "It is."

"I made a mistake, but this is the beginning of fixing it. I wouldn't do that again."

She couldn't tell if he believed her, and that hurt, too. She wondered if she and Neil would ever be able to get past this. To be able to co-parent, without it coming between them. And when she thought of being so attracted to him? Wondering where that might lead? It made her embarrassed. Of course nothing could ever work between them. There was too much water underneath that bridge.

"What about you, Neil?" she asked, forcing a steadiness into her voice that she didn't feel. "How are you feeling about this?"

"You mean having a daughter?"

She nodded.

"It's a shock, I'm not going to lie. I can't promise I'll be any good at it, and that's all I've been thinking about since meeting her."

She clasped her hands together, missing his touch already. But these were things that needed to be said. And they needed to be said without her heart being swayed by desire.

"I understand that," she said. "I had the same kind of doubts for a long time. I still have them, if you want to know the truth. Sometimes I think I don't have the slightest clue what I'm doing, but I've always tried to lead with my heart where Mary is concerned. It's gotten us this far."

The muscles in his jaw bunched again. "I can tell you I'll try to do the same."

"But what about the risks you take, Neil?" Her voice wavered a little because she hated the question. It had the potential to undo all of this, if they let it. It was the same question she'd never gotten the answer to when she'd gotten pregnant. She'd been too afraid to ask, because she thought she'd already known what he'd say. This time, she had to ask, and she had to ask straight-out. Cora had to know if he was going to prioritize being a father. And that meant some changes for him. Some major changes.

Scrubbing a hand through his hair, he stood and walked over to the window. "It always comes down to this, doesn't it? With you, my parents. It's not about the risks, it's not about those things. It's about how they make me feel."

She watched him. "And how do they make you feel?"

"Alive," he said simply. "They make me feel like I don't have one foot in the grave."

"You're not even thirty. I don't get how you can feel like that. Or how you could've felt like that as a teenager."

He turned, his expression sharp. "I do. And I did. Don't you get it, Cora?"

She sat forward in her chair, looking up at him. Aware that they were finally getting into the deep stuff. The stuff they'd never had the courage or maturity to approach before. And it felt like she was standing on the edge of a precipice, looking down into a dark hole.

"Tell me," she said. "Explain this so I can understand."

He rubbed his chin, looking tired all of a sudden. There were dark smudges under his eyes that she hadn't noticed before. She was tired, too. It seemed like she'd been doing a lot of lying awake at night and staring at the ceiling lately.

Taking a visible breath, he crossed his arms over his chest. His T-shirt stretched over his shoulders, and thick veins stood out on his biceps and forearms. His stance was stiff, his body rigid. This was not a comfortable subject for him, it was obvious. Neil wasn't the type to open up easily, or at least, he'd never been when they were together. The fact that he was talking to her now was significant, and she fought the urge to get up and go over to him, just to be closer.

"I had a hard time when I was a kid," he said, his voice low. "I was lonely and isolated, and I grew up watching my parents negotiate life, negotiate their *marriage*, like it was a transactional relationship. I never saw them show much emotion. Even when I was sick or hurt. Or when I was in love with someone they didn't understand."

She gazed up at him, her pulse skipping.

"They didn't talk to me," he continued. "They never knew me. They still don't know me, and that feels so wrong, so uncomfortable, that sometimes I want to crawl out of my skin when I'm with them."

"But they love you," she said. "That's obvious."

"Yes, they do. And I love them. But there's a numbness when it comes to my family that has shaped the person I am. I don't want to be numb. I want to *feel* things."

"And that's why you take risks," she said evenly.

"That's why. But I also know the things I do only provide physical sensations, adrenaline, a temporary high. The emotional stuff?" He shook his head. "That scares the shit out of me. I've never learned how to connect with that part of myself, and I'm sure a therapist would be able to explain all of this in a way that makes more sense, but I've done a lot of thinking on it, and I at least understand that part."

She looked down at the kitten, and stroked his silky black fur. Drawing some comfort in the slight weight of him in her lap, of his warmth and gentle breathing. When she looked back up at Neil, it was with an ache in her throat.

"So," he said, his voice low. "When you ask if I'm going to stop living my life the way I always have because I'm a father now, I really don't know. I'm not sure how to live it any other way. Letting myself feel what I need to for Mary seems a hell of a lot riskier to me, and I know how screwed up that is. My relationship with you..."

He paused, and she could almost feel the blood pumping through her veins. A low swish that made her hyperaware of her own body. Of her fingertips touching the kitten's fur. Of her back resting against the rigidness of the chair. Of the breaths she was taking, in and out, slow and easy.

"Your relationship with me, what?" she said.

He watched her, then took a step forward. Then another, until he was standing close. So close that she could see the exact color of his eyes, the warm honey in them.

"It changed me," he said. "When you left... I don't think I've ever admitted until right now how much it changed me, Cora."

And there was the chasm between them. Yawning wide and deep. Her guilt for leaving, and his anger that she went. She didn't know if he was ever going to feel okay about it, no matter how much they talked, or how much time passed.

She put the groggy kitten down in his bed by the table, and stood. She couldn't sit there and look up at Neil any longer without feeling like she was going to come apart. She needed some agency. She needed to feel strong, even though she also felt broken at the same time. She'd lived with so many mistakes over the years, so much regret for how she'd done things. And it was simply taking a toll. She just wanted to feel like she'd done something right for once.

"Leaving changed me, too," she said. "I can tell you how it was, I can put it into words, but I could never explain how I really felt. How lost I really was."

"Why didn't you at least let me know that you were okay? If you were planning on coming back, or if you just needed some time? I would've given it to you, you know."

"I didn't know that. I was operating on the assumption that you were going to leave, too."

He frowned, his face stormy like the ocean outside. Like the clouds overhead that seemed full of unending rain, pushed along by relentless wind.

She raised her chin. "You can't deny that, Neil. Whether or not you were really going to leave Christmas Bay, whether you were really going to leave me, you led me to believe that by the things you said and did. How was I supposed to know you would've stayed and that I could've counted on you? I'd just found out I was pregnant, that I was going to be responsible for another life. I couldn't take the chance of depending on someone who wasn't going to be there. Of getting my heart broken, and having to deal with that kind of trauma on top of taking care of a new baby. I just couldn't. I didn't have the bandwidth."

He shook his head. Started to say something and then stopped. He was so tall, so imposing. So sexy, that she had to focus on her breathing and composure, for fear he'd be able to see that she was actually shaking.

"You're right," he said, his voice dangerously quiet. "I told you I was going to leave. I own that. And I own the kind of kid I was. One that didn't necessarily scream responsible. But didn't I show you how I felt? When we were together? I thought you would've been able to feel it. I thought I did a pretty good job of that part."

She knew exactly what he was talking about. Their physical chemistry back then had been electric. He'd shown her things that still made her cheeks hot when she thought about them. About those nights by the river when the midnight air had been chilly on their naked skin. He'd awakened a desire in her, a spark, that crackled to this day. And he was right—their love language had been much more physical than anything else. Even when they'd had long talks, and they *had* talked, she couldn't remember ever really opening up to him. Or him to her. She guessed she could blame their young age for that clumsiness in their relationship.

But now… Now they were opening up and then some. She felt like he could see right into her. And the knowledge shook her, because if he could see into her heart, there could be no more walls, no more hiding to keep herself safe.

She licked her lips and gazed up at him. "I felt it," she managed. "But I needed to hear it, too."

"And what about now? Do you need to hear it now?"

Her heart thumped in her ears. She nodded, unable to take her eyes off him. He had her transfixed. "Yes."

"Will you believe me? Will you trust me, Cora?"

He had to know it was a lot to ask. Maybe too much.

He reached up and cupped her cheek in his hand. Moved his thumb gently over her cheekbone. She closed her eyes for a second, trying to find that composure that was everything to her, but she knew he could feel her trembling anyway. She could barely keep her knees from knocking together.

He leaned close, and she opened her eyes again, locking gazes with his. Those brown sugar eyes that had always had the power to transport her to another time and place. To let her escape her reality for a short while, and make her feel like she was someone special to him.

And then, his lips were on hers, and she was reaching up to put her arms around his neck. Pulling him closer, closer, because she didn't think she'd be able to take it if her body wasn't pressed against his, if she couldn't feel the beating of his heart.

He wrapped an arm around her waist, and she breathed him in as his mouth moved over hers. She'd missed him. She'd missed him so much deep down, but without letting herself think of him, because that would've been a betrayal to Max, whom she'd also loved. But she'd loved Max in a different way. Neil had literally felt like a part of her, and when she'd left him behind, it had felt like that part had been severed.

Now her body was alive with renewed feeling, with tingling and heat and pleasure, because he was touching her again. He was kissing her again. He was holding her again.

He moved his fevered lips down her neck, and she tilted her head to the side, closing her eyes, losing herself in the desire she'd been fighting since the day she'd laid eyes on him again.

He slid his hand up the back of her sweatshirt, and she felt it splayed there against her spine. Right below her bra strap, where his thumb flirted. It was like he was an eclipse—the moon overshadowing the sun, and she couldn't see anything anymore, not logic or wisdom, or anything else except how he was making her feel.

And then she took a breath, a deep breath that filled

her lungs and awakened her brain, and she pulled away a few inches to look up at him.

He was breathing heavily, holding her so close that she could feel his belt pressing into her lower belly. He smelled so good, so familiar, and she bit her lip to try to snap herself out of whatever this was. She needed some time, some perspective, to figure out how she really felt. And she'd never get perspective kissing him. Not in a million years.

"What's wrong?" he asked, his voice gravelly.

"Neil…aren't you scared? Aren't you scared of this?"

"I'm scared shitless."

She felt the corners of her lips tug into a small smile. That pretty much summed it up for her, too. "Then why are we doing it?"

He pulled away. Just enough to create some daylight between them. "Good point."

The house was quiet except for the wind whistling outside the windows and the rain tinkling against the glass, like sand blowing against it.

Taking his hand out from underneath her sweatshirt, he rested it on her hip instead. It left her cold. She wanted him, and she didn't *want* to want him. Or anyone, for that matter. Letting herself kiss him like this was absolute insanity.

Suddenly, she wanted nothing more than to sit with Poppy over a hot cup of cocoa, their childhood favorite, and let her cousin talk some sense into her. Surely she wouldn't approve of this, if for no other reason than Cora's heart was so tender right now. Vulnerable. She *knew* Mary wouldn't approve. In fact, the thought of her daughter knowing anything about this afternoon filled her with dread. Just how would she explain *this*? And would Mary even be open to listening to an explanation?

"This is complicated, for sure," Neil said. "I'm sorry. I shouldn't have kissed you."

"I didn't exactly stop you."

"So we both agree that it's a bad idea. Right?"

"I mean, are either of us ready for anything more? Have we changed that much from when we were together?"

Would she be okay with Neil only sharing a part of himself, and holding the rest back? Because as far as she could tell, that was what he was doing. He still hadn't been able to give her an answer about anything, even though he'd asked her to trust him.

He frowned. "Are you asking if I want a relationship?"

"I'm asking if you want more than a one-night stand."

"I care about you. I've always cared about you, so yes. I want to be able to raise our daughter together."

It wasn't what she meant. And to her, the word *care* fell far short of the word *love*, which she knew she was getting dangerously close to.

"So," she said evenly. "We can agree that parenting Mary would probably be easier and a lot less complicated without anything else between us."

His expression was dark. "I guess that's what we're saying."

"It's the smartest thing. I mean, considering our history. Considering where we both are in our lives…"

"Right. Smart."

They stood there watching each other with the dull roar of the ocean outside the house. She let her gaze drop to his chest, where his T-shirt fit just right—the soft, worn cotton stretched over his lean muscle. It made her forget for a second what her reasoning was for pulling away just now. Her mind literally went blank.

"So," he said, leaning against the counter. "I guess I should ask what that question was."

She stared at him. "Question?"

"You said you came over to ask me a question. And we got a little...sidetracked."

"Oh. Yes." She wondered again how good an idea it was to invite him for Christmas. But they were going to be in each other's lives. For Mary's sake, they needed to find a new normal. One without tearing each other's clothes off would be best.

Putting her hands in the sweatshirt's front pocket, she took a breath. "Yeah, I was talking to Mary the other day about Christmas. And we were just wondering if you'd like to come over to our place. We'd love to have you."

He raised his brows. "For Christmas?"

"I'm sure you probably already have plans with your parents. But Mary would really like you to come if you're free. Even if it's just to stop by so we can give you your present."

"You got me a present?"

"It's nothing huge, but yeah. We went shopping the other day. Mary picked it out."

"That's sweet. I don't know what to say."

"Say you'll come." She hadn't meant to try to convince him. She'd been planning on just the opposite—throwing out the invitation, and letting him decide on his own. No pressure. But all of a sudden, the thought of having him for Christmas morning, getting to see him with his daughter on her favorite day of the year, was something that she was longing for.

He smiled. "Actually, there's nothing I'd like more."

"Really?"

"Really. My parents are leaving for a cruise to Puerto

Vallarta next week, I usually work over Christmas, so we've done our own thing for the last few years."

She frowned at that.

"It's okay, really. I have this tradition that I like, it makes me happy. Kind of reminds me what the season is all about. Corny, maybe, but true."

"What's that?"

"I serve Christmas dinner to the homeless at the community center."

Cora's heart squeezed. "That's...that's wonderful, Neil."

"It's not a big deal."

But it was. It was a lovely thing to do, an important thing to do. Because Christmas Bay was such a small town, with cold, wet winters, it didn't historically have a lot of people experiencing homelessness, but there were starting to be more and more, just like there were everywhere. It was incredibly sad, and Cora had always been proud of her hometown for offering help, and a leg up to folks who needed it the most.

"I don't have to be there until late afternoon," he continued, "so I'll be free early on. I'd love to stop by. Are Beau and Poppy okay with this? I don't want to crash your morning."

"You're not crashing anything. Everyone wants you there. And Poppy is making her famous cinnamon rolls, so you're in for a treat. They're delicious."

"Okay," he said. "It's a date, then."

She smiled, her stomach dipping. "It's a date."

Chapter Thirteen

"Bro," Jay said, a soda in his hand. "Allison is up front. She wants to see you."

Neil lowered the pad of paper to his side, and stared at his friend. He'd been working on inventory of the firehouse supplies, but at the mention of Allison, he wanted to lock himself in the garage. Immature? Yes. But true.

"Did you tell her I was working on equipment inventory?" he asked. "Come on, help me out here."

"I did, and she still wants to see you. She brought something for the Toys for Tots barrel, and she looks pretty good, if you ask me." Jay shrugged and took a sip of his soda. Then burped. "Wow. I gotta switch to iced tea."

Neil groaned.

"Dude," Jay said. "I don't know what the problem is here. She's hot."

"I'm just not up for anything right now."

"So you've said." Jay narrowed his eyes. "That's not it, though. You're not up for anything with *her*, specifically. But you *are* interested in Cora Sawyer. Am I right, or am I right?"

Neil set the pad of paper on a stepladder next to him, and tugged on the collar of his uniform, even though it was already unbuttoned. "Is it warm in here, or is it just me?"

Jay grinned. "Oh, it's just you."

"It's not funny."

"It's kind of funny."

"How?"

"You always get the girl, man. Always. Us poor slobs have to witness it on the daily, and now you've got too much to handle. I don't feel sorry for you."

Neil threw him a look.

"Now isn't the time," Jay said. "because you have to go break her heart and everything, but I want to know what's going on with Cora. Seriously, you can unload on me. I'm your guy."

Neil headed to the door that led into the station. "When and *if* I decide to unload anything, I'll keep that in mind. But honestly, there's nothing to talk about."

That was an outright fabrication, but he didn't have the energy to open up to Jay at the moment. He had too much on his plate to have a heart-to-heart with anyone.

"I don't believe that!" Jay shouted after him.

Ignoring him, Neil opened the door leading into the station, and was met with a blast of warm air. The captain had recently lost thirty pounds and had started running half-marathons, so he was always freezing. Consequently, he drove everyone else out of the building when he turned the heat up. Luckily it was an icy day, but Neil was still hot. Still on edge. He couldn't wait to go home and take a long walk on the beach in a T-shirt. His poor mom was always complaining about hot flashes—he wondered if this was what one felt like.

Resisting the urge to tug on his collar again, he turned the corner to see Allison standing beside one of the station Christmas trees, looking beautiful in a sparkly red sweater and tight-fitting jeans. Her hair was down today, and cascaded past her shoulders in dark, silky waves. Neil could understand why Jay thought he was off his rocker for not being interested in a woman like this. But his heart, as much as he didn't want to admit it, and wouldn't admit it—especially to Jay—was already taken. A fact that he still hadn't come to terms with yet. Neil was good at denial. And when it came to Cora, it was the only thing getting him through his day-to-day duties at work. It was the only thing allowing him to get any sleep at all. But at some point, he was going to have to face this. He was going to have to deal with what was happening between him and Cora. And now he was going to be spending Christmas at her place. *Christmas.*

His head was spinning.

"Neil," Allison said with a tentative smile. "Hey."

"Hi, Allison. What's up? Jay said you wanted to see me?"

She nodded, brushing her thick mane of hair over her shoulder. "Yeah. You know, I had to come by to drop off my Toys for Tots gift, and I thought I'd say hello."

He smiled. He hoped he didn't look as uncomfortable as he felt.

"It's good to see you," he said.

"I felt bad about how we left things."

"How we left things?" he repeated, not knowing what she meant, exactly. There wasn't really anything to feel bad about. They hadn't fought, hadn't even argued that much. But he knew she probably thought he was a jerk. And maybe he was. Maybe Jay was right. Neil had never treated the women he'd dated unkindly, far from it, but he'd been emotionally barren with them as a whole. And now it was finally catching up with him.

"Well," Allison said, crossing her arms over her chest.

"I was angry with you for a few days. I thought it was pretty obvious."

Now he really did feel like a jerk. He hadn't noticed, because he'd been so occupied with thoughts of Cora.

"Oh," he said. "I'm sorry."

She waved a hand. "No, no. It's okay. I've thought a lot about it, and I mean, I did like you. I liked you a lot, but you know, you always had a wall up. You never let me get past it. But I don't think it was me, I think it's every woman, Neil. You keep people out, and I know you well enough by now that I can see it's been a pattern your entire life."

He stared at her. She wasn't pulling any punches. And she was also one hundred percent right.

"I just needed to see you to tell you that," she said. "Because it was important for my healing process. I didn't want to hold on to it."

"No," he said slowly. "I'm glad you got it off your chest." Actually, he could've done without hearing it, but if it made her feel better...

She licked her cherry red lips. They matched her sweater. She looked fancy and festive, and completely over him right then.

"I heard that you just found out you have a daughter," she said evenly. "I met her the other night?"

News always traveled fast in a small town, but that was fast even for Christmas Bay.

"Yes. That was Mary."

"She's pretty." She paused, looking up at him with eyes that were very cool. Much cooler than he'd ever seen them before. "It's none of my business, but as a daughter whose dad was never around, I'll just say it anyway... I hope for her sake that you grow up a little, Neil."

He blinked at her. It was the final punch to his chest.

"Are you saying I'm going to be a bad father?" he asked.

"I'm saying it's a possibility if you don't start letting people in where it counts."

He was having trouble processing her words, much less opening his mouth to argue. Clearly, she was still angry and had wanted the last word. She'd cared about their relationship, or what she thought was a relationship, much more than he'd known. So, yeah. He was a jerk.

Without another word, she turned on her heel and walked past the overflowing Toys for Tots barrel, and out the door. And most likely out of his life for good.

He stood there staring after her. With a brand-new heaviness to his bones. Because she was right, he had the potential to give his kid some major issues for life.

Unless he just stepped back, and loved her from a distance, that is.

"You *kissed*?"

Poppy's eyes were so wide that it looked like they might pop out of her head. She set her cup of hot chocolate on the coffee table, and pulled her feet up underneath her. Then scooted closer to Cora, who also had her feet tucked underneath her. This was how they used to sit as kids, talking about boys. Cora guessed some things never changed.

"Tell me everything," her cousin said.

Mary was at the fire station, taking care of Harry. Who didn't need to be taken care of so much anymore, but she loved going over there, and it seemed like the entire firehouse liked having her. As long as Neil was alright with it, she was alright with it, too.

She leaned over and set her cocoa down next to Poppy's and took a deep breath. "Yeah. We did."

"When? I can't believe you waited this long to tell me."

It had only been twenty-four hours, but Cora understood what she meant. She'd been dying to talk to her cousin about this, but she'd had to wait for the right time.

"Things have just been so crazy around here. The shop is so busy with Christmas coming up…"

"I know, it's going to be here before we know it. But get to the good stuff."

"Well, I was driving over to Neil's to invite him for Christmas morning yesterday when I was running errands…"

"Ahh. Go on."

"It was raining so hard, and he invited me in for coffee. His house is so cute, Poppy. Right on the beach, and it's that cottage style that you like so much."

Poppy patted her hand. "Focus, Cora. The good stuff, remember?"

"Right. Well, we were just talking. But it was different. We started talking about things that we'd never talked about before, because we were too young or scared, or whatever. But I ended up asking him if he was going to be around for the long haul. If he was going to change his lifestyle to be a dad. It's not that I want him to change who he is, or what he loves. But I want to know that I can count on him if he's going to help raise Mary."

"You don't have to explain," Poppy said. "I know what you mean. What did he say?"

"He asked me to trust him. And if we can trust each other. I was the one who left back then, after all, no matter what my reasons were. But he never answered the question."

Poppy frowned.

"And we just…kissed."

"You just kissed. Just like that?"

Cora nodded. "I know. It sounds sudden, and I guess it was. But it also wasn't. I don't know how to describe how it feels being around Neil again after all this time. It's like we just picked right up where we left off. With all the teenage angst and attraction, and all of it. It's weird. It's like no time has passed at all, but at the same time, so much time has passed that I know in my heart he has to have changed where it counts."

"You mean being reliable?"

"I mean being present. I'm hoping reliable, too. And I'm not talking financially, I know he'll be there for Mary to help support her in that way. I'm talking emotionally. It's so important that I can trust him with her heart."

Poppy chewed the inside of her cheek. "You don't think he'd just cut and run, do you?"

"I don't think so. But I could see him justifying things to himself. Like maybe she'd be better off without him. Especially since they don't really have a relationship yet."

"But he asked you to trust him."

Cora nodded, running her hands down her thighs, just so she had something to do with them. "Yes, he did."

"So this is going to take a leap of faith, right?"

"Right."

"But the question is, are you at a place where you can do that? Especially since you're still grieving Max."

Cora swallowed hard. She kept thinking of Max, kept wondering if she was a horrible person for kissing Neil. For feeling the things she felt for Neil, period. The truth was, she was still too upside down to know anything at all.

Poppy leaned forward. "Hey."

"Yeah."

"It's going to be okay, you know. It will."

"I'm scared that I'm going to encourage Mary to love him, and then... I don't know. I just don't."

"You can't control what Neil is going to do, or what he won't do. All you can do is be there for your daughter. And there's nothing wrong with encouraging her to love, by the way. Loving and possibly losing, is all part of life, right?"

Cora knew this was true. But knowing it was true, and actually being able to accept it, was something different altogether. It would take some faith, yes. It would also take strength. She knew this was a perfect opportunity to show Mary how strong they could both be. And sometimes that meant taking a leap. And sometimes that meant falling and being able to get back up again.

She just wasn't sure her heart could take any more pain.

"It was so sweet of you to come and pick us up to do this, honey," Neil's mother said, walking beside him, her boots crunching in the gravel. "But what's the occasion?"

He turned to her and smiled. "It's Christmas, Mom."

His dad was walking up ahead, scouting for the best tree on the U-cut lot that Neil had seen on the way into Eugene. Asking them if they wanted to cut their Christmas tree this year had been completely spur-of-the-moment, and he still wasn't quite sure what had come over him. They never had a live tree, they always got a giant prelit one at Costco every few years and it sat in their foyer, covered in themed colors and decorations. They'd never cut their own as long as he could remember.

But Neil guessed that was the whole point. Getting them out of their comfort zone. Showing them how fun it could be picking out a tree and cutting it down, and putting it in water and having that wonderful pine scent fill the room.

He'd rediscovered it himself this year, and he wanted to share the experience.

"This one looks good!" his dad shouted from about forty feet ahead. He was pointing to a huge blue spruce that probably wouldn't fit in the White House, let alone their foyer.

"Oh, Richard. That's way too big!"

"No, honey. It's perfect, we can cut a little off the bottom."

She turned to Neil, her soft blue hat pushed far up on her head. He wasn't used to seeing her in hats. Usually, she complained they messed up her hair, but she'd dug one out of her closet before climbing into his truck. He didn't know if Mary was the reason, or if it was his dad's heart attack, or if they were simply more aware of getting older, but the change in both his parents was evident.

"He's very excited about this, Neil," she said quietly. "He's always wanted a live tree, but I veto it every year."

"I didn't know that."

"When I was a little girl, baby spiders hatched all over our tree. It was like *Charlotte's Web*. They were everywhere, on the curtains and the TV and on little webs behind the couch. I was so traumatized, I never wanted a live one again after that. Did I ever tell you that story?"

"You did." He smiled. "I love the *Charlotte's Web* part."

She smiled too, and put her hands in her puffer jacket's pockets. Her suede coat had the day off, thank goodness. She looked cozy and happy for the first time in a while.

"This is nice," she said. "Being out here with you."

"It is nice."

"Is this why you like to camp? Or…whatever it is you do in the wilderness?"

He laughed. "Yeah, I camp. Being outside has always made me feel bigger. Does that make sense?"

She glanced over at him. "Yes, I think so. But I'd like it better if you didn't pair being outside with those other things."

"I get it."

"When you're a parent, you worry. You never stop worrying, it goes with the territory."

He stepped over a few branches on their way to where his dad was standing impatiently, and thought about that. Even though he was in the most tender stages of getting to know Mary, he understood where his mom was coming from. He used to be annoyed by her hovering, seeing it as disapproval. But now he saw that it was simply concern. He hadn't been able to—or hadn't wanted to—put himself in her shoes until now.

He slowed. Then came to a stop and turned to her. "I'm sorry, Mom."

She stopped, too. "For what?"

"For not hearing you."

She watched him, her breath puffing from her mouth in silver clouds. "I never thought you'd say that. I'm surprised."

"I'm not too stubborn to admit when I'm wrong. It's the getting to the part where I know I'm wrong that takes a while."

She smiled. "That means a lot. But you're not the only one who's been wrong. Your father and I could've done a better job trying to get to know the man you've become, instead of wanting you to be someone you're not. You gave me that advice about Cora the other day. I've been thinking about it ever since."

It was significant. It was the closest she'd ever come to

validating the feelings he'd had as a little kid, and it hit him square in the chest.

"I'm sorry it's taken so long for us to get to this point, Neil," she continued. "I've been doing a lot of soul-searching since your dad got out of the hospital, and so has he. Since getting to meet Mary. We were wrong to discourage your relationship with Cora."

Neil blinked down at her. It wasn't anything he could've prepared himself for, this admission. He knew that Cora had impressed them at dinner the other night, but this was more than he'd let himself hope for.

"Seriously?" he said.

"Well, I think we were right to be concerned about it, obviously. She ended up pregnant after all."

He nodded.

"But we were wrong to judge her for who she was, what she didn't have. That was wrong, and I've felt bad about that for a long time. I just haven't been able to come to a place where I could admit it without seeming trite."

"So...you don't think she wants money anymore?"

She waved her hand. "I never really thought that. I was just anxious about her coming back in general. But now I see that it might be good for you. I know it's been good for your dad and me."

"But will it be good for Mary?"

"What do you mean?"

"I mean, I love her already. I'm really worried I'm going to mess this up."

"Oh, honey," she said. "All parents feel that way in the beginning. If you didn't, I'd be concerned."

"That doesn't make me feel any better, Mom."

She laughed.

"Will you two hurry up!"

His dad was practically chafing at the bit, ready to use the saw they'd been given at the gate, and Neil waved to him.

"We'll be right there!" Turning back to his mom again, he put his hands in his pockets. "I'm serious, though," he said. "Allison came to the station yesterday, and said some things…"

"Who's Allison?"

"This girl I'd been dating."

"But not anymore?"

"No."

"You never tell us what's going on in your life. I can't keep up."

"Well, I haven't felt like you really wanted to know."

Her cheeks flushed. "I always want to know, Neil. I must've been doing something wrong to make you feel that way."

"I'm sorry, Mom. We're kind of a hot mess."

She smiled, but it was small. "So what did this Allison say?"

"It wasn't a huge thing, but it hit a nerve. She said I needed to grow up for Mary's sake. Which, yeah. I get it. But having a kid is a monumental task, it's not just a matter of snapping your fingers and being up to the job."

"Oh, sweetheart," she said, patting his arm. "You're going to do just fine."

He felt the muscles in his jaw bunch as he looked down at his boots. He'd love to believe that. But he wasn't sure it was that easy.

"You overthink too much," his mom said quietly. "You always have."

"I'm getting frostbite waiting for you two slowpokes!" his dad yelled, his voice echoing through the trees.

"Well," Neil said. "I guess that's a wrap for this heart-to-heart."

"Patience is not his strong suit. He's dying to cut something with that saw. You'll probably need to oversee it, I don't trust him."

Neil turned toward his dad, but stopped when she put her hand out to stop him.

"I'm glad we talked, honey," she said. "I want to know what's happening in your life. I feel like we've missed a lot over the years."

He looked down at her. Their relationship had always been complicated, but he loved his mom. It made him sad that what she'd said was true—there had been a lot missed. On his end, and on hers.

"Is this because of Mary?" he asked.

"Well, yes. She's definitely changed our perspective. Finding out that you have a granddaughter all of a sudden, it's hard to ignore the mistakes you feel like you made with your own child. But it's more than that. We're getting older, your dad was lucky with this heart attack. Life is too short not to try to fix those mistakes. We love you, Neil."

Hearing these things from his mother wasn't commonplace. As a matter of fact, he couldn't remember the last time she'd told him she loved him. He knew, of course, but hearing it, even as a grown man, packed a punch.

He pulled her into a hug. "I love you too, Mom."

"Frostbite!" his dad yelled. "Over here! Happening right now!"

They both laughed. And finally headed his way, walking closer than before.

Chapter Fourteen

Cora unlocked the front door of the antique shop, looking out the window at the people walking down the sidewalk. It was a beautiful morning—cold, but clear, and there was a Salvation Army Santa on the corner ringing his bell. She could hear it from where she stood—a reminder that Christmas was only a week away.

She smiled and turned the open sign over. They were announcing the winners of the Christmas window contest today, and Mary was on pins and needles. The word on Main Street was that she had an excellent chance of taking first place. But so did Frances, the reigning champ. Justin had pretty much conceded, saying that Mary's Harry window was just too cute for his toolbox theme to compete, but Cora wasn't so sure. He had a lot of loyal customers who'd be casting their votes.

Looking at her watch, she took a sip of her coffee and wondered if Neil was working today. She'd just made a fresh batch of Christmas cookies, and Mary had decorated them about an hour ago. She sighed. There was absolutely no reason to bring him more cookies, except that it was a chance to see him again, and seeing him again was all she could think about. Not the smartest thing if she was going to try to put the brakes on whatever this was.

She leaned against the doorframe and watched Justin turn the Christmas lights on in his store window. He waved, and she waved back. She'd felt so much peace these last few weeks, even bordering on happiness for the first time since Max had passed. She kept coming back to the fact that she was still grieving, so how real could this be? It felt wrong, but at the same time, it felt good and right having Neil close. It was like she'd been on a raft for months, and now she had solid ground underneath her again. Was it just an illusion? Her heart grasping at a way to survive the pain? She just didn't know.

She was still contemplating that when she saw a shiny Mercedes pull up to the curb in front of the shop. She took another sip of her coffee and watched the driver's side door open and a woman step out into the bright December sunshine. Her stomach dropped when she recognized who it was.

Vivian Prescott. Looking beautiful in a red wool coat and formfitting jeans.

Cora stared at her. Was she here to visit the shop like she'd said she wanted to? Or maybe she just had some Christmas shopping to do downtown? Cora knew she shouldn't feel so nervous at the thought of seeing Vivian again, but she did. It was obvious that Neil's parents weren't the same people that she'd known—or thought she'd known—when she was seventeen. But they were still his parents, and she was intimidated by them. It was that imposter mom syndrome she'd always had—not feeling like she was old enough or good enough, or wise enough to be raising another human. And she couldn't help wondering if they felt the same way.

She watched as Vivian stepped onto the sidewalk, and

looked up at the antique shop sign above the door, shielding her eyes from the sun.

Cora set her coffee cup down and wiped her suddenly clammy hands on her jeans.

The older woman headed for the door, and pulled it open with a cold blast of salty sea air. Her sleek hair blew in front of her face and she pushed it away with a black-gloved hand.

She looked around the shop, and when she saw Cora standing there, she smiled.

"Vivian," Cora said. "How are you?"

"Hello, Cora, I'm doing well. This place is adorable, I can't believe I haven't been in before."

Vivian had said she liked antiques at dinner the other night, but she struck Cora as more of a Macy's kind of lady. But it was a nice thing to say, regardless.

Vivian turned to the front window, her brows raised. "Is that the famous Harry window?"

Cora laughed, and felt a little of the tension ease away. "It is. They're announcing the winners today over the radio. Mary is beside herself."

"I bet. What time?"

"Noon." Cora looked at her watch. "Only a few hours away."

"Richard and I will be crossing our fingers. Obviously, this is the best window in town."

"I don't know. Have you seen Coastal Sweets' window?"

"I haven't, but I was planning on going there next for some stocking stuffers. And Richard has to have his peanut brittle. They've got a good window too, huh?"

"Frances wins nearly every year."

"It can't be cuter than this one."

Cora smiled, and Vivian patted her hair into place, looking a little awkward. They stood there for a minute, the Christmas music coming from the speakers up front the only buffer between them. "I'll Be Home for Christmas." Cora's favorite.

"Well," Vivian finally said. "I actually came to bring you something."

Cora watched curiously as the other woman opened the snap on her designer handbag, and pulled out a small package wrapped in tissue paper.

"Here," Vivian said, handing it to her. "I thought Mary might want this. It's really for both of you."

"Oh… Thank you so much. Should I open it now?"

"Yes. It's for your Christmas tree."

Cora tore open the tissue paper. And there in her hand, was an ornament. A silver bell that looked like it had just been polished, and was clearly very old. It was lovely.

"Oh, Vivian," she said. "This is beautiful."

"It was my mother's. Her mother gave it to her when she was little, and she gave it to me. And now…well. I want you and Mary to have it."

Cora looked up at her, her eyes stinging. It was such a tender gesture, so unexpected, that it took her off guard.

"This is too much," she managed. "I can't…"

Vivian reached out and closed Cora's fingers over the bell. "You can, and you will."

"I don't know what to say."

"Say that you'll give Richard and me another chance."

Cora watched her, momentarily at a loss for words.

"I know we made you feel things that I'm ashamed of now," Vivian went on, her cheeks flushed. This wasn't easy for her, it was obvious. But she was plowing ahead anyway, and Cora admired her for it.

"It was a long time ago," Cora said.

"It was, but it feels like just yesterday to me. It must feel that way to you, too."

Cora nodded. That was true, it did.

"We love our son very much," Vivian said, her voice soft. "And we haven't understood him well. Or maybe we haven't tried to understand him. The things he did back then, and still does, we have a hard time with. But we're trying to be better with Neil. Does that make sense?"

"It does."

"And we never should've judged you like we did. I know you felt it."

There was no use denying it. Vivian knew it was true, so Cora just stood there, her knees feeling like Jell-O. She never thought this day would come. She knew she'd eventually see Neil again—knew that those feelings from the past would probably come bubbling up to the surface. But she never thought his parents would accept her, truly accept her. Especially after what she'd done. It was an emotional moment, and one that made it hard for her to look Vivian in the eyes, for fear her chin would start quivering.

She swallowed hard and forced a smile. "I did," she said. "But now that I'm a mother myself, I understand that you only wanted the best for Neil. I'm sorry I ran away like I did. That was wrong."

"We were partly responsible for that. You didn't feel like you could trust Neil, and you probably didn't trust us, either. And why would you? I'm guessing you were terrified of us."

Cora laughed, unable to help it. And Vivian gave her a slow smile.

"I'm right, aren't I?" she said.

"Well…"

"Be honest."

"Yes."

"See?"

They stood there, and the moment felt so surreal, that Cora had to bite her lip just to ground herself a little.

"Can I ask you a question?" Vivian said.

"Of course."

The older woman watched her closely, her eyes warm. "Did you have much help? When you left here?"

"From my family?"

Vivian nodded. Cora had told her that she'd worked after Mary was born, but hadn't gone into detail. She wondered how much, if anything, Neil had told his parents about the years after she'd left Christmas Bay. Vivian was obviously curious, and not in a judgmental way, either. It made Cora want to sit down and have a coffee with her. Neil's mother, of all people. She still couldn't believe it.

"Financially," she said. "My parents helped me afford childcare so I could work, but emotionally...no. That was a different story."

Vivian frowned. "They disapproved?"

"They did. But they also weren't around enough to know much about my life—they were going through a divorce, and were fighting all the time. My grandpa was the one who was there for me. But even with his support, I couldn't stay here. I just wanted to run away. To become someone that nobody knew. I guess a lot of that was panic, a lot of it was stubbornness. A ton of it was immaturity."

"You were still a girl yourself."

Cora nodded. The acknowledgment from Vivian felt good. The understanding tone felt even better. Like a hug that she'd been waiting a long time for.

"What about now?" Vivian asked. "Are you close with your folks? Are they close with Mary?"

It was a painful question. Even now, in her late twenties, Cora struggled with it. And maybe that was because Mary was getting older, and her childhood was passing by in a flash, and her grandparents didn't know her at all. For Cora, that was far more hurtful than them not knowing their own daughter.

She shook her head. "No. I'd never tell Mary this, but I think they've always been embarrassed that I was a teenage mother. I mean, they send cards on her birthday and Christmas, but I don't think she'd recognize them if they bumped into her on the street. I've forgiven them for a lot of things, but I just can't find the grace to try to have a relationship with them when they've ignored her like they have."

"I'm sorry, Cora."

"She has her aunt and uncle, though. And that's a blessing. And now she has you and Richard…"

"She certainly does." Vivian smiled. "What about your husband's parents? Are they in the picture?"

"They passed when he was young."

"So you didn't have anyone, really. When you left here."

"I had Mary."

Vivian took a visible breath. "It must make it hard for you to put your faith in Neil now. The fact that you've been hurt so deeply."

It was true. Cora nodded slowly.

"He's scared, too," Vivian continued. "I'm not sure if he'd want me sharing it, though. Well… I know he wouldn't, he already thinks I interfere in his life too much as it is. But as a mother, and now as a grandmother, I can't stand the thought of a relationship between you two not working for a second time around because you don't know how he really feels."

Cora stared at her.

Vivian's perfectly tweezed brows raised. "Am I right in thinking that you might want a relationship again?"

"Oh… Well…"

"I could see something between you the other night, Cora. You can tell me."

Could she? Vivian was being very sweet, very motherly, which was like kryptonite for Cora. But did she really believe that she wouldn't tell Neil? Cora was having a hard enough time with her feelings for him without him knowing about them, too.

But Vivian was looking at her intently and it was obvious that she'd decided in the last few minutes that she was going to try her hand at matchmaking. Cora knew she was going to be facing a tough adversary in Neil's mother if she didn't cooperate. Which was funny. Her own mom had never cared at all who she'd ended up with. But she'd been furious when she'd gotten pregnant. Cora had never understood why—she hadn't pretended to be interested in any other part of her existence, only that one.

"I don't know," she said carefully. "It's complicated."

"I understand. I do. But if there's any chance of a happily-ever-after this time, I'm going to do all I can to help."

Cora gave her hesitant smile. "What does that mean?"

"It means you both had the cards stacked against you before. I'm simply saying this time should be easier. If that's what you and Neil decide you want." Vivian smiled back, a twinkle in her eyes. "Which brings me to my next question…"

"She did what?"

Neil stood next to Cora, leaning against the ice-skating rink railing, and watched Mary whiz by for what must've been the twentieth time. She was still riding the high from coming in first in the chamber of commerce's window decorating contest and had wanted to celebrate.

He was proud of her. Not only was she the reigning champ at decorating Christmas windows—taking the baton from Frances O'Hara, who had conceded with grace and humility, and also a bag of congratulatory gummy worms—she was also good at ice skating. Really good, and before Cora had just told him what his mother had done, all he'd been thinking about was taking her on a father-daughter ski trip. She'd probably be a natural.

Cora looked over at him, her green knit cap pulled low over her eyebrows. Her nose was red from the cold, her cheeks pale, making her freckles stand out. She looked so pretty that she nearly stopped his heart. He had to force himself to look back at the ice-skating rink and the constant parade of kids skating past, so he wouldn't stare at her.

"She didn't tell you?" Cora asked.

"She said she might stop by the shop to take a look around, but she never told me she was bringing you the ornament. She loves that thing, I'm surprised she let it go. She's really warming up to you and Mary."

"Maybe a little too much."

He glanced over at her and smiled. "How so?"

"I think she wants us to get back together."

And then he couldn't help but stare. "I'm sorry, what?"

"I know. This whole time I thought she hated me. But she's been nothing but sweet and… I don't know. Motherly."

"I've noticed the same thing. This is not the mother who raised me. This is more like a grandma."

"Exactly."

He watched her, trying not to fixate on how plump her lips were.

He cleared his throat. "Why do you think she wants us back together?"

"She came right out and said it. More or less. She said if that's what we want, she wants to make it easier for us this time around."

"Oh God. What does that mean? I'm afraid."

"Well, for starters, she invited Mary and me over for a special dinner at their place. Before they leave for their cruise this weekend. You're invited, too."

He raised his brows. "A special dinner?"

"That's what she said. She said she's going to make her mom's fettuccini Alfredo for Mary, and they want to give her their Christmas present."

He pinched the bridge of his nose. "I love that they're excited about Mary. I love that they're excited about you. But her trying to get us together is weird. We're adults, we've got a daughter. We're beyond this, right?"

"Well, yes. But it *is* kind of sweet, you have to admit."

"I guess. But what if Mary gets wind of this? She's made it pretty clear that she doesn't want anything going on between us. What then?"

"I think your mom would know better than to involve Mary."

"Would she?"

Cora chewed her lip, contemplating this.

"Look! I can skate backward!" Mary shouted, whizzing by again, her stubby braids sticking out underneath her hat.

They both waved, and Neil was struck by the fact that they did it simultaneously. Easily. Just like a married couple. It was a simple thing—waving to their daughter as she skated past, but it made him feel like such a *dad*. His heart squeezed and he wondered if Cora felt it, too.

She glanced over at him. "What?"

"Nothing. Just kind of...enjoying the moment. Being here together, with Mary. That's all."

She smiled, and there was an electricity that passed between them. It was a familiar kind of heat, only it felt a little different today. Deeper, more meaningful, and he wasn't quite sure why. It was possible that every outing they went on, every moment they shared was bringing them closer together. Making the fear and questions harder to see, and bringing the joy to the surface. At least, it was a nice way to explain it. It could be that he was just insanely attracted to Cora, and there was nothing between them but chemistry and history.

Somehow though, as her gaze dropped to his mouth and lingered there, he didn't think that was it. It was something more—something that made him want to reach for her, to hold her close and not let her go. Maybe his mother was right—maybe the second time around could be easier if they just gave in to whatever this was and stopped fighting it so much.

"Hey!" Mary yelled, skating by again. "Watch this!"

They both turned to see her do a little hop on her skates, from one foot to the other, then she beamed at them before skating away.

"She's pretty good on those things," he said.

"She's got a pair of roller skates at the shop. She's on them all the time, so I'm not surprised she's taken to this so well. She's always moving, always going. I can barely keep up with her."

"She's a great kid, Cora."

She moved a little closer, until her shoulder was touching his. He could feel her warmth through his jacket and his stomach tightened. He wanted to kiss her again. He wanted to put his hands in her hair and up the back of her sweater, and feel her bare skin sliding underneath his fingertips. He felt like a teenager again. He should go straight back to his house and take a cold shower—that was probably the smartest thing. But suddenly, he let himself imagine doing all the things that had just crossed his mind, let himself go to a place that he'd been afraid of visiting since she'd been back, and his heart beat heavily at the thought. What if? What if she wanted those things, too? What if they had some kind of future that wasn't just about co-parenting, but actually becoming a family of some kind? A special little unit that wasn't perfect, but didn't have to be, in order to be full of love, full of joy.

He forced his gaze back to the ice-skating rink, and the sight of his daughter making another round. She was keeping an eye on them, he could tell. And what would Mary think of anything happening between him and her mother? He already knew the answer to that. It was an age-old obstacle facing single parents who might want to get back into the dating world. Kids came first, as they should. And a preteen who wasn't ready for her mom to be involved with anyone, would probably get the last word.

"You're awfully quiet all of a sudden," Cora said. "Is everything okay?"

"Fine."

She waited for a few beats, probably wondering if he'd elaborate, which he didn't. They'd already decided that pursuing anything wasn't a good idea, so why was he ruminating on this? He knew why. He just wanted her, that was all.

"So," she said. "What are your thoughts about this dinner of your mom's?"

He shrugged. "It's okay. She can think she's match-making, but we're one step ahead of her. I'm just happy to have you and Mary spend a little more time with them. Get to know them better. And honestly, I'm getting to know them better, too."

"I'm glad, Neil."

"I guess it's never too late, right?"

She leaned into him. It was sweet and familiar, even though the last time they'd stood side by side like this was almost a decade ago. He wished he could put his arm around her. He wished a lot of things.

Instead, he leaned away a little. Just so he wasn't touching her anymore.

It was the only thing he knew how to do.

Chapter Fifteen

"What about this one? Do you think he'd like this?"

Mary stood in the middle of aisle two at Judy's Bark and Meow and held up a little toy mouse on the end of a string. They'd been doing some Christmas shopping, which of course, wasn't complete without a few presents for Harry, at least as far as Mary was concerned.

Cora smiled and put a bag of dog treats shaped like bunnies into the cart for Roo. Then remembered how much she loved them, and grabbed two more. When you had a dog that weighed over one hundred pounds, cute bunny-shaped treats didn't last very long.

"It's adorable," she said, trying her best to ignore her aching feet. They'd been out since ten that morning, and it was almost dinnertime. She was toast.

"Do you think this, or the balls with bells in them?"

"He might bat those behind the couch and lose them. The mouse would be easier to keep track of."

Mary frowned, considering this. "That's true."

"Did you text Neil back? He wanted to congratulate you again on your Harry window. He was so impressed by it, honey."

"I did. And Justin texted, too. He was glad that I'm

going to donate the prize money to the animal shelter. It makes me happy to give it to them."

Cora's heart squeezed. "It makes me happy, too."

"Wouldn't it be cool if we were rich, Mom? And we could do stuff like this all the time?"

"It would be nice to be able to help like that. But you don't have to be rich to help. Just look what you're doing."

"I know, but it'd be awesome to be able to do it a *lot*. I wonder if Richard and Vivian give lots of their money away. I wonder if they like to help people like that?"

A few weeks ago, Cora wouldn't have known the answer to that question. But now, she had a pretty good idea that Neil's parents probably did good things with their wealth. They definitely had a facade, and appearances were important to them, but they were good people deep down. She felt it. They'd raised their son to be a good man, and that didn't just happen by accident.

"I think they probably do," she said.

Mary put the toy mouse in the cart next to the treats. "Mom. Guess who else sent me a message on Instagram? You're never going to guess."

"I don't know. Who?"

"You have to guess!"

"I don't know. Harry Styles."

Mary smiled and rolled her eyes. "Mom, come *on*."

"Okay, sorry. Harry Potter."

"Mom."

Cora laughed and put her arm around her daughter's shoulders. She seemed happy lately. It was nice. Cora wasn't sure what to attribute it to, but she had a feeling that part of it was Neil. She could relate.

"Okay, seriously," she said. "Who messaged you?"

"Riley Abbot. Can you believe it?"

"She did? What did she say?"

"She was like, all nice and everything. She said how cool the window was, and we started talking a little bit."

"Honey, that's great. See? She's not so bad, right?"

"I mean, she's still kind of snooty. But she said her parents are getting a divorce and her dad is moving out after Christmas, and she's been really sad lately. Maybe that's why she wasn't nice at school. Maybe it wasn't me after all."

Cora kissed the top of her head. "I think that's probably a good assumption."

"What does *assumption* mean?"

"It means when you think something is true."

"I feel bad for her," Mary said. "It sucks not having your dad around."

Cora frowned. Losing Max was a constant wound. A constant hurt that might ease for Mary over time, but would never go away. Grief was a heavy burden.

"But," Mary continued softly, "it's nice having Neil here. He's a pretty good dad, too. Don't you think?"

Cora hugged her again, her heart aching. But at the same time, it was incredibly full. She was grateful for Neil. She was devastated about Max. It was the constant push and pull that had her unable to sleep at night without dreaming vividly of them both.

"He is," she said. "He's a good dad."

"I still feel guilty saying that. Calling him dad, I mean. Even though I don't call him that to his face and everything."

"You don't have to feel guilty, sweetheart. You can love them both. Caring for Neil doesn't mean you care for your dad any less."

"Even if I called him 'dad'? I mean, someday?"

"Even if you called him 'dad.' There's room in your heart for both of them."

Mary smiled. She seemed satisfied with that, at least for now. But it was obvious that she wanted Neil to occupy a special place, and she was having trouble with exactly what that place would be.

Mary began pushing the squeaky cart toward the check-out lane. Cora followed her, and thought this was progress. No matter how long it took her daughter to find a place for Neil, the fact that she wanted him there, was a very good thing.

Now, if Cora could only accomplish the same thing, they'd all be happy.

"Could you put this over there under the tree, darling? I don't want Mary to miss it."

Neil's mother handed him a present for Mary. *Another* present. So far there was a growing pile under the pretty blue spruce that they'd cut down the other day, and Neil worried it was too much. He looked down at it and frowned.

"Mom…"

"I know what you're thinking. But this is the first Christmas we've gotten to spend with her, and we just got a little excited, that's all."

"You can be excited without spoiling the tar out of her."

"That's what grandparents are supposed to do!" She gave him a little wink, which was completely unlike her. It was like she'd been aging backward these last few weeks. The other day she'd emailed a link to an article about Disneyland, and the best times to go. He'd blinked at it, wondering if she'd been hacked. It was hard to picture his parents traipsing around Disneyland, but here they were. Apparently, it was on their radar.

"Now shoo," she said, sweeping her hands toward the tree. "They're going to be here pretty soon, and I want everything to look perfect."

"Everything does look perfect, Mom. Try not to stress so much. They're easy to please."

"But what about Cora? Do you think she's going to like what we're having for dinner? Did you ask her if pasta was okay?"

He laughed. "You never care this much about what *I* like for dinner."

But she seemed happy—rushing from room to room making sure everything was in order. Dinner was almost ready and the entire house smelled like Italian food. Neil's stomach growled as he walked over and set the present down with the others. Mary had her pile, of course, but Cora also had a pile. Who knew what kinds of things his mom had bought, but she'd been shopping the better part of a week.

Rubbing the back of his neck, he stepped back and stared down at all of it.

"Mom," he said. "I don't know that—"

But he was cut off by the sound of the doorbell ringing—a deep gong that reverberated throughout the large house.

"Honey!" she said, heading toward the kitchen. "I have to check on the bread, can you answer the door? I'll be right back."

"Sure."

He watched her disappear into the kitchen, the delicate scent of her perfume trailing after her. His dad was nowhere to be seen. She'd sent him upstairs to change a few minutes ago. Apparently, his ugly sweater from his company's Christmas party a few nights ago wasn't going to cut it.

Neil walked over and opened the door to see Cora and Mary standing on the stoop. Mary was holding a Tupperware container, and smiled up at him. Then came in for one of her signature hugs.

"Hey there," he said. "Come on in, you two. Dinner's almost ready. Mom is in the kitchen, she's taking drink orders. Cora? Want a glass of white wine?"

She smiled, unbuttoning her long rain coat to reveal a soft gray sweater dress underneath that clung to her curves. She wore a berry-red scarf draped loosely around her neck. Her lipstick matched, and her skin was glowing. Winter looked good on her.

"I'd love one," she said.

"What about you, kiddo?" he asked, looking down at Mary. "Want a Shirley Temple?"

"Ooohh. What's that?"

"Sprite, grenadine and cherries. It's really good."

"Yes, please." She handed him the Tupperware container. "Here you go. Christmas cookies. I decorated them myself."

"Oh wow. I love your cookie deliveries."

She smiled, looking proud of herself. "We dropped some off for Frances and Justin, too. They like the gingerbread ones, but I like the sugar cookies because of the frosting."

"Well, naturally."

Cora looked around the foyer, her eyes wide. "Neil, this place…"

"Yeah," he said quietly. "It's a lot."

"No, it's lovely. It's just huge."

"Yeah," Mary said. "I'd be afraid I'd get lost or something!" She looked around eagerly. "Do they have a dog or cat?"

"Sadly, no," he said. "Harry is the only pet in our family at present."

"So that means you're keeping him?" Cora asked. "For sure?"

"Looks that way. I'm not sure I could unload him now if I tried. The little stinker is attached."

"I think you're the one attached to *him*," Mary said with a smile.

"Maybe you're right, smart aleck," he said, reaching down to poke her in the belly.

She laughed, and he wondered what her baby giggles had sounded like. If she'd been quick to smile as a toddler, or quick to cry. There was a momentary pang of regret for not knowing those things, for missing them completely, but it was followed by a genuine feeling of joy that she was here now. That it wasn't too late to get to know her. He was grateful for that, and surprised that the usual flash of anger at Cora had eased to a mere flicker. He wondered if over time it would disappear completely. If he was on his way to forgiving her and moving on because of all the good things that she'd brought back with her. That she was sharing with him now.

"Is that who I think it is?"

They turned to see Neil's dad walking down the stairs, dressed in a powder blue cashmere sweater, with a white collared shirt underneath. His gray hair was neatly combed, and he wore a warm smile that matched his eyes as he took in his granddaughter. Mary was the newest love of his life.

She ran over to give him a hug. Neil could tell his dad adored her hugs just as much as he did, and he watched them, standing close to Cora. Appreciating the moment for what it was. Soaking it in.

"I like that Christmas sweater of yours," his dad said, tweaking Mary's nose.

She wrinkled it, and Neil could tell she was loving the grandfatherly attention.

His dad turned to Cora then, and kissed her on the cheek. "Hi there, Cora. I'm so happy you could come."

"Thank you for inviting us. Your house is just lovely."

"It's alright. I'm ready to downsize, but Vivian likes the view. Now Neil has the best view on the coast, as far as I'm concerned."

"It's pretty good," Neil said.

"If you'd let us buy the lot next to you, we could build and be just a stone's throw away."

Neil gave Cora a quick look. He wondered if she'd ever seen *Everybody Loves Raymond*. It was the first thing that came to mind—the idea of his parents living so close and his mother just popping in on a whim. He loved his mom and dad, but he'd definitely have to move.

Her lips tilted knowingly. Like they were sharing an inside joke. This was happening more and more lately, him feeling like she knew what he was thinking. It was nice. And it was also a little sobering because if she knew what he was thinking, she'd also know how much he wanted to kiss her again.

"Well, hello there!"

They all turned to see his mom sweep into the room, making a beeline for Mary. Another hug, another kiss on top of her head. Mary was eating it up.

"Cora," his mom said, turning to take Cora's hands in hers. "I hope you like fettuccini as much as Mary does."

"Oh, I love Italian food. It smells so good in here."

His mom smiled. She'd always been a wonderful cook, but she'd been doing less and less of it lately. More often than not, Neil would just meet them at an upscale restaurant, or they'd go to the country club for lunch. He missed his mom's dinners that she'd made when he was a kid. The conversation had been sparse, but the food had been plentiful, and even if she hadn't told him she loved him very often, he could feel it in her cooking.

"Did Neil get your drink orders?"

"White wine for Cora," Neil said. "And a Shirley Temple for Mary."

"Attagirl," Neil's dad said. "Want to help me make it? We'll put extra maraschino cherries in."

"*Ooohh* yeah."

His dad grinned and held his hand up for a high five. Mary slapped it, and they headed into the kitchen like they'd known each other forever. Neil was amazed at how fast they'd taken to each other.

Cora stared after them. "I think they're going to be besties."

"You should've seen Richard this morning," Neil's mom said. "All excited that you both were coming over. I don't think I've ever seen him like this."

"I *know* I've never seen him like this," Neil said.

"Well, I need to go check on dinner and grab Cora's wine," his mother said, wiping her hands down her red apron. "I'll be right back. You two sit down, relax. Neil, why don't you turn on some music for Cora?"

He and Cora exchanged another look. The matchmaking was in full swing, his mom wasn't wasting any time.

She disappeared into the kitchen, where he heard his dad telling Mary about Shirley Temple, the actress.

Neil smiled over at Cora, who was looking up at him with those pretty eyes.

"Music," he said. "I seem to remember you liked the old stuff. Mötley Crüe? Def Leppard? Think my mom would mind if we cranked the stereo?"

She laughed. "Only if we started dancing on the tables. I wouldn't mind an eighties dance party, I know Mary wouldn't."

"I think it's high time that she's officially embarrassed by her parents. Have you started turning the music up when you drop her off at school?"

"I never did, that was Max's department. He…"

At the mention of her late husband, her voice trailed off.

He waited for a few seconds, and then walked over to her. Took her hand in his. Felt how soft her skin was. Her nails were a perfect shade of pale pink, and he wondered if she'd painted them before she came over. If she wanted to look nice for him, if she'd been thinking about him as much as he'd been thinking about her. And if she had, what exactly did that mean? What were they going to do about this, if anything at all?

"I'm sorry," he said.

"It's not your fault."

"But I might be making you feel bad, or guilty, and I would never want that."

"I do feel guilty, but that's me, not you."

"Why, though?" he asked, his voice low. "I mean, I get it. But we haven't done anything except kiss. You haven't done anything wrong, Cora."

She looked up at him, and her eyes were sad. He hated the look in them. Like she might be regretting that kiss.

"It's more than a kiss. You have to know that, just like I do."

Yes, he knew. It was the elephant in the room.

She glanced over her shoulder to make sure they were still alone. He could hear his parents and Mary in the kitchen. Pots and pans banging. Occasional laughter. A timer going off. It felt so right, so normal, that he wanted to lean into it. To this happiness, or peace, or whatever it was. But at the same time, there was a voice in the back of his head whispering that it couldn't last. If he was smart, he would heed that warning.

Cora looked down at her hand in his. She tightened her fingers around his, holding him in place for a second longer. And then she let go and stepped back. Enough so he couldn't reach for her again.

"I'm so confused," she said, shaking her head. "What are we doing, Neil?"

He couldn't answer that because he didn't know what the hell they were doing, either. All he knew was how he felt, and how he'd been feeling. He understood her confusion because he was entrenched in his own.

"I don't know," he said.

"I'm so happy we're spending time together. And it's good for Mary, of course. But we're playing with fire here. Nothing's really changed...has it?"

"You're saying you don't trust me."

"No, that's not what I'm saying. I trust you with Mary, I trust that you want to do the right thing. But with us..."

"You don't trust me. Just say it, Cora."

"Well, no. You don't have a great track record. And neither do I, as far as staying put when things get messy is concerned."

"We've grown. Things have changed. *We've* changed."

"But what does that mean? That you want to give this a chance?" She waved her hand in a wide arc. "Whatever it is? Is this the beginning of us wanting a relationship? Or is this the beginning of us wanting sex? Because there's a big difference. Your heart is on the line, and so is mine."

This was the first time since they were seventeen that they'd talked about a relationship of any kind. When they'd talked about it as kids...well. That had ended badly. With Cora running away, and him burying his head in the sand. Using all his dangerous hobbies to take his mind off her. To fill the void that she'd left behind. And he realized that was exactly what he'd been doing—filling the void.

He turned away from her, unable to look her in the eyes. He didn't want her to see how he was really feeling, which was scared to death. Because right then, he was tempted to say something like, *Yeah. Let's try this and see where it takes us. Let's give it a shot. Let's show our daughter that we didn't give up on each other.*

He frowned, looking out his parents' giant living room windows to the view beyond. Their house sat on a hill above the expansive neighborhood, and looked out at the purple mountains in the distance. The sky was starting to turn a bubblegum pink, the wispy clouds a buttery yellow. A sky swirling with heavenly colors that suddenly hurt his heart. He swallowed hard. Money couldn't buy happiness, but it sure as hell could get you the nicest house on the block.

"Neil," Cora said softy behind him. "Talk to me."

He crossed his arms over his chest. "I don't know what you want me to say."

"I want you to tell me what you want."

The words resonated with him. It was the question he'd been avoiding for twelve long years. Twelve years of wanting something that he could never articulate. Of feeling so empty that he'd started blaming other people for not being good enough in a plethora of different ways. His parents for being too controlling, ex-girlfriends for being too needy... When the problem had always been him, and what was missing in his life. *Cora.* Cora had been what was missing.

Slowly, he turned around. He looked down at her, his chest feeling uncomfortably tight. She was so pretty, she was so sweet. His girl. She hadn't been for a long time though, but she could be again. If he was brave enough to take that step.

He took her by the hand. "Come here," he said, his voice gravelly.

"Where?"

"Over here."

He led her through the living room and into his dad's study. He'd always loved this room because of the books that lined the walls from floor to ceiling. Most of them were nonfiction. But some of them were classics, and he remembered getting lost in here as a kid. Losing himself in the stories and the papery smell, and the possibilities. He'd always been a dreamer, and he'd never felt his mom and dad had gotten that about him. But maybe they'd understood more than he'd given them credit for. They'd been right to worry about him, because he'd been floating, unmoored through life for a very long time now. He had a good job, a stable existence. But he was lost. And now, there was a very distinct feeling of being found again. By a little girl who was still a stranger to him, but whom he'd actually die for. And by a woman who'd held his heart in the palm of her hand since high school.

He left the study door open a crack so he could hear

his mother call them for dinner. It would be soon now. He didn't have a lot of time to say what he needed to. The thoughts that had crystallized in his brain, and were waiting for a release through the spoken word. Through physical touch, which had always been his most successful form of communication where Cora was concerned.

He looked down at her. Put his hands on either side of her face, sweeping his thumbs over her cheekbones. Her eyes were bright, questioning. But she didn't move, didn't protest the secrecy of the moment. Maybe she was craving this release just like he was.

"You asked me what I want," he whispered. "I want you. I've always wanted you."

She stared up at him. Her lips were so plump, so kissable. Her skin so soft against his. He wanted her, but that was an understatement. He craved her. She was his other half.

"Neil…"

"You don't have to say anything right now. I just want you to know how I feel. I was a coward when you left. I should've gone after you. I should've found you. I loved you, Cora. I've never felt the same way about anyone else."

Her eyes, those gorgeous baby blues, grew glassy with tears. But she didn't cry. She swallowed visibly, and turned to kiss the palm of his hand that still cradled her cheek.

His heart labored in his chest at the feel of that kiss. He'd opened the door. Now he was going to have to convince her to walk through it. To trust him. But did he trust himself? Was he a man who'd come far enough to learn from his mistakes and to grow from them? He guessed time would tell. But he was going to try his damnedest because he knew what was on the line.

"And Mary?" she asked.

"I'm not going to pretend that I know what I'm doing. But I'm going to be there for her. If that means making some adjustments in my life, then I'm good with that."

She smiled. He thought she looked relieved. She definitely looked beautiful.

"It might take a while for us to figure this out," he continued. "But I want to try, if you do."

She gazed up at him for a long moment, and he gazed back. For a few seconds it felt like they were in their own little world. Being transported back to a time where they were younger, more innocent. With their whole lives ahead of them. Again, he wondered what would've happened if she hadn't left Christmas Bay. But he didn't want to ruminate on that anymore. What was done was done, and he wanted to move forward. Try to leave their mistakes in the past. It was time.

Slowly, he leaned down, drawn in by the color of her eyes—they were midnight blue in the dim light of the study, the room of books and dreams. He hovered over her mouth and she parted her lips just slightly. He could feel her soft puffs of breath, the warmth in them, and it made his gut tighten with desire.

And then he was kissing her. Moving his mouth over hers and feeling her lean into him. Reaching up to put her arms around his neck. Pressing her hips into his. His heart slammed in his chest. What he really wanted to do was push her up against the wall, and hear her say his name. But of course, this was only a stolen kiss. A few seconds, and he would need to pull away again. To regain his senses, and let his blood cool some.

"Mom?"

Neil felt Cora jump before he could even process what

happened. She jerked away so fast that he stepped forward, momentarily caught off-balance.

Cora's hands flew to her mouth as she looked past him.

He turned, dreading what he was going to see there. Knowing that it was going to change things before they'd even started.

Mary stood a few feet away, in the doorway of the study, the light of the Christmas tree glowing softly behind her. It was a deceptively gentle sight. Because the look on her face was one of pure betrayal. Neil could remember feeling some of his strongest emotions as a preteen, when nothing made sense, and everyone seemed to let him down in spades. It was a tumultuous time, full of angst, and if he hadn't already known that from experiencing it himself, he would've been able to tell just fine by the look Mary was giving him now.

"What are you *doing*?" she cried.

"Honey," he said. "We can explain."

"Don't call me honey! Like, you don't get to call me that *ever again*."

"*Mary.*" Cora had recovered enough to take a firm tone.

"What, Mom?" Her eyes flicked back to her mother. Her cheeks were bright red, Neil couldn't even see her freckles anymore. This was bad. This was really, really bad.

"What's going on in here?" his mom said, appearing behind Mary and craning her neck to get a better look.

Neil sighed.

"Mary!" his dad called from the living room. "Did you find your folks?" He appeared cheerfully behind Neil's mom in the doorway. Apparently, they were going to have an audience for this. "I had to put the bread in a little longer… What's happening in here?"

Cora smoothed the front of her dress that didn't need

smoothing, and looked like she was trying very hard to hold it together.

"They were, like, *kissing*," Mary said. "Gross."

"Mary," Cora said. "Stop."

"Kissing?" Neil's mom said, her eyebrows raised hopefully.

"Kissing?" his dad said. "Who was kissing?"

"Richard!" his mom said. "Neil and Cora. Who else?"

"I can't believe you two," Mary said. "You're like *teenagers* and stuff. Worse than teenagers."

Neil's mom put her hands up. "Let's just all calm down."

"Tell *them*!" Mary said.

Neil rubbed his temple.

"I don't understand what's happening," his dad said, looking confused. It would've been funny if it wasn't such a train wreck.

"What don't you understand, Richard?" his mom asked. Neil thought she was being extraordinarily patient under the circumstances. "They still have feelings for each other."

Mary stared at Cora. "I *knew* it. I knew you liked him. What about Dad?"

"I'll always love your dad, Mary."

"It sure doesn't look like it, Mom."

"Mary," Neil said. "I'd never try to replace your dad."

She crossed her arms over her chest and glowered at him. Her lips practically disappeared.

"Let's look on the bright side," Neil's mom said. "We're a family again, right?"

"We were a family before, Mom. Cora and I don't have to be together for us to be a family."

"Vivian," his dad said. "You were trying to meddle, weren't you? Is that what this dinner is about?"

Her cheeks colored. "Well, no! I wanted to spend time with Mary and Cora."

"Be honest."

"I am being honest."

Cora cleared her throat and looked at her shoes.

"Mom," Neil said.

"Okay. *Okay*, is that so bad? That I want to make up for the mess we all made back then?"

Mary looked up at her. "Are you saying I was the mess?"

"Honey! Of course not!"

"You wanted us to come over because you wanted them to get together?" Mary asked. "Eww."

"Mary," Cora said, "it's not like we're two strangers off the street. We're your parents."

"I *had* a dad, and now he's gone, and I like Neil and stuff, but he's not my dad, not like that!"

Fat tears were streaming down her cheeks now, and it was taking all Neil's self-control not to cross the room and take her in his arms. If he did, she'd probably kick him in the shin.

All of a sudden, the smoke detectors in the kitchen went off.

"Damn!" his dad said. "That'd be the bread. I hope everyone likes it charbroiled."

"Mom, I want to go home," Mary said with a sob.

"Mary…"

"Oh, honey. Please don't go," Neil's mom said.

Neil pushed past everyone. "I'll go get the bread." He could smell the smoke from the kitchen and it set his teeth on edge. For him, it was the smell of everything going south in a matter of seconds.

He grabbed an oven mitt off the counter and pulled the bread out—black and smoking like Pompeii. Then he got a stepladder from the pantry, and climbed up to the smoke detector to turn it off. The house went blessedly silent and he took a deep breath. The smoke filling the kitchen stung his nose and eyes, and he looked toward the study where his parents were still in the doorway talking in low tones to Mary and Cora.

He should've waited to talk to Cora. He should've known this would happen—he'd been dying to kiss her again. *Wrong time, wrong place, dumbass*, he thought sourly. The worst part was that he'd broken the delicate web of trust he'd built with Mary over the last few weeks. She was still grieving her father—who knew how long it would take for her to come back around?

Still, as he climbed down off the stepladder, he wondered if this had been inevitable. Would she ever come to a place where she was ready to see her mom with someone else? At least while she was still a kid? He wasn't so sure. She'd loved her dad fiercely, and was protective of his memory, as she should be. And he'd stepped all over that in one careless moment.

Cora walked out of the study behind Mary, who wouldn't look at him. She was looking at the carpet, her lips still pursed.

"We're staying for dinner," she told him. "I know Mary is upset, and I promised her we'll talk about it when we get home. But your parents went to all this trouble and we're going to stay and eat. Isn't that right, Mary?"

"Right," she mumbled.

Neil's mom looked at him, her brows knit. His dad had his hands in his pockets, glancing awkwardly from Mary to Cora and back again. The tension was so thick, Neil wondered if it would be better if they didn't force Mary to stay when she didn't want to. But he wasn't going to second-guess Cora's decision. She was clearly in charge here, her voice gentle but steely at the same time. It was one of those parenting moments where he felt painfully out of his depth.

"Well," his mom said, clapping her hands together. Unlike Cora's, her voice was trembly. "Let's eat, shall we?"

Chapter Sixteen

Cora stood in front of the window of the antique shop and chewed on her fingernail. She hadn't bitten her nails since Max had been in the hospital. And before that, she hadn't bitten them since she was a teenager. But she was worried, and she'd started nibbling at them without even realizing it.

Poppy walked up behind her. "She'll be back any minute. She probably stopped at Coastal Sweets for some gummy worms. You know how Frances likes to chat."

Cora looked at her watch. Mary was going on half an hour late, and it was almost dusk. Which, granted, wasn't super late, but Mary knew she wasn't allowed to stay out past dark. She'd walked down to Donut Country to meet Riley Abbot for a hot chocolate. Which was very sweet, considering she'd thought Riley hated her a few weeks ago. Cora was happy they were connecting, especially since Riley was having such a hard time at home, but Mary still wasn't speaking to her, and everything had Cora on edge since their ill-fated dinner at Vivian and Richard's the night before.

"She's not usually late," she said. "Even when she's upset."

Poppy frowned. The old-fashioned streetlamps had

winked on five minutes ago. The wreaths hanging from them swung in the coastal wind that had just picked up. A light mist was beginning to fall, which made Cora's stomach even tighter.

"Why don't we go get our jackets," Poppy said, "and we can walk down to the donut shop. I bet we'll run into her coming home."

Cora looked at her watch again. Only a minute had passed since the last time she'd looked. "No, you and Justin have that Christmas party tonight, and you're not even ready. You go ahead."

"I don't like to leave you like this."

"I'm okay." Cora forced a smile. "I promise I'll keep you updated. And you're right, she's probably on her way."

Poppy stood there for a few seconds, hesitating. "Are you sure?"

"Positive. Go."

"Okay...if you're sure. I'll just be upstairs getting dressed." Poppy gave her a quick hug. "Don't forget to let me know when she comes home. If we need to, Justin and I will leave the party. It's pretentious anyway. I mean, my dress has *sequins*."

Cora gave her a look. "You know you're dying to wear that dress. You'd better get going or you're never going to have time to curl your hair."

Her cousin gave her one more squeeze, and then headed for the stairs leading up to the apartment. Cora watched her go, biting her lip. She didn't want to ruin Poppy's night—no matter what she said, she'd been looking forward to this party for weeks. It was being thrown by an old colleague of hers at the TV station where she'd been a weekend anchor, and all her friends were going to be there. Justin was going to wear a tux. It was a *big dill*, as Mary would say.

At the thought of her daughter, she looked out the window again. It was close to being dark now. This wasn't like Mary.

Her phone dinged from her back pocket and she sagged with relief. It was probably Mary. Maybe with a good excuse for not coming home on time.

But when she pulled it out and saw Neil's name on the screen, her stomach sank.

Hey, just checking in. Is she still mad?

They'd been texting since last night. Since they'd kissed again, and everything had gone to hell in a handbasket. But that wasn't quite true, because things were also wonderful, too. Cora was falling in love again. She was scared to death, but it was happening, whether she liked it or not. The timing was strange, but then again, she was starting to think that it might be meant to be. That maybe Max had had a hand in this small happiness, that he was sending her a sign in Neil.

But at the end of the day, if Mary wasn't on board, Cora knew it wouldn't work. If she couldn't accept this, if it was too painful for her, then it would have to wait. Or it might not happen at all. As drawn to Neil as she was, Cora was okay with that, because Mary came first.

She typed out a quick response, her eyes blurry from sudden fatigue. She told him Mary hadn't come home yet and that she was worried. But she didn't say anything more because this could all be a false alarm, and she didn't want to freak him out.

He texted back immediately. I'll be right over.

She stared at it, relieved. She'd spent so much time facing things alone, that this felt good. She hadn't asked him to come, he'd just known she needed him—that their daughter might need him, too.

Swallowing hard, she typed out thank you. Then went behind the front counter to grab her raincoat and a hat. She wondered if Poppy was right—maybe Mary had stopped by Coastal Sweets on the way home. Maybe Frances had seen her. Maybe she was even there now...

She dialed the candy shop's number and waited for someone to answer.

"Coastal Sweets, this is Frances."

"Hi, Frances," she said. "This is Cora Sawyer."

"Cora! How are you, honey?"

A lump rose in Cora's throat at the sound of Frances's motherly voice. It wasn't just the immediate situation with Mary that had her tied in knots. It was her grandfather's passing, her move back to Christmas Bay, losing Max, questioning whether things would work with Neil... It was all of it, and Frances's voice warmed her through.

She switched the phone to her other ear. "I'm doing okay... Frances, listen, the reason I'm calling is that I'm looking for Mary. She went to Donut Country a while ago to meet a friend, and she hasn't come home yet. I was wondering if she might've stopped by your place?"

Frances made a tsking sound on the other end of the line. "Oh... I haven't seen her. I have a bag of gummy worms waiting for her, though. I set them aside after the last order came in. We can't keep them in stock around here."

Cora's heart sank. She was going to need to go out looking for Mary after all, and the reality of that turned her stomach.

"Okay. Well, thanks, Frances. I appreciate it."

"If she comes in, I'll tell her she needs to go straight home."

"Thank you."

"Merry Christmas, sweetheart."

"Merry Christmas to you."

She hung up the phone with suddenly shaky hands.

Putting her jacket on, she kept an eye on the window, hoping to see Mary run up at any second. Instead, she saw Neil making his way down the sidewalk, his hands deep in his jacket pockets, and his shoulders hunched against the mist.

She walked over to unlock the door, and he brushed past, scrubbing a hand through his hair. "Geez, it's cold out there."

"I know. It's cold and dark… Where could she be?"

"We'll find her. She couldn't have gone far."

Cora bit the inside of her cheek. "Maybe. But what if she did? What if she ran away or something?"

"I doubt that. She loves you way too much. You have a great relationship, and she wouldn't do that to you, Cora."

"She loves me, but she's furious with me. I've never seen her this upset, and that includes when she found out that I never told you about her."

He frowned. "And she's not answering her phone?"

She shook her head.

"Does she have her location on?"

"She's supposed to, but I checked, and it's turned off."

He pulled her into a hug. "We'll find her, baby. I promise."

It was the first time he'd called her "baby" since they were teenagers. She leaned into him, trying to hold on to what he'd just said—that Mary wouldn't do something as drastic as run away. But eleven was a tricky age, and she'd been through a lot recently. Cora tried not to be the parent who said *my kid would never*, because she knew everything was a possibility—even things you were pretty sure your kid wouldn't do.

"Come on," Neil said. "Let's go."

He took her hand, and she followed him out the door. She locked it behind them, and was immediately met with the heavy mist and fog that was so characteristic of winter in Christmas Bay. Normally she liked the weather because it only made her feel cozier staying inside. It made the Christmas lights seem brighter on the trees and wreaths, and on the little cottages lining the beach. But tonight felt colder than usual, and she blinked as the mist clung to her hair and eyelashes.

"Donut Country is open until seven," she said. "Maybe she's still there."

They walked down the sidewalk, the light from the shop windows glowing softly through the night. Her elbow bumped against Neil's, and it was a comfort. Like Frances's voice earlier, it was a reminder that she wasn't alone. She and Mary had people who loved and cared about them here. They had family here.

She put up the hood on her rain jacket, and turned to Neil. "Were you working?"

"I'm going on shift in about an hour. But I can show up later if I need to. We'll find Mary first."

She nodded. His voice was calm and even, and she was grateful for that. They kept walking, and she looked over at the shops as they passed. They were cheerful and bright. So many of them had participated in the chamber's window decorating contest, and Mary had been the one who'd won. Cora was so proud of that. The animal shelter was even going to have a little ceremony where Mary would officially present her check to them. It was going to be right after Christmas, and Mary wanted to invite everyone. She'd specifically asked if Vivian and Richard could come. Of course, that was before. Before the kiss heard around the world.

Cora sighed, her breath puffing from her mouth in a cloud. There weren't very many people out tonight. Even the ever-present tourists had decided to call it a day, and the shops were starting to close up. Lights were being turned off and signs brought in from the sidewalk. Most people probably wanted to spend the evening in front of a fire or a movie, or both. At least, that's what Cora would be doing tonight if her daughter wasn't off doing who knew what, who knew where.

She squinted at Donut Country a few blocks down, worried they might decide to close early too, but their neon-blue open sign was glowing through the gloomy evening. Cora hoped against hope that Mary and Riley were still there talking, having lost track of the time, like kids so often did.

Neil put his arm around her. "Hey," he said.

She looked up at him.

"I'm sorry about last night. I'm sorry it went south like it did."

"Me too. But at least we finally started talking, finally started being honest with each other. That's a good thing."

"I meant what I said, you know."

"About being in it for the long haul?"

He nodded.

"Good," she said with a small smile. "Because I was afraid this latest drama would scare you off."

"She's a kid. She's figuring it out. It's not going to scare me off. If anything, it's making me want to work harder to get closer to her."

The words, spoken so casually, meant everything to her.

But it was hard to lean fully into the moment, because it also felt delicate. Like it could be broken into a thousand tiny shards at any minute. Things were upside down with Mary, which meant they weren't right with Cora, either. That's just how it was, and how it would always be.

As they got closer to the donut shop, Cora's belly tightened. What were they going to do if she wasn't there? Call the police, she guessed. Ben Martinez was the police chief, and he was a nice guy. He'd know where to look, what to do next. But she hoped and prayed it wouldn't come to that. Did a child have to be missing twenty-four hours for a report to be filed? She had no idea if that was true anymore.

Neil reached out and opened the door to the little shop. A bell tinkled above them, and it smelled warm and sugary inside. Cora looked quickly around, hoping to see Mary sitting with Riley at one of the tables, but her stomach sank when she realized her daughter wasn't there. There was only an elderly couple drinking a cup of coffee, and a mother with a toddler sitting next to the window.

"I'll ask if they've seen her," she said quietly. "Maybe she just left."

Neil nodded, and she walked up to the counter, waiting for a teenage girl in a white apron to come over.

"Hi," Cora said. "I was hoping you could tell me if you've seen my daughter? I think she was in here with a friend tonight?"

"Sure," the girl said. "What does she look like?"

"She's eleven. Blonde, thin, lots of freckles. Her friend has long, reddish hair."

"Yeah, they were here. They sat and talked for a long time." She frowned. "She looked like she was upset, she was crying a little."

Cora frowned. It was worse than she'd thought, and

she'd known it wasn't great. "Okay, thank you. Can you tell me when they left?"

"About an hour ago. Before the weather turned bad."

Cora glanced over her shoulder at Neil, who was watching from a few feet away. His body looked stiff, his arms crossed tightly over his chest. She wondered if he was thinking the same thing she was—that they should probably call the police soon.

She turned back to the girl behind the counter. "Thank you. Listen, if they come back in by any chance, could you please tell them to come home? My daughter's name is Mary and her friend's name is Riley. It's getting late and I'm very worried."

"Okay, sure. I'm sorry."

Cora managed a smile and walked back over to Neil. "I'll call Riley's folks. I was hoping I wouldn't have to. I guess they've got some problems at home, and I don't want to get her in trouble…"

"I know," he said. "But it's time."

He put his hand on the small of her back and pushed the door for her again, and they walked back into the ominous, misty evening.

"Let's go back to the shop and make sure she's not there," she said. "And then I'll call Riley's mom before I call Chief Martinez."

"Sounds good," Neil said.

They walked back down the sidewalk, and this time Cora stared straight ahead, ignoring the deceptively cheerful Christmas lights, the warm displays in the windows, and concentrated on picturing Mary safe and sound. Maybe if she pictured it hard enough, she could manifest it into being. Never in her life had she wanted something more. It was the same feeling she'd had when Mary was a toddler, and they'd been shopping in a department store. She'd turned around and her daughter was gone. She'd never forget how frantic she'd felt, how instantly terrified. Tonight was like that. Only worse, because now she was beginning to entertain the idea that Mary really might have run away. It wasn't likely, but it was possible. And right now, all she cared about was possible.

Neil's phone dinged from his pocket, and Cora looked over anxiously.

He pulled it out, but frowned when he saw the text on his screen. "Just my folks. They're at the airport getting ready to board. They wanted to know if I've talked to Mary yet."

Cora chewed the inside of her cheek. *If only.* They were almost back to the shop, and she could see the lights inside were dimmed now. Poppy and Justin must've left for their party. She'd have to call them later if Mary didn't show up. Beau would need to know too, of course. It would be an all-hands-on-deck situation. Something that she hoped wouldn't come to fruition, but the fact that the lights were off wasn't a good sign. Unless Mary was up in her room. Her room was her safe haven.

She dug her keys out of her pocket and opened the front door. And there, sitting on the windowsill, was Mary. She was looking out the window at the harbor, with Roo at her feet.

Cora clutched her chest. "*Mary.* Where have you been? We've been worried sick!"

Mary turned, and it was obvious she'd been crying. Her eyes were red, her face blotchy. Roo stood up and shook, then lumbered over to lick Cora's and Neil's hands.

"I texted you, Mom."

"No, you didn't. And I've been calling, you haven't answered. And your location is turned off."

"Sorry. I didn't mean to worry you, but I texted. It must not have gone through. But I'm not a little kid, I can take care of myself. I'm, like, almost thirteen. Riley's parents are fine with her being out after dark."

"We aren't Riley's parents. And you are not almost thirteen, you're eleven, young lady. You're too young to be walking around town after dark. We almost called the police."

Mary's face screwed up. "Oh, geez."

"If you have kids of your own someday, you'll understand." Cora wanted to cringe, she sounded just like her own mother. But it was true, and now she at least had some empathy for what her parents went through with her.

"I thought you guys would be too busy with each other to even notice," Mary said sullenly.

"Mary," Neil said. "You know that's not true."

"How do I know that? Because if you cared at all about what I think or how I feel, you wouldn't, like, keep *kissing* all the time."

"We do not kiss all the time," Cora said. "And you matter to us more than anything else."

"Right, Mom."

"Honey…" Cora sighed, frustrated. Mary was clearly testing her, which was normal for a lot of kids, but not really normal for Mary. They were in unchartered waters here. Cora wondered if they might end up being one of those mother/daughter pairs who were always at each other's throats during the teen years. Never really understanding where the other was coming from. It was a depressing thought.

Mary scowled, crossing her arms over her chest.

"Can I say something?" Neil asked Cora under his breath.

She nodded. Maybe he'd be able to reach her. She was willing to try anything at this point.

"Mary," he said, stepping forward. "I messed up before, and I've been really afraid I'm going to mess up again."

Mary looked over at Cora warily, like she was being ganged up on. Which was exactly the problem. She had two parents, not just one, who loved her and wanted the best for her.

"And I guess I have messed up," he continued, coming to a stop a few feet away from her. "I wouldn't ever want to be a wedge between you and your mom."

She looked up at him, her expression dark. Cora knew if she wasn't careful, she could eventually lose her to this anger. Cora had let her own parents go for some of the same reasons, and it was a terrifying thought.

"You've been through a lot in the last year," Neil said. "You've lost your dad and your grandpa, you've had to move to a new town and go to a new school. You've had to get to know me, and see that I still have feelings for your mom. And I understand how hard and confusing that probably is. All of it."

"It is," she said, her eyes suddenly filling with tears.

He kneeled down on one knee so they were eye to eye. Cora could feel the tension between them—Neil trying to reach out, and Mary trying her hardest to be unreachable.

"If you don't want your mom and me pursuing any kind of relationship right now, I'll walk away. I know she feels the same way. If it's too hard for you, if it's too soon, it's done."

Mary looked from him to Cora, and back again. Clearly, she hadn't expected this. The power being put squarely into her hands. The ability to make a decision when so many things had been out of her control lately. It was a powerful moment, Cora could see it in her eyes. Neil had to know it could be a toss-up, that he could lose Cora in the process, but he loved his daughter enough to do it anyway.

She sniffed and stared at him. "Really?"

"Really."

Cora's heart beat heavily. She had a sinking feeling that her love for Neil, this new flame burning inside of her, was going to have to be snuffed out in order for any kind of normalcy to come back to her daughter's life. That was just how it was going to have to be for now.

Mary uncrossed her arms, and looked down at her tennis shoes.

"Do you want us to stop?" Neil said matter-of-factly. Leaving no room for questions or interpretation.

She looked up at him, clearly conflicted, clearly still angry. "I don't know. I don't want to make you guys sad. But… I just don't know."

He waited a few seconds. Then patted her knee. "Okay, then." He stood up and turned to Cora. She watched him, her breathing shallow.

"I'll call you tomorrow," he said. "See how you guys are doing. We can talk about this later."

"Alright," she said. But she knew, just like he probably did, that there was nothing to talk about. This was too much of a weight on Mary. It could change next week or a year from now, but as it stood right then, it was just too much. She and Neil needed to make the decision for her. At least until they knew she was okay enough to decide for herself.

As he passed by, Cora could smell his faint aftershave.

That musky, sexy scent that was so Neil. She got butter-flies. And then a lump in her throat knowing this was it.

He reached out and squeezed her hand. How she wanted to fall into his arms and follow her heart. But that wasn't life, it just wasn't, and her grief and Mary's grief, along with so many other things, had to be considered.

And then he was out the door and disappearing into the Christmas mist before she could say anything.

Mary stood up, and Roo walked back over to her, nudging her hand with her nose. Mary rubbed her soft ears and gazed at Cora apologetically. The anger was gone. All of a sudden, she just looked deflated.

"I'm sorry, Mom."

"I know, baby."

"I made him leave."

"He left because it was the right thing to do. You need some time to figure out how you feel."

"He's a good dad."

Cora's chest tightened. "He's trying to be."

"I don't know why I didn't come home tonight."

Cora walked over to her daughter, feeling deflated, too. She was tired and sad, and wasn't in much of a holiday mood. But Christmas Eve was only a few days away, and she needed to rally. Mary was counting on her, and they had a lot to be thankful for.

"I understand that you have feelings that are over-whelming right now," she said softly. "But you have to let me know where you are. You can't do that again, it scares me too much."

"I'm sorry I'm so mad all the time."

"You're not mad all the time. But when you do get mad, I want you to talk to me. I'm not saying I'll get it right away, but I'll try."

"And Neil, too?"

"Neil, too."

Mary chewed on her bottom lip, her freckles standing out on her nose and cheeks. She looked so young right then, so small.

"Grandma and Grandpa sent me a text earlier," she said. "They're going on their cruise. They wanted to make sure I was okay."

Cora tried not to look surprised. It was the first time Mary had called them that. It sounded nice. Sweet and effortless. Maybe they were making progress after all.

"You should text them back," she said. "They'll be happy to hear from you."

"They're nice, aren't they?"

"They're very nice."

Richard and Vivian had risen to the occasion. They'd changed where they'd needed to. And it was obvious they were over the moon about Mary. That was the most important thing. But Cora also felt accepted, loved even, and that was a wonderful feeling.

Mary walked over and hugged her, resting her head on Cora's chest. Her hair was still wet from being outside in the mist, her jeans damp.

"I love you, Mama," she said, her voice muffled against Cora's jacket.

"I love you too, sweetheart."

Chapter Seventeen

"Are you sure, man?" Neil's buddy Josh asked over the phone. "It's gonna be pretty epic."

Neil stood outside the front door of Gran's Diner with his jacket zipped all the way to his chin. It was frosty this morning, a little icy. Definitely Christmassy with the cars and trucks passing on Main Street sporting wreaths tied to their grills. With the twinkle lights strung over the businesses glowing through the murky light.

Everything looked cheerful, but Neil still felt lost—a loose buoy in a stormy ocean. The night before with Mary had been hard, unsettling to say the least. So when Josh had called asking if he was still coming on the paragliding trip after Christmas, he'd felt at peace saying no. It was the first step in being around for Mary. Maybe it would be from a distance for a while, but that was alright. Eventually they'd settle into their new normal, and he'd ease into his new life as a father. This small concession felt good, it felt responsible. He'd still adventure, but he'd adventure with Mary in mind, and that was the right thing to do.

"No, dude," he said. "I'm going to stick around here for the holidays. Sorry to bail."

"That's alright. Just holler if you change your mind."

"Have fun. Be safe." He sounded like his mother right

then, and he thought that was kind of ironic as he turned to the road, watching for Cora's car.

"Will do. Later."

He hung up and put his phone in his back pocket. She'd be here any minute. They'd decided to meet and talk about Mary, but what they were really doing was putting an end to this romance. Stopping it before anyone could get hurt. It would be amicable, of course, because by now they knew they loved each other. And they wanted their daughter to be happy. But most importantly, Neil had given Mary his word.

He stood there, his jaw bunching. Yes, it was the right thing to do. But it didn't make it any easier, and as Cora pulled into the parking lot, he had the uncomfortable feeling that they were coming full circle. Just a few weeks ago he'd waited for her to show up at Gran's Diner, too. Little had he known what was going to unfold in that short amount of time. They *had* come full circle. Only it wasn't the ending he'd hoped for. He longed for Cora even now as she climbed out of her car, her blond hair pulled into a sleek bun. A soft red scarf draped around her neck, and her jeans riding sensually low on her hips.

His throat grew dry as she walked up to give him a hug.

"Hey," she said.

"Hey."

They watched each other for a long moment, the waves crashing in the distance. The ever-present sound of the ocean calming him when nothing else could.

"Are you hungry?" he asked.

"No. But I'll have some coffee."

"Me too. Maybe the caffeine will wake me up."

"You didn't sleep?"

"Well, Harry's taken to sleeping on my face, so no. But there are other reasons…"

She frowned. "Neil…"

"I know what you're going to say." He smiled down at her, and then leaned down to give her a kiss on the cheek. She smelled so good. For a second all he could think about was trailing his mouth down her neck, kissing the warm hollow of her throat. Loosening her silky hair from its tie. Taking her in his arms and never letting her go.

Maybe someday…

"Let's go in," he said. "It's freezing out here."

Pulling the door open, he waited for her to walk past, and then followed her inside. This diner had been around a long time, and probably hadn't changed much since the seventies when it had opened. Consequently, it was one of Neil's favorite places. And it always smelled like pie in here, even at nine o'clock in the morning.

A friendly server seated them by the window. When they were alone again, their menus sitting expectantly in front of them, Cora cleared her throat.

"You said you knew what I was going to say…"

He clasped his hands on the tabletop. Very formal. Very businesslike. After all, they were getting down to the nitty-gritty of trying to walk away from each other. At least for a while. Maybe forever.

"I think we both know Mary isn't up for any more complications right now," he said quietly.

She nodded, her eyes sad. "Yes."

"So we're on the same page, I guess. We knew it might not work, so it's not much of a surprise."

"No," she said.

"But it was nice while it lasted."

She gave him a small smile. "All five minutes of it."

"But that kiss…"

She reached out and put her hands over his. He didn't think he'd ever get used to the feel of her skin on his. It would probably always make his heart pound, even if he lived to ninety.

"I'm glad it happened," she said.

"Even though…"

"Even though."

They sat there for a minute, quiet, until the server brought their coffees. The steam curled into the air, the scent warm and familiar.

Cora leaned back and picked up her cup in both hands. Then took a long sip before putting it down again.

"Do you still think it's a good idea for me to come for Christmas?" he asked.

"Of course. I'd be so sad if you didn't, Neil."

"I just don't want to confuse Mary any more than she already is."

"But you're her father. She wants you there. And I want you there, too."

He nodded. Neil had always considered himself pretty tough. He didn't let people in easily, and when he did, they had to work to stay there. Sitting here now, with the frost sparkling outside, and the Christmas lights twinkling around the diner's windows, he didn't think he'd ever felt so raw in his life. He'd invited Cora in, and she'd wrecked him. Not her fault, not his, either. But the pain was a reminder of why he'd kept the memory of her at a distance. He was going to lose her again, and that was almost too much to bear.

From across the room, someone pushed Play on the jukebox and the sweet sound of "Christmas (Baby Please Come Home)" filled the small space.

He watched her. This woman that he'd loved for so long. She smiled, and her eyes were misty, like the weather outside. They'd both come home. Their daughter was home too, and Neil knew it was something to be thankful for. Everything else, including the longing he and Cora had for each other, would have to take a back seat for now.

For now, they'd just be thankful for what they had.

Cora walked out of Coastal Sweets with a bag of candy in her hands. The very last of her stocking suffers, and bought not a minute too soon, since it was Christmas Eve, and the little candy shop had been about to close.

But Frances, always sweet, had invited Cora in and promised to stay open as long as it took for her to find just the right assortment. Which didn't take long because most of her purchase was different-flavored gummy worms for Mary.

She walked down the sidewalk now, clutching the bag against her chest, and reaching up to tug her knit hat farther down over her ears. She'd bought some peanut brittle for Richard, and some dark chocolate for Vivian, for when they came back from their cruise, and she'd bought a little teddy bear holding a huge sucker in his paws for Neil. Silly, maybe, but it had spoken to her, and she'd picked it up and put it on the counter before she could think too much about it.

That was what she'd decided to do over the last few days. Not worry so much about the little things. Yes, she and Neil had agreed to walk back a potential relationship, but that didn't mean she couldn't tell him how she felt. Even if they weren't together, she still loved him.

There was a comfort in that decision, a settling of her heart, and as she walked back toward the antique shop where he was going to meet her in a few minutes, she chose to be happy that they were in each other's lives. It wasn't the romance that she'd let herself hope for, but it was something, and something was better than nothing at all.

Cars passed by in the foggy evening, the drivers giving her a little wave. The sidewalk was fairly empty though, as most people were inside with their families by now, enjoying dinner or an early church service, or whatever holiday traditions they observed. For Cora's family, that would mean dinner *and* a church service, followed by dessert in the little apartment above the antique shop, and Beau reading *The Night Before Christmas* underneath their grandpa's old electric throw. She couldn't wait.

Still, as excited as she was, she hoped Mary would come around. Ever since the other night when she'd stayed out with Riley, she'd been quiet and withdrawn. Spending more time than usual in her room. She seemed sad. But it was a different kind of sad—it was more like a weight on her slight shoulders.

Cora walked along, lost in her thoughts, going deep into her memories of Neil, and of Max, and of Mary as a baby. Of her grandfather who was no longer here physically, but whose spirit she felt with her every day. She breathed in the damp coastal air. Smelled the saltiness and listened to the ocean crashing in the distance. She was home. And she was so glad to be home.

When she finally looked up and saw the antique shop a block away, she stopped, frozen in place.

Smoke coiled from the rooftop, and her heart, which had been so light a second before, felt like a brick against her rib cage. Was she seeing this right?

A fire. And Mary was the only one home.

* * *

Neil stood on the sidewalk, his arms full of presents that he'd come to drop off before tomorrow morning. He'd probably gone overboard, but he honestly hadn't been able to help it. This was his first Christmas with his daughter, and he hadn't known what to get, so he'd followed his parents' lead and had gotten it all. He refused to feel guilty about that. Next Christmas he could exercise some self-restraint. This year he was going all out.

Smiling at the thought, he looked down the street, waiting for a glimpse of Cora. She'd just texted saying she was almost done at Coastal Sweets, and she'd be heading back in a few minutes. She'd said Mary was in her room, but he hadn't wanted to have her come all the way down and unlock the shop's door, so he'd decided to wait for Cora instead. Plus, that would give him a minute or two alone with her, and that wasn't a terrible thing, was it?

He rearranged the presents in his arms, and stood there, his breath puffing from his mouth. But when he smelled the familiar, tangy scent of smoke, he stiffened.

Setting the presents down, he walked out from underneath the shop's awning and glanced up the street, then down the other side, looking for the source of the smell.

But before he could turn around again, a woman came running out of Brother's Hardware.

"Fire!" she cried, pointing to the antique shop. "Oh my God, it's a fire!"

Neil stepped farther back and looked up. Sure enough, smoke was billowing from the roof. A dragon that he'd come face-to-face with so many times before. But this time, someone he loved was in that dragon's lair, and his stomach twisted.

"Call 911!" he yelled over his shoulder.

Turning at an angle, he lunged toward the door, and hit it with a crash. The glass shattered and flew everywhere. He felt shards of it bounce off his face, land in his hair, go down the back of his jacket.

He shook it off and ran through the darkened shop, hearing Mary yelling from upstairs.

"Help!" she screamed. "Help me!"

"I'm coming, Mary!"

He tore up the stairs, and prayed the door to the apartment wasn't locked. He'd have a much harder time with a dead bolt over seventy-five-year-old glass. But when he grabbed the handle, it turned easily in his hand. It wasn't hot yet, which meant the fire was probably contained to one area of the apartment. But fire was an unpredictable beast, and he clung to the hope that it would stay relatively small. Or at least small enough to be able to get his daughter out before she was hurt. Or worse.

He pushed the door open and was met with a wave of heat. The kitchen was on its way to being fully engulfed. The fire snapped and popped, but the path to the bedrooms was clear.

"Mary!" His voice boomed, and the sound of it, tinged with panic, scared him. He wasn't prone to panic, even in the worst fires. But this was different, and every muscle in his body screamed to have Mary safe in his arms.

"Dad!" she yelled back. "I'm in here!"

He ran to her bedroom and hit the door. She was on the floor, huddled near her bed. Her eyes were huge. The dog, Roo, was trembling beside her, her long tongue lolling and the whites of her eyes showing.

He grabbed onto Roo's collar in case she decided to bolt. He hoped she wouldn't, because she was big, and he couldn't carry her and Mary both, if it came to that.

He leaned down in front of Mary, who was clearly terrified. He knew he had to be calm and measured with her, but they didn't have much time. He wasn't sure how long it would be until the entire apartment was on fire.

"Are you alright?" he asked, looking her quickly over for any burns.

She nodded.

"I know you're scared, honey, but we have to go."

"I can't!"

"You can, Mary. I've got you."

"What if we die?"

"We're not going to die. It's going to be alright, but we have to move. Look at me." He touched her chin until her eyes met his. "We can't stay here. We have to go, do you understand me?"

She nodded.

"Okay, get up."

She did as she was told, clinging to his arm.

He reached over and grabbed a T-shirt from her bed. Wetting it down would be best, but this was better than nothing. "Hold this in front of your face, okay?"

He coughed, the smoke and heat burning his throat. Mary coughed, too.

"I've got Roo's collar," he said. "You keep holding on to my arm. Do not let go, do you hear me?"

She nodded.

He led her to the doorway, and saw that the fire had grown. The path to the fire escape was blocked with flames, their tongues licking and pulsing, ravenous for more fuel. The only way out was the way he'd come in—down the apartment stairs. And that was exactly where the fire was headed.

Gripping Roo's collar, he looked down at Mary. "We're going to make a run for it. Can you do that?"

Tears were pouring from her eyes. Probably from fear, definitely from the smoke, which was as black and thick as tar. The rest of her face was concealed by the T-shirt. Roo barked frantically, on the verge of panic. She was trying to twist away from him, and he just hoped her collar would hold.

"I'm sorry, Daddy," she cried. "I'm sorry."

He had no idea what she meant, what she was apologizing for, but his heart broke at the sound of her voice. At the terror there.

"Hold on to me, honey," he said, coughing. "It's going to be okay."

"Do you have Roo?"

"I have her."

"Don't let her go!"

"I won't."

"I'm scared. I can't breathe."

"I know it's scary. But we need to head for the door. Just hold on to me. Are you ready?"

She nodded.

"Go!"

Together, they ran through the gauntlet of smoke and sparks coming down like rain. Neil's eyes burned, his chest feeling like it was being squeezed in a vise. When they finally got to the door, Roo skidded to a stop with a yelp, trying to pull out of her collar.

"Roo!" Mary cried.

"I've got her!"

The door yawned open in front of them, and he pushed Mary out first. He looked down the staircase, and two firefighters appeared in full gear. One of them was Jay, he could tell by his bulk. They were a sight for sore eyes.

"Everyone's out!" he yelled down to them.

Mary clung to his arm.

"I'm right behind you," he said, to her. "Be careful on the stairs. Go to Jay, he'll take you to your mom."

"But what about you?"

"Roo's too scared, I have to carry her. I'll be right there."

With one more agonized look, she headed down the stairs and into Jay's arms. Even though he could feel the heat from the fire behind him, even though it was hissing eerily through the apartment, relief washed over him.

He leaned down and picked Roo up, careful to get a firm hold. "It's okay, baby," he said. "I've got you."

It looked like they were all going to make it out okay. The biggest tragedy of his life narrowly averted. Thank God.

He held the dog against his chest, his arms and shoulders straining with the weight of her, and he stepped forward, feeling for the top step with his foot.

And then he heard the old ceiling beams moan. The sound sent chills into his scalp. He looked up with only one thought going through his mind. An old firefighting motto his captain had taught him as a rookie...

Never count your blessings until you're out.

Chapter Eighteen

Cora couldn't breathe. She couldn't hear anything except for the swoosh of blood in her veins, the frantic pounding of her heart. Someone had her by the shoulders so she couldn't run toward the burning apartment, even though she was screaming for them to let her go.

The lights of the firetrucks and police cars flashed through the dark, misty night. Christmas Eve. Although she was barely aware of the holiday at all.

"My baby's in there!" she sobbed. "My baby!"

The arms around her held her tight. And from somewhere far away, she realized it was Beau. His cheek pressed against hers. Begging her to stay with him, it was going to be alright, they were going to get Mary out.

She pounded his chest with her fists, but still he held her. There was a crowd on the other side of the barrier. Friends, neighbors, tourists. All watching in horror as the second story of the old building went up in flames. Cora's childhood. Her grandfather's pride and joy. The place where her little girl had been safe and warm, waiting for her to come home after picking up the last of her stocking stuffers.

Cora sobbed, choking on the smoke, the smell of charred wood and brick. The pulsing red and blue lights hurting her eyes, piercing her heart. She'd just lost her grandfather. Endured the death of her husband. She couldn't lose her daughter. It was unfathomable, it was unthinkable. And as she twisted in Beau's arms, with a strength born of pure panic, someone yelled into her ear.

"They have her, Cora! They have her! They're coming out with her now."

Cora stared into the dark entryway of the antique shop's shattered front door. And sure enough, like a scene out of a movie, a tall firefighter appeared with Mary in his arms. She was terrified and crying, but otherwise looked okay.

Cora sagged against Beau. She closed her eyes for a second. "Thank you," she said. "Thank you, thank you."

"Mom!"

Opening her eyes again, she saw Mary running toward her. She held her arms out, and her daughter fell into them. She smelled like a campfire.

"Are you alright?" Cora asked. "Are you okay?"

Mary nodded, pulling away to look up at her. Her freckled cheeks caked with tears and soot. "Dad is inside. He's inside with Roo. The roof came down, we heard it."

Cora looked up, frantic for any sign of Neil.

There was commotion everywhere. Firefighters shouting to each other, water gushing from giant hoses, police officers keeping people back. But all Cora could think of was Neil. Mary's father. Her first love.

"Neil," she said under her breath. "Please…"

Mary hugged her tight, and someone draped a blanket over them. The warm tears on her face met the freezing Christmas Eve air, and she realized she couldn't stop crying. She was shaking, her knees having trouble keeping her upright. And still, the same word reverberated in her head over and over again. *Please*…

And then, there he was. Stepping through the shattered door, cradling Roo in his arms.

Cora heard herself sob with relief. Heard Mary squeal at the sight of her father. A hero to them both. The crowd behind them whistled and clapped, and the feeling of complete and utter joy was so overwhelming, that Cora felt dizzy with it.

For the second time that night, she uttered a thank-you.

Their home was gone. Everything they owned was probably gone, too. But she was the luckiest woman in the world.

Neil carried two steaming cups of cocoa in from the kitchen. Extra marshmallows, just like Mary had asked for.

Leaning down, he set them on the coffee table in front of her and Cora, who were cuddled up on his parents' sofa underneath the softest, coziest blanket in the house.

He sat down and put his arm around his daughter. She was safe. And he'd never been so thankful in his life.

He felt Cora watching him, and his gaze met hers over the top of Mary's head. His parents had insisted they stay at their place in Christmas Bay for as long as they needed. Along with Beau and Poppy, of course. But Beau had been spending more and more time at Summer's place, and they were about to move in together officially. Justin Frost was planning on asking Poppy to marry him on New Year's Eve, a sweet secret that somehow she knew nothing about, but everyone else in town seemed to be privy to.

So that just left Cora and Mary, and even though Neil appreciated his mom and dad's offer, he had no intention of letting them stay at their house if he could help it. If Mary and Cora agreed to it, he wanted them at his place. It was small, but there was plenty of room for the three of them. Well, four of them, if he counted Roo. And Harry would make five. Roo and Harry might not love each other at first, but it would be a baptism by fire. No pun intended.

"How's your shoulder?" Cora asked, her voice low. Mary wasn't asleep, but her eyes were clearly heavy as she blinked across the room at the Christmas tree. She'd been through a lot, and it was one o'clock in the morning. They'd all been sitting here decompressing for the last hour or so, trying to wind down from the trauma of the evening.

The Christmas tree sparkled by the window, its pine scent filling the room. Only the gifts he'd brought over, and the ones from his parents sat underneath it—a reminder that all their presents from the apartment, all their belongings had been burned—but Neil had promised he'd make up for that. As soon as the stores opened the day after Christmas, they'd be first in line.

Mary had just smiled, and shook her head. Looking more grown-up all of a sudden. Wiser somehow.

No, she'd said. *I'm just happy we're all together. Stuff is stuff, right?*

He knew she'd probably change her mind once she realized the only clothes she had left were the ones on her back. That was okay. It would take a while for all of them to realize just what they'd lost. And what they'd found.

He smiled at Cora. "It's alright. A little sore, but I'll live."

The roof had indeed collapsed. But Neil had only gotten the tail end of it, and had even managed to keep Roo securely in his arms when a chunk of ceiling had hit him in the shoulder. All in all, the apartment had been pretty much gutted by the fire. The result of a candle burning in the kitchen that was too close to the curtains over the sink. Mary had lit it not long before Cora had headed back to the antique shop from Coastal Sweets, and it had gone up like dry kindling. Neil was still surprised the damage to the building had mostly been limited to the apartment. From the early looks of it, the antique shop was alright. Lots of smoke and water damage to the antiques, some structural damage, but the integrity of the historic shop was still intact. A blessing, all things considered.

When they'd gotten to his parents' house, he'd set Cora and Mary up on the couch to rest before he'd made them something to eat, but Mary hadn't been able to stop crying.

She'd said she was sorry over and over again. She'd been so hysterical that Cora had had to hold her against her chest, rocking her like a baby until she could breathe again. Neil had wrapped his arms around them both, and they'd just sat like that for twenty or thirty minutes. Not saying anything else. Just being together. Just forgiving each other. Just loving each other through it.

His daughter looked up at him now, her eyes red-rimmed. "I had a present for you," she said. Her voice was hoarse and froggy from the smoke. "It was all wrapped and everything."

"Oh, yeah? I know I would've loved it."

She nodded. "It was a baby picture of me. I found a cute frame and stuff. It was for that bookcase in your living room."

"Aww, honey." He swallowed hard. "I definitely would've loved that."

"I'm sorry."

"It was an accident, Mary."

She looked at Cora. Then back at him, her eyes full of hurt. "I'm sorry about the fire, too. I'm sorry about that dumb candle. But that's not what I'm talking about."

He brushed her hair away from her face, and Cora laid

her hand on Mary's knee. They waited while she took an audible breath. It was shaky.

"I'm sorry…" she said. "About not wanting you guys to be together."

Neil caught Cora's gaze, before looking back down at Mary.

"You don't have to be sorry about that," he said quietly. "Your mom and I both understand why you feel the way you feel."

"But you don't," she said.

"What are you saying, sweetheart?" Cora asked.

Mary licked her lips. "I'm saying that I was afraid if you got together, I might disappear. That you might not care as much about me anymore, if you had each other. I know it's stupid, and I was going to tell you that I changed my mind, that I'd be happy to have my mom and dad together, and then the fire happened." Her eyes filled with tears. "It was going to be a cheesy Christmas present from me. My blessing and stuff."

Cora wrapped her arms around Mary and held her close. "Oh, honey. That's the sweetest thing. But you know you could never disappear, right? That could never happen. You're the light of my life."

"And you're the light of mine," Neil said, his throat tight. "I love you very much, Mary. I know things are new between us, but that love is real."

She wiped the tears on her cheeks. "I know it is. I just hope it's not too late. You know, for you guys. I hope I didn't ruin it."

They sat there for a long minute, holding each other. Grateful the fire hadn't been worse. Grateful for so many things. Neil knew this was the honeymoon phase, that the adrenaline from the fire would eventually wear off and reality would set in. But for him, that feeling of gratitude went about as deep as anything he'd ever felt before. It wasn't going anywhere. It wouldn't disappear, just like Mary could never disappear. After all, she'd called him "Dad" tonight. It was what his heart had been waiting for. There was no going back.

"You didn't ruin anything," Cora said, kissing her on top of the head.

Mary looked up at him then. Questioning.

He leaned back so he could see them both better. His daughter, and the woman who was the love of his life. He'd spent a lot of time pushing that feeling away, because the knowledge scared him. But there was no point in denying it anymore, no point pushing anything away. That love was here to stay. It didn't mean it would be easy, or that it would last even, but for right now, all he wanted in the world was to explore it. To feel it. To let it saturate him through.

"I know it's kind of backward," he said. "Usually you date someone, get married and have a baby. But your mom and I started with the baby and are going from there…"

Cora's lips, those pink, lovely, kissable lips, stretched slowly into a smile.

"So," he continued. "What do you say about coming to stay at my place for a while? For as long as you both feel comfortable. I mean, I could honestly use the help with Harry, he's a pain in the butt."

Mary grinned.

"And then," he said, looking at Cora again, "your mom and I could go on a few dates. Roll the dice and see what happens. See where we end up as a family… What do you say to that?"

"Can we, Mom? Please?"

Cora bit the inside of her cheek. "Neil, this is pretty sudden for you…"

"Only twelve years. Come on. Give it a shot?"

Mary clasped her hands in front of her chin, giving her mother a puppy dog look. Neil had to admit, it was pretty good.

"If it doesn't work," he said, "then we know we're lousy roommates. And by then the apartment will be remodeled and you can move back in if that's what you want. In the meantime, we can just see where this adventure takes us…"

Cora's eyes were warm and sexy, reminding him of when they'd been so young and in love. He could get lost in those eyes.

"You do love your adventures," she said softly.

He smiled. Feeling the love and peace of the season fill him up. He knew Christmas would never be the same again. Because this year he'd been given a second chance. He'd been given a family—his own perfectly imperfect family.

And that was the most thrilling adventure of all.

Epilogue

Cora rubbed the small of her back. She was only five months along, but she was finding that her second pregnancy was a lot harder on her back than the first one.

Neil came up behind her and pushed her hair away from her neck, kissing her there, and then biting her playfully for good measure.

"Gross!" Mary said from across the antique shop. But she was laughing, setting out cookies on the long table with her best friend Riley. "Will you two *stop*?"

"I know, I know," Neil said. "But your mom's kind of irresistible in this ugly Christmas sweater."

"Hey," Cora said. "You love it."

"No, I love you. The jury is still out on the sweater."

"Be nice," Mary said. "I got her that sweater when I was, like, five. My dad helped me pick it out and everything."

"In that case, it's perfect."

Mary smiled. "Thought so."

"Honey," Cora said, looking at her watch. "We're opening the door at five. The caterers are bringing dinner in half an hour. You still need to set the rest of the desserts out, I'm getting nervous it's not going to be ready in time."

"It's okay, Mom. We've got it under control, don't we, Rye?"

Riley nodded, pushing her thick red hair over her shoulder. "Yeah, like, don't worry, Mrs. Prescott. We're on it."

Neil leaned close to her ear. "I've heard that before. It's okay, babe. We'll be ready, and it's gonna be great."

Cora smiled, standing on her tiptoes to kiss him on the cheek. She was still learning to trust him when he said things like that. She was still learning to trust, period, but she was getting better at embracing the gifts she'd been given. At not worrying so much that they were going to be taken from her at any minute. At living every day with purpose and intention and gratitude.

It had been exactly one year since the fire had gutted the apartment above the antique shop. She and Mary had moved in with Neil, only intending for it to be temporary, but it hadn't been. They'd gotten married in a small ceremony on the beach last spring, with all their friends and family cheering them on, and she'd gotten pregnant shortly after. They'd just found out they were having a boy. Max Beauregard Prescott. Beau said he was fine with getting the middle name honor, because Max had gotten the first. But if it had been anyone else, he would've thrown punches for it.

Cora rubbed her belly now, watching her little family put the food out. Joking, laughing, getting ready for their new Christmas Eve tradition. Tonight, with a tree sparkling in the window and icicle lights hanging from the awning outside, they were going to be serving their very first meal to community members in need. It had been Mary's idea. Taking Neil's tradition of serving Christmas dinner to the homeless, and moving it into the warmth of Cora's grandfather's antique shop. Cora thought her grandpa would be so proud of this. To have all three of his grandkids home again, running the shop, living their lives to the fullest. It was what he'd wanted most for them.

And here they were.

As for the empty apartment above the shop? She, Beau and Poppy had decided to start offering one-year leases at a reduced rate to young, single mothers who were trying to get on their feet again. That had been Neil's idea. And they had all loved it immediately. Their very first renter was upstairs now—a twenty-two-year-old with a sweet toddler named Jack. She'd just gotten her GED, and had been offered a job working evenings at Cartwrights Market. She was interested in business and management, the same courses Cora was enrolled in at the community college. Mary was going to help babysit after school.

Cora watched Riley and Mary head to the refrigerator in the back to get the pies they'd made yesterday, and her eyes stung with tears. It was a pregnancy thing, she told herself. Hormones. She cried at the drop of a hat lately, but Neil would just smile and kiss the tears away.

It's okay to be happy, baby, he'd say.

And she'd just lay her head against his chest. Thinking of how much love she'd had in her life. Of who she'd loved, and who she'd lost. She knew she'd carry that love with her all her days, and that it had helped shape the person she'd become. It had shaped Mary, too. And she was so proud of Mary.

Neil grabbed his truck keys from the counter. "I'm going to pick my parents up. They're bringing the fettuccini."

"Okay," she said. "I love you."

He leaned down and gave her a long kiss on the lips. He smelled musky and warm. He smelled like her husband, familiar and true. He always told her he wasn't going anywhere. But Cora thought maybe she was the one who was finally staying put. In her heart, in her soul, she was finally home.

"I love you, too," he said.

And it was the sweetest sound in the world.

* * * * *

Catch up with the previous installments in
Hearts on Main Street
Kaylie Newell's new miniseries for
Harlequin Special Edition

Poppy's story
Flirting With the Past

and Beau's story
His Small-Town Catch

Available now, wherever Harlequin books
and ebooks are sold!

Get up to 4 Free Books!

We'll send you 2 free books from each series you try PLUS a free Mystery Gift.

FREE
Value Over
$25

Both the **Harlequin® Special Edition** and **Harlequin® Heartwarming™** series feature compelling novels filled with stories of love and strength where the bonds of friendship, family and community unite.